THE RED ROAD

THE RED ROAD

A Novel

JENNI WILTZ

Decanter Press

PILOT HILL, CALIFORNIA

This is a work of fiction. Names, characters, businesses,
organizations, places, events and incidents are either the
product of the author's imagination or are used
fictitiously. Any resemblance to actual persons, living or
dead, events, or locales is entirely coincidental.

Published in the United States by Decanter Press.
First Edition
For more information, contact us:
publisher@jenniwiltz.com

Publisher's Cataloging-in-Publication Data
Wiltz, Jenni.
The red road: a novel / Jenni Wiltz.
350 p. ; 22 cm.
ISBN 978-1-942348-00-9 (pbk)
ISBN 978-1-942348-01-6 (ePub)
ISBN 978-1-942348-02-3 (Amazon)
1. Teenage girls — Fiction. 2. Family problems — Fiction.
3. Coming of age — Fiction. 4. High schools — Fiction.
5. Interpersonal relations — Fiction. I. Title.
PS3623.I48R43 2015
813'.6 — dc23   2014918224

DEDICATION

For Mom and Dad

CHAPTER ONE

Wednesday, March 26

FOUR METAL SPEAKERS BLARED INTO the courtyard. Emma watched the perforated cones pulse in rapid succession, strained by the exuberance of a mariachi band. She tried to remember how to describe the tempo of a piece of music. Beats per measure? Time signature? She couldn't remember anything from the two years she'd taken flute. If pressed, she could pick out "Lean on Me" on the piano, but that was all. She hated "Lean on Me." And she hated the ranchero music the school played during lunch.

A handful of Mexican boys got up to dance, pulling their girlfriends behind them. Emma picked one couple and watched their sensual sway. The boy wore pointy cowboy boots and a lizard belt. When he smiled, his teeth shone cloud white against his brown desert face. He danced with a girl wearing a midriff shirt, the fingers of his right hand resting on the waistband of her jeans. Half an inch up and they'd be on her bare skin.

Emma sighed. The only thing that touched her bare skin was the too-tight elastic of her bra and underwear, a situation unlikely to change anytime soon. She swallowed hard to push down the pang of jealousy burning in the back of her throat.

Emma and her friends occupied their usual table at the far end of the courtyard. On one side, Rachel Cooper sat with pale legs folded to her chest, a waterfall of red hair shielding her face from the sun. Emma sat on the other side. Next to her, Via Mebrete bounced her right leg with a rhythm that would have put a drummer to shame. "What's for lunch?" Rachel asked, pointing at Emma's brown bag. "You know I eat vicariously through you."

Rachel's parents had divorced sophomore year. She and her mom lived with an aunt and uncle, but were thinking of moving in with her grandma instead. If they did, it would be the third place Rachel had lived in less than a year. Her mom worked two jobs, one at a motel and one at a gas station, because Rachel's dad, a lawyer, had all the money. Emma wondered what he did that was so bad Rachel's mom couldn't stand to be married to him anymore.

She opened her sack lunch, packed with a turkey sandwich, a sliced Granny Smith apple, two oatmeal cookies, a can of lemonade, and a paper napkin folded in half lengthwise. Her mom had wrapped the refrigerated soda can in foil so its condensation wouldn't liquefy the napkin.

"Your mom is so cute," Via said. "Mine gives me loose change and tells me to go to the cafeteria." She nudged the cardboard tray that held soggy fries, a plastic cup of apple juice, and a hamburger. "They don't even have pickle relish in there."

Via's family was in even worse shape than Rachel's. Her parents had split up before she started kindergarten, when her dad left to join a group of fellow Ethiopian expats in Washington, D.C. He'd sent Via a postcard with a picture of Kennedy's grave for her tenth birthday. She had no idea if he was still there.

Every time the subject of fathers came up, Emma was the odd man out. Her dad had taught her to throw a football (she sprained a thumb), ride a bike (she fell off, mostly), and put things on the grill (there was a picture of her, shirtless, at age three, using tongs to turn hot dogs over the flame). He remarked on all unforeseen events by saying, "What are the odds? It's like Lou Gehrig getting Lou Gehrig's disease." She couldn't imagine life without him.

"I don't know," Emma said. "Sometimes I'd rather have a hamburger."

"I can't remember the last time my mom made me anything," Rachel said. "She keeps her purse in the oven."

"Don't your aunt and uncle cook?"

"They like Hot Pockets."

At the far end of the courtyard, behind a folding table draped in plastic, a student council representative sold prom tickets. Emma watched Rachel's gaze drift toward the line of people waiting to buy. It happened every time there was a formal dance. Rachel picked out a mark and found a reason to stand by his locker. She twirled her strawberry curls, put on two coats of mascara, and waited for an invitation. It always came. She'd been the only freshman to attend the junior prom.

On good days, Emma tried to convince herself she could do the same. Awake or asleep, though, the dream always ended when she saw her face in the mirror. She lifted her hand and tapped the massive zit on her chin. *Yep*, she thought. *Still there.*

A breeze whipped through the courtyard, shuffling papers and stealing loose napkins. Via zipped up her hoodie. "We have a chem test tomorrow, you guys."

Rachel groaned. "I'll lose four hours of study time at work."

"A few hours of slave labor at the Falafel Hut isn't worth failing this test."

"That's slave labor *plus tips*. I have a car payment, you know."

"I'm not taking any chances." Via shoved her chemistry binder at Emma. "Quiz me."

Via's loopy letters filled every college-ruled line from edge to edge, exhibiting a reckless disregard for margins. Emma scanned her notes and tried to think like a teacher. "The change in potential energy of a chemical reaction is a reflection of what?"

"Are you trying to fucking kill me? Give me a warm-up question first."

Rachel sighed and rolled her eyes.

"Sorry," Via said. "I forgot you joined the morality patrol."

"It's a youth group."

"You mean it's where Tim hangs out." Like Rachel, Via had a car and an after-school job. She also had a CV, two letters of reference, four art shows under her belt, and this past Halloween, she'd driven to Santa Barbara by herself just to go to a party. On the scale of bravery, Emma topped out at killing small spiders.

"Moving on," Emma said, turning the page in Via's binder. "What is a coulomb?"

"A unit of electric charge."

"Correct."

"Okay, now ask me a harder one."

Emma looked at Via's drawing of an electrochemical cell and blanked on the difference between electrolytic and voltaic cells. Tomorrow's test, covering electricity, voltage, and half-cell potentials, was going to be hell. The whole year had been hell. She'd already suffered through seven and a half months of Honors English, AP Chemistry, AP US History, third-year French, pre-calculus, and PE. She did homework every weekday until bedtime and all day Sunday.

It wasn't enough.

On the university-prep track, getting straight A's was the equivalent of treading water in a shark-infested sea: You used up all your energy maintaining the status quo and the sharks still got you in the end. The good schools *expected* perfect grades. Unless you also led a successful crowd-funding campaign to build a girls' school in Uganda, discovered the cure for cancer as part of your science fair project, and spent weekends teaching foster children to read, you were average — borderline disposable. Some days it was all Emma could do to remember to bring her math book home. *Maybe the students who get accepted are all mutants,* she thought. *With adamantium skeletons that can stand up to the weight of all those expectations.*

"You guys," she said. "I'm scared."

"Of what?"

"The SAT, college, scholarship applications, all our regular homework." Emma brushed her fingertip over a word carved in the table's wooden surface — NORTE. Her nail slipped easily into the shaft of the *t*. "I'm signed up for five AP classes next year."

Via shrugged. "We were scared of this year, too, but we're surviving."

Emma's eyes drifted back to the Mexican kids. None of them brought their books to lunch. They smiled and laughed like they were actually having fun. She, on the other hand, would have an ulcer before she could vote. "I don't think it's supposed to be this way. We shouldn't just be wishing it was over."

"I don't wish that," Rachel said.

"Why not?"

"Because I'm not valedictorian yet."

As valedictorian of her middle school, Emma had been given a $25 savings bond and told to make a speech at graduation. Before going on stage, she threw up in the bathroom twice, leaving a speck of celebratory pre-ceremony canapé on the hem of her dress. The experience resulted in no net gain of which she was aware. "You have a 4.0," she said. "You do lacrosse and tennis and you're on the yearbook staff and the leadership committee. You volunteer at the soup kitchen. Your transcript is perfect."

"It's not enough," Rachel said softly. "You know that."

Emma looked away. Her own transcript was pockmarked with two B-plusses for the first semesters of chemistry and pre-calculus. She pictured a pair of Old West gunslingers, aiming for each other's hearts beneath the blazing sun of high noon. She, not Rachel, was the one who fell backward, clutching a gaping hole in her side. "We're sixteen. We're supposed to be having fun."

"Fuck fun," Via said. "I'm going to Amherst."

Rachel glared at her and took a deep breath.

"Here." Emma shoved her bag of apple slices toward Rachel. "Eat. My mom gave me too many."

As Rachel reached for a slice, a group of tall boys wandered into the courtyard. There were five of them, all on the water polo team. The tallest, Dan MacLeod, wore knee-length green shorts, a black T-shirt, and black plastic flip-flops. Even when it was forty degrees outside, Dan wore the same black plastic flip-flops. He had a weird backpack, too, a striped woven sack with thin rope straps.

He sat next to her in AP Chemistry, but never seemed to have the requisite supplies. At the beginning of the year, she'd become his go-to paper provider, and he'd agreed to be her lab partner. Lucky for her, he was the most precise measurer she'd ever met, and that included her mom, who was like Attila the Hun with measuring cups.

Everything had been fine until February 8, when he'd leaned over their lab table and asked if she had a hot date for Valentine's Day. Her pencil had slipped, and instead of entering "NR" for the cross of Pb with $Pb(NO_3)_2$, she'd blistered through the page with the tip of her Ticonderoga. "What did you say?" she asked.

His dark hair had flopped over his eyebrows, almost reaching his cheekbones. "Here," he said. "Let me do that. You're messing it up again." Since that moment, she'd been haunted by the implications of his question. No one had ever asked her out and she'd assumed no one ever would, not while she had baby fat and bad skin.

One day during sophomore year, class president Javier Benavides had flung an arm around her after biology class. Javier's friend asked, "Hey, is this your new girl?" Javier had raised both hands quicker than a cowboy in a calf-tying contest. "No way," he'd said. "These are the ones you save for marriage."

Emma had no idea what that meant, aside from the fact that it was mortally embarrassing for Javier's name to be linked with hers in any romantic context. She was dating kryptonite — until February 8 at 11:42 a.m., when Dan had joked about her having a date on Valentine's Day.

This was no small thing.

She watched Dan and his friends walk toward her table. They were heading for the main hall, its doorway just behind her. She liked the way he walked, with slightly turned-out legs that weren't bowed but definitely weren't straight. He had smooth lips, while hers were always chapped. It didn't seem fair.

She tried to smile, in case he looked at her. The boys shuffled by, talking about the match on Saturday. He didn't see her. He didn't even look in her general direction.

Story of my life, she thought.

CHAPTER TWO

Wednesday, March 26

THE SMELL OF WARM SESAME oil wafted from the kitchen to the dining room. It reminded Emma of Chinese food, even though she knew that wasn't what they were having. The culprit had to be stir-fry. Her mom was obsessed with stir-fry. Somehow, she'd been fooled by the labels on the frozen bags that claimed there were different flavors: Spicy Szechuan, Veggie Delight, Mandarin Lo Mein. They all tasted like sawdust.

Emma turned back to Mr. Lopez's study guide. There was a lot of ground to make up on tomorrow's chem test — her last quiz had scored a seventy-three percent. There was an English paper due on Friday, plus a French vocabulary quiz, and her nightly batch of pre-calculus problems. If she devoted an hour to pre-calc and three hours to chemistry, the rest could be dealt with tomorrow night. Three hours of chemistry felt like a death sentence, but she had no choice. That seventy-three was entirely due to partial credit for showing her work.

She remembered the Mexican kids dancing in the courtyard at lunch. What did they do after school? She didn't even know. Three years on the university-prep track meant that she and normal kids were developing into two different species, like Darwin's finches. Separate them for too much longer and they'd lose the ability to communicate, let alone produce viable offspring.

Emma shoved her study guide away in disgust.

"Everything okay over there?" her dad asked.

He sat in his recliner, a threadbare pile of rust-colored velour her mom had tried to throw away when they moved out of the old house. He held a shoe in one hand and a brush with no handle in the other.

"Yeah. It's just chemistry."

He pushed back his gold-rimmed glasses. "What are you studying?"

"Half-cell potentials."

"I don't even know what that means."

"Dad, you took chemistry." She glanced at his textbook, still sitting in the oak bookcase in the living room. She'd consulted it in December, when her shitty book failed to explain orbital diagrams in plain English.

"That was a long time ago. I think they made it harder, just for you."

"Do you remember anything about half cells, osmosis, and diffusion?"

"You'll ace it. You always do."

Something hot and bright crept up from the pit of her stomach, a rush of panic she'd been feeling for two years now, ever since they'd moved into this house.

Before the sliding kitchen chairs had put the first scratches in the hardwood floor, her dad's boss at SeedCorp had announced the company was moving to Tennessee. They'd offered to hold his job, but the Malo Verde housing market made a quick sale impossible and they couldn't afford to sell at a loss. At least that's what he'd told his boss.

Dad, she'd said, *please don't make me leave my school. I like the teachers and the counselors and the university-prep program here is so strong.* The problem was she'd never met her guidance counselor and had no idea what other schools' programs were like. The only reason she said it was because she was afraid.

In that moment, her grades went from a present to a penance.

While Emma struggled with geometry and biology, he'd struggled to update a twenty-three-year-old resume. Despite hundreds of applications and dozens of interviews, no one hired him. "It's my age," he said, running his fingers through hair the color of fireplace ash. One year went by and then another. To keep the house, they gave up everything that could be given up. Her mom took on freelance bookkeeping work for a neighbor's daycare business, and they'd limped along as best they could. Then, two weeks ago, her dad had landed a job as a census taker. It was temporary, but better than nothing.

Tomorrow was his first day.

"You'll do fine, Em," he said. "You've never disappointed me yet."

Her mom came out of the kitchen with a dish towel clutched in her hands. She smiled and swept long golden-brown bangs behind her ear. In direct sunlight, her hair looked almost red. Her eyes were like that, too, changing from brown to hazel depending on the light. "You guys ready for dinner?"

"I'm always ready," her dad said.

Her mom's eyes traveled down his arm to the shoe in his hand. "You're not wearing those tomorrow, are you?"

"I am."

"Roger, you're going door-to-door. Your feet will be killing you. Just wear tennis shoes like everyone else."

He looked at the shoe, shined to help camouflage the worn patches near the ball of the foot. "I'm wearing these."

"You don't work for SeedCorp anymore."

"I know where I work, Sharon."

Her mom tossed the dish towel over her shoulder, lips moving in silent retort.

Emma glanced at her dad to make sure he hadn't seen her mom's gesture. "Come on. Last one to the kitchen has to clear the table."

Her thirteen-year-old sister, Mattie, waited for them at the small table in the breakfast nook. Thin, blonde, and blue-eyed, she already had a boyfriend. Martin Rodriguez, a basketball player who lived two blocks away, presented her with a new stuffed animal every week.

"Hey, Em," Mattie said. "Can I borrow ten dollars?"

"I don't have ten dollars."

"I told you not to ask your sister," her mom said.

"What's it for?" Emma asked.

"The girls are going to the mall on Friday after school."

"So go, but don't buy anything."

"I have to."

"No, you don't."

Her mom carted four plates to the table, two in her hands and two balanced on her forearms. "Who needs milk?"

"I do," said Mattie and her dad, at the same time.

Her mom filled each glass halfway before sitting down. When they were all seated, hands folded in their laps, her father began to say grace. "Come, Lord Jesus, be our guest," they chanted. "Let these gifts to us be blessed. Amen."

When he finished, he looked around the table.

"What?" her mom asked.

"Soy sauce?"

"You haven't even tried it."

For a moment, no one moved. Then her mother sighed, got up, and grabbed the bottle from the pantry. Her dad picked it up and turned the bed of rice and broccoli into something that resembled an oil spill. He scooped up a dripping mouthful and nodded in approval as he chewed. One drop trickled out the side of his mouth and he tried to lick it up with his tongue.

"You have a napkin," her mom said.

"Oh!" He faked surprise when he picked up the folded paper napkin beneath his knife and spoon. "That's what these things are for."

Mattie giggled. "Dad, you're funny."

"What did you do in school today, Matt?"

Her sister pushed a piece of broccoli to the side of her plate. "We had a debate in English class about John Steinbeck and whether his representation of farm workers was fair."

Emma's father nodded. "Which book did you read?"

"In Dubious Battle."

He looked to Emma. "You've read that one, haven't you?"

"No."

"I thought you read it a few years ago," her mom said. "You complained about it."

"That was *The Pearl*, Mom. We read it in eighth grade."

"What didn't you like about it?" her father asked.

"I don't remember. I was thirteen."

"It must have been different for Steinbeck. Not like it is now."

Her parents' eyes met across the dinner table. Sometimes one or both of them would slip and say something about gang members or farm workers, both code for "Mexicans." Before she was born, Malo Verde had been a coastal farm town where they grew lettuce and broccoli and artichokes and strawberries. Now, it was a stronghold for drug smugglers, gangs, and former inmates of the nearby state prison. Locking them up had little effect since the gang leaders they wanted to impress were all in prison anyway. On the wrong day (or sometimes the wrong week), the headlines made Malo Verde sound like Iraq, but with fog.

"Dad," Mattie said. "Are you excited about tomorrow?"

"I am."

"What do you have to do?"

"They'll hand out our assignments in the training session."

"I hope you get a good one."

"It's going to be a big day for you, too, Em."

"Oh?" Her mom tilted her head, one golden earring sparkling in the light.

"Chem test," she answered.

Her dad carted another forkful of soy-soaked rice to his mouth. "Have you given any more thought to Cal Poly?"

"Dad, they require two years of a performing or visual art."

"But everything else you have is so good. They can't turn you down."

"They can. Those are the rules."

"Can you do something this summer? And then next year?"

"No, Dad, I can't." Her schedule for high school had been full since eighth grade. Just thinking about it liquefied the contents of her stomach. "I'll already have AP Government, AP English, AP French, AP European History, AP Physics, and maybe calculus. Plus the SAT and finding scholarships."

She said the last part softly, hoping he might not hear.

From the moment she'd learned the alphabet, he'd promised to put her through college. "Any school you want," he'd said. "You get the grades, and I'll handle the rest." But that was before SeedCorp, before unemployment, before her mom started jotting down the phone numbers of bankruptcy lawyers. The one time Emma had mentioned loans, her dad shook his head. "Loans are for the kids who get Cs. You'll do better than that."

What if I can't? she wanted to say.

"Can I have more milk?" Mattie asked. "This stir-fry is spicy."

"It's not spicy," her mom said. "And we're almost out."

Mattie set down her glass, a meniscus of milk resting at the bottom. "Being poor sucks."

"We're not poor." Her mom sat straighter than the rest of them, holding the knife and fork with her fingertips, the way rich people did in movies. She held a pen the same way, as if the lightest pressure was all she needed to produce elfin-perfect cursive. Emma, a lefty, clutched all pencils and utensils in a sweaty death grip.

"Then what are we?" Mattie asked.

"Lucky," her dad replied.

Emma looked past her mom to the stack of bills sitting in the basket on the kitchen counter. There were three unopened envelopes that hadn't been in the stack yesterday. *Are we?* she thought.

After dinner, Emma carted the dishes to the sink, where her mom scrubbed them and loaded them in the dishwasher. It seemed weird to Emma that her mom washed the dishes before putting them inside a machine designed to do the exact same job, but adults did things that made no sense all the time. Just yesterday, Mrs. Evans had worn pantyhose with sandals. If it were up to her, Emma decided she'd never own a pair of panty-hose and she'd never wash anything twice.

She watched her mom's quick fingers swipe food scraps from the plates to a mesh grate set over the drain. The garbage disposal had stopped working a year ago and there was no money to fix it. Every night, her mom cleaned the grate with her hands and a sponge.

"Mom," Mattie called from the couch. "What channel's *Wheel of Fortune* on?"

"You know what channel," her mom replied.

"I'm going to check on the roses," her dad said. A minute later, Emma saw him through the back window, carrying a spray bottle and a pair of shears. Six manicured bushes lined their backyard, all with finger-width thorns ready to inflict grievous harm on any cats that fell off the fence.

"Em," her mom said, wrist-deep in lemon-scented suds. "Do you need the table to study tonight?"

"Chemistry test, remember, Mom?"

"Would it help if there was pudding?"

Emma smiled. "It always helps if there's pudding."

"Mom, come on," Mattie called. "*Wheel of Fortune*'s starting."

Her mom pulled out a metal bowl and a hand mixer older than Emma. She poured a package of store-brand pie filling into the bowl and added the rest of the milk. Now Emma knew why her mom hadn't let Mattie have a second glass at dinner.

I'm such an asshole, she thought. *All I do is complain, and all Mom does is think about how to make it better for us.* "Thanks, Mom," she said, slipping away into the dining room. Her chemistry book was right where she'd left it, spine flat on the linen tablecloth. "I hate you," she said. "Everyone hates you. You know that, right?"

The chemistry book, unperturbed, flashed its cover art at her: red, yellow, and green molecules with white swoosh marks behind them, intended to make it look as if they were zooming across the cover. "You're not even that fast," she said.

CHAPTER THREE

Thursday, March 27

"ISOTONIC MEANS EQUAL CONCENTRATIONS of solute. Hypertonic means high solute concentration. Hypotonic means low solute concentration." Emma chanted it like a mantra as she walked into class and sank into her plastic seat. This was it — the last chemistry test before the final. Mr. Lopez erased the board, his arm swiping right to left. When he finished, the tops and bottoms of numbers floated, dismembered, on the vacant field of green.

Emma took a deep breath and pulled out her scientific calculator, her father's old Texas Instruments from college. The buttons were as yellow as a coffee taster's teeth and the plastic cover split like a fat man's pants, but it still had the original user's manual in the inside pocket. She could have cheated and written notes to herself, thumbing through the pages during the test, but she didn't.

Things, she believed, carried some essence of their owners.

On her right, Dan MacLeod twirled a dull-tipped yellow pencil in his fingers. He wore his usual black plastic flip-flops, board shorts, and black T-shirt. Today, his hair looked gelled. It created a perfect arc over his eyebrows, swooping down at the end of his brow and curving up over his ear. His long legs stretched halfway beneath the desk in front of him. They were smoother than hers. *So not fair*, she thought.

"You ready for this?" he asked.

"No."

"You always say that when you've spent, like, a thousand hours studying."

"Then how come you're the one who gets the A?"

He shrugged his wide swimmer's shoulders. "Natural talent."

"Your talent is dull," she said, pointing at his pencil. "It needs sharpening."

"I like doing it in the middle of the test. Gives me an excuse to get up and stretch."

"More like cheat off Angela Hong in the front row."

"That hurts. You know I only cheat off you."

Emma reached into her backpack's front zipper pouch and pulled out her spare pencil. White with red strawberries, it was a souvenir of her father's days at SeedCorp. "Here. It's bad luck to start a test with a dull pencil."

"Says who?"

"Confucius."

He held the pencil beneath his nose. "Is it scratch and sniff?"

"It is now."

"You're mean today. I like nice Emma better."

She thought of the English paper she had to write that night, the French quiz tomorrow afternoon, and the long-ass book she had to start reading for her history report. "Nice Emma's gone away for a while."

"Anything I can do to help bring her back?"

Emma shifted in her seat, the plastic creaking like the floor of a haunted house. If she actually asked him for something, he might say no. If that happened, she wouldn't be able to look him in the eye until June. She knew who she was and what she looked like. "No. There's nothing."

"Hey, Highlander," one of the water polo boys called. All the team members had nicknames, just like the pilots in *Top Gun*, her mom's favorite movie. "Paper me."

"Shit," Dan said, turning to her. "Can you help me out?"

Emma passed him a piece of paper. He leaned back and passed it to his teammate, one long arm stretching across a desk and a half.

I'm smaller than that desk, she thought. *I'd fit inside so easily.*

Mr. Lopez cleared his throat to get their attention and she banished all thought of Dan's arms in light of the coming ordeal.

● ● ●

The test contained multiple-choice, fill-in-the-blank, and free-form problems that ranged from difficult to apocalyptic. In Emma's experience, teachers who wrote their own tests underestimated students' ability to see through their strategies. For multiple-choice questions, the right answer was always there, as was a diametrically opposite wrong answer. There was usually a long-shot or humorous answer thrown in because the teacher was tired.

The fourth answer was the one to be careful with. It made sense, and distinguishing it from the right answer required the ability to remain confident in one's first impulse. Confidence wasn't Emma's strong suit, which meant she had to rely on deduction, induction, reduction, and a plea to the non-denominational patron saint of AP Chemistry.

By the time Emma carried her test up to Mr. Lopez, there were only two minutes left in the class period. When the bell rang, she picked up her backpack and headed into the hall. "How was it?" she asked, as Rachel and Via shuffled out of the classroom behind her.

"Brutal," Via said. She dropped her backpack and reached inside for a hair clip. With deft fingers, she wound her fluffy black strands into a bun. "My brain's so fried my hair hurts."

"But you were done way before both of us," Rachel said.

"I left some stuff blank."

"Why?"

"I didn't feel like begging for partial credit."

Emma shook her head. "I'm only passing this class because of partial credit."

Via shrugged. "The real world doesn't give partial credit."

"This isn't the real world," Rachel said. "This is high school."

"What was number nine?" Via hoisted her backpack and shrank visibly beneath its weight. "I spent ten minutes on that fucker and still don't know if I got it right."

Out of the corner of her eye, Emma saw Dan's woven backpack as he left the classroom and walked down the hall in the opposite direction. He didn't want to be seen with her — not even to return a pencil. "21.6 grams," she answered.

Rachel bit her lip. "Are you sure?"

"Pretty sure."

"Goddamn it," Rachel swore.

Via grinned. "Say it a little louder. I don't think Tim heard."

Rachel whirled, her red curls twirling like maypole ribbons. Tim stood behind her, one hand tucked into the front pocket of his skin-strangling Wranglers. His face was darker than his blond hair or green eyes. Emma didn't see how you could trust anyone that tan.

Rachel's voice flew up an octave. "Hi, Tim."

"Hey girl," he said. "What are you up to?"

"Just got out of chemistry."

"What do you have next?"

"Spanish. How about you?"

"Shop."

"Are you going to PathFinders this week?"

That was the name of Rachel's youth group. Emma was secretly glad Rachel never asked her to go. When she was seven, she'd gone to church with her grandma. The minister asked everyone to find a particular sentence in the Bible, which she'd tried to do and failed. There was something inherently dishonest about a book with no page numbers or table of contents.

"That depends," Tim said. "Will I see you there?"

"You will if you give me a ride."

Via crossed her arms over her chest. "What happened to *your* car?"

"It's — "

"Missing? Vanished? Gone to join your sense of self-respect?"

"Broken." Rachel's glare reminded Emma of a gum commercial, the kind where invisible things like breath and wind sprouted ice crystals.

"Let's go," Emma said, nudging Via with her shoulder. "We have to get ready for PE."

Over Tim's shoulder, she saw a group of Mexican boys turn the corner into the hallway. They wore saggy black jeans and T-shirts, with stacks of gold chains twined around their necks. She wondered if they were actually in a gang, or just dressed like it. Three years ago, a gang initiation had left eight innocent bystanders dead. Five of them had died at Samaritan Hospital, less than a mile from her house. The mug shots they'd showed on the news looked like two-thirds of Emma's freshman class. After that night, even white reporters had learned to roll their r's when they pronounced a suspect's name.

"I should go, too," Rachel said.

"I'll walk you to class," Tim replied.

He raised his arm to put it around Rachel's shoulders. Before she could duck into his embrace, the Mexican boys passed behind him. A thin boy with sharp cheekbones and two gold chains said something in rapid Spanish. The only word Emma understood was "*madre.*"

As he passed, the other boy shoved Tim's raised elbow out of the way. Tim's elbow jerked forward, catching Rachel on the side of her head. "Ow," Rachel said. "What was that for?"

Tim spun in a half-circle, fists balled in front of his chest.

The Mexican boy stepped back and mirrored Tim's posture. Emma saw four tattooed dots at the base of his thumb and forefinger. She knew what it meant. Before her mom had canceled cable, she used to watch *Lockup* on Friday nights.

"Watch where you're going, homes," the Mexican boy said. His friends fanned out and stood with their feet spread. One was tall with pale skin and acne scars, one had a widow's peak, and one had a moustache.

"I'm talking to my friends," Tim said. "You got a problem with that?"

"Maybe I do," the Mexican boy said.

"Tim, come on," Rachel said, wrapping her fingers around his arm.

Suddenly, Emma's skin fit too tightly over her pulsing veins. She backed into the wall and touched it with her fingertips. Her mom would have said not to, that the germs on its surface outnumbered students in the school, but she had to know there wasn't anyone behind her. She glanced at the boys surrounding Tim, their jaws loose and smiling. They weren't scared at all.

"Well, maybe," Tim said, "you need to keep walking."

"Is that what you're going to do, homes?"

"I'll show you what I'm gonna do." Tim put his arm around Rachel, who stutter-stepped under the weight. "That all right with you?"

The Mexican boy grinned. "Keep walking, then, homes. Maybe I'll be behind you." The boys standing behind him laughed. "Maybe we all will."

"You jaggers don't scare me."

The smile fell from the boy's face. "The fuck you mean, you jaggers?"

Something tingled behind Emma's ears — a whisper of hair, dislodged by the beating of her pulse.

"Stay away from me," Tim said. "Stay away from all of us."

"Or what?" The Mexican boy balled his fists and settled into his knees.

One of his friends, the one with the moustache, said, "Do it, man."

"Tim," Rachel whispered.

A wave of heat crested inside her, forcing sweat through the skin of her palms. She remembered what her mom had said after the city's seventeenth homicide of the year, in March: *Never look them in the eye. Never talk to them. Just let them kill each other.*

The Mexican boy pulled back his fist.

Tim pushed Rachel out of the way.

Emma shrieked and reached for Via's hand. Via grabbed Rachel and they stood flat against the wall, strung together like a daisy chain.

The Mexican boy's haymaker whooshed through the air. Tim ducked, aiming a punch at the other boy's ribs. The Mexican boy caught Tim under the chin as he straightened up. Emma watched Tim's head snap back. A drop of spit, oblong like a galaxy, flew out of his mouth.

"What's going on out here?" Mr. Lopez hurried to the doorway of the chemistry classroom. He stepped into the hallway, arms held out from his sides, and inserted himself between the fighters. "All right, break it up, come on."

Tim stood up straight, one hand holding his jaw. The Mexican boy laughed and retreated into the protective circle of his friends.

"You two, come with me," Mr. Lopez said, pointing at each combatant and jerking his thumb down the hall. "You can explain yourselves to the principal."

"But he didn't do anything!" Rachel said.

The Mexican boy's friends hooted and whistled. Without turning around, their friend held up his left hand and flashed a sign: four fingers held straight up, the thumb pulled back.

"Come on," Emma said. "Let's get out of here." She pulled their human caravan down the corridor. As she slalomed past cheerleaders and football players and gamers and gangsters, she felt it: the quick pang of panic, now compounded by guilt. A voice inside her head taunted her: In Tennessee, they got in trouble for moonshine, not gang signs.

CHAPTER FOUR

Thursday, March 27

THE LOCKER ROOM SMELLED OF pine and vanilla. The vanilla came from a body spray, something cheap and bright that made Emma think of unicorn barf. She liked the pine better, with its earthy tang of damp and salty places. Her favorite smell was a sweaty penny in her palm, or the scent of her hands in elementary school after she'd played on the jungle gym or twirl bar.

She waved her hand in front of her eyes to dispel the noxious vanilla cloud, then exchanged her sweater and jeans for a T-shirt and knit shorts stamped with the school mascot, the Minuteman. The logo featured a square-faced man holding a rifle, wearing tight white pants and a black tri-cornered hat. At football games, their mascot used to hold a wooden cutout painted black to look like a rifle. Parents got mad because it sort of did look like a rifle, and now the mascot didn't hold anything.

Beside her, Via laced a pair of scuffed tennis shoes in preparation for field hockey. Emma had signed up for badminton instead. Too many girls came to afternoon class with bruised and bloody shins to make Emma want to have anything to do with hockey. Her calves were the only body part she was proud of, the only part that didn't jiggle.

"So," Via said, wrapping the laces around her fingers to pull them tighter. Her nails were perfect ovals, filed religiously every night. "What do you think they'll do to Tim?"

"He'll get suspended, maybe?"

"He doesn't deserve it."

"He threw a punch."

"What's he supposed to do, let those other guys wail on him?"

"No," Emma said. "Yes. I don't know." Heather James walked down the aisle between them. Emma leaned toward her locker to avoid getting bitch-slapped by Heather's enormous backpack.

"If self-defense is a valid strategy in court, it sure as shit ought to work here." Via touched her toes, then flat-handed the ground with her palms. "I'm out of here. Have fun flinging cocks, or whatever you do in that dumb-ass sport you signed up for."

Emma pulled her knit shorts an inch below her natural waistline. The longer they were, the more of her doughy thighs they hid. She walked to the gym alone, still disoriented by the almost-fight. She'd been sure someone would end up with broken bones, all because Tim and a Mexican boy couldn't navigate the niceties of personal space.

It wasn't just a boy thing, either. She was forever angling her body sideways to avoid the press of the popular *chola* girls. They walked in rows five girls wide, like they owned every inch between the plastic baseboards. Her backpack had been knocked clean off her shoulder twice last week.

In the gym, she found a match-up list taped to the bleachers and scanned for her name: West vs. Becerra, Court 3. She picked up a racket and birdie from the tub near the door and went to stand on the court. Next to her, Rafael Dominguez and Juan Sanchez began their match. She noted where they held their rackets and how far apart they spaced their feet. Rafael, graceful and athletic, never missed a return. He'd been in her world history class last year, but they never exchanged a word.

"Hey," she heard. "Are you West?"

Emma turned to see a short, pudgy girl with a flat face and curly black hair, the top half pulled into a ponytail. She had drawn-on eyebrows and four gold hoops in each ear. "I'm Elvira." The girl pronounced her name El-vee-ra, with an accent on the vee and a trill on the r. Emma saw her eyes drift toward Rafael, who slammed his racket like he was playing whack-a-mole. "Damn," Elvira said, licking her lips. "Let's not keep score, okay?"

Emma volunteered to serve first and barely cleared the net. Elvira hustled, but couldn't get there in time. The birdie fell to the polished hardwood floor. "*Chinga la madre,*" Elvira said. She rested her weight on the racket and bent to retrieve the birdie. With a glance at Rafael, Elvira lifted her arm and tossed the birdie over the net. "Service."

Now it was Emma's turn to dash forward and swing the racket in vain, air whooshing through its plastic strings. "Man, we really suck at this."

"Still better than field hockey."

"I know, right?"

Elvira's eyes tracked Rafael as he jumped to return a volley. A thin coating of perspiration shone on his forehead. "Sweat looks so much better on guys."

Emma offered a noncommittal "mmm." She'd never seen Dan break a sweat. Water polo matches happened on Saturday mornings. In order to attend, she'd have to ask her parents to borrow the car. They'd want to know why, and she had no good reason other than to see Dan in a Speedo. It wasn't something she could say to her dad. Still, she decided to play along. Let Elvira think she was one of the normal kids — endowed with a C average, five real dates under her belt, and a clear picture of what a sweaty guy's chest looked like. "Totally," she said.

"Sometimes I ditch class in the afternoon to watch the guys' soccer practice. Most of the time, they take off their shirts."

The mechanics of ditching class were foreign to Emma. "Where do you go?"

"The bleachers behind the tennis courts."

"How can you even see the soccer field from there?"

"I have good eyesight."

"I think I need glasses."

"They'd make you look smart."

"I don't want to look smart."

"Are you going to the prom?"

"No."

"Me neither." Elvira stared at Rafael's sweat-haloed brow.

"Out of bounds," he called, hopping back as the birdie plunked down on his side of the white painted line. "Fuck." He lifted the hem of his shirt to wipe his brow and Elvira's eyes glazed over.

"Still with me?" Emma asked.

"Uh-huh." Elvira grasped the net with pudgy fingers, each encircled by a gold ring.

"Did you hear about the fight?" Emma asked. "It was right in front of my class before this."

"Oh?" Elvira didn't sound impressed. "Who with?"

"A guy my friend wants to hook up with and a Mexican guy."

"What Mexican guy?"

Emma frowned. Her school had nine hundred members of the junior class alone, and it seemed like most of them were Mexican guys. "I don't know."

"Was he wearing red?"

"Why?"

"It's a thing. Like a dare."

"What kind of dare?"

Elvira's eyes traveled from Rafael's brow to his hands. "You know how it is."

But Emma didn't know anything other than what she saw on the news, which was all bad. "No, I don't know."

"I hate it," Elvira said softly, turning her back on Rafael. "I don't feel like playing anymore."

Emma looked over her shoulder. Mrs. Patterson was nowhere to be found. Most of the other girls were already sitting on the floor and gossiping. Some of them had rolled up their sweat pants as if the gym were a tanning salon. On the next court, Rafael and Juan engaged in a sudden-death volley, shoes shrieking against the hardwood.

Elvira shuffled to the bleachers and sat down. Emma sat beside her silently, unsure what to say. It wasn't until she got dressed in the locker room that she realized Elvira had a red bandanna tied around her half-ponytail.

CHAPTER FIVE

Thursday, March 27

A WISP OF STEAM SWAYED LIKE a belly dancer above the platter of pork cutlets. A second bowl, with peas and butter, waited in the microwave. Her mom reached into the cabinet for four glasses. "Get the milk," she said. "I heard the truck outside."

Emma couldn't imagine doing her dad's job. Counting the number of people in the entire country involved trusting them to a degree that she found unnatural, if not impossible. She watched her mom scoop peas onto each plate, portioning out equal servings faster than a lunch lady. A blue undertone made her skin look translucent, like the diamond in her wedding ring. On her other hand, she wore her mother's ring, a skinny diamond with pointed ends perched on a thick gold band. Every memory she had of her mother was bookended by those rings, glinting in the sun as she reached out to catch Emma on a slide or push her on a swing.

"Give your father more butter," her mom said.

Emma flung a spoonful of sun-bright margarine onto his peas just as his key slid in the lock. "Hi, Dad," she said, licking the spoon and smiling as he came around the corner. He raised his hand to high-five her, the traditional father/daughter greeting in the West household.

The thunder of quick footsteps on the stairs brought Mattie, hurtling toward him. "Dad! Happy first day at work!" He grunted as he caught her and wrapped her in a hug. "How was it? Were the people cool?"

"Hang on," Emma's mom said. "Let's sit and say grace first." They took their seats at the table, hands folded over napkin-clad laps. Four voices repeated the old Swedish blessing that was the first rhyme Emma ever learned.

Mattie flipped her blonde hair over her shoulder. "Okay, now you can tell us."

Her dad chewed his first bite slowly and took a sip of milk. "Well, they gave us a list of people who didn't send in their paper survey. We have to knock on their door three separate times to try and complete the interview."

"Why three?"

"If you only try once, they might be at work or something."

"Three seems like a waste of time," Emma said.

"The census is important," her mom said. "It's how I found your great-great-great-grandfather." Her mom's desk was full of folders with notes on her family tree. The branches usually dead-ended with names like "Preserved Smith" and "Mollinex

Ratcliffe," Puritans whom Emma imagined as Hester Prynne's next-door neighbors.

"Speaking of the family tree." Her dad smiled, deepening the creases beneath his cheekbones. After one day in the sun, his skin already looked darker. "Em, did we ever tell you who you're named after?"

Emma blinked. "Someone from our tree?"

"My great-grandmother, Emma Christina."

Her mom's notes only covered her side of the family. Her dad's side, generations of silent Swedish farmers, remained undocumented and undiscovered. "Why did you pick her?"

"She came to America with her brothers when she was seven. She was the only one who got to keep her name." He forked the last piece of his cutlet. "Everyone called her brother 'Frank.' I never knew his real name was 'Svante Enoch' until he died."

"Why didn't they keep their names?" Mattie asked.

Her dad shrugged. "Too hard for the immigration officers to say. Emma's is the only real family name left."

Emma gulped. As if she didn't have enough weight on her shoulders, now she had to live up to a relative brave enough to leave her country forever at the ripe old age of seven.

"What about me?" Mattie asked. "Who am I named after?"

"Well, we were going to name you after my favorite baseball player, but then you were a girl."

"Wait." Mattie put down her fork. "You named me after a boy?"

"We figured, why change a perfectly good name? So we called you Matt. Well, we put 'Mattie' on your birth certificate. The nurse convinced us."

Mattie's eyes clouded like glass in the "before" picture for a dish soap commercial. "But what if your favorite player was named Walt or something?"

Their father grinned. "Waltina. Has a nice ring to it."

Mattie held out her hands, one toward each parent. "Never tell this story again, okay?"

"It's nothing to be ashamed of. Mattie is a beautiful name."

"You wanted me to be a boy!"

"But you're you," her dad said calmly. "I wouldn't trade you for anything." This was how he handled any explosion of female ire — he only got calmer, softer, gentler. Emma wondered how big the hole inside him was, the one where a father envisions playing catch with his son.

"So how many people live on our street?" Mattie asked.

"I don't know," he said, scooping peas onto his fork. Two of them plummeted back to the plate as he raised the fork to his mouth. "They didn't assign me to our street."

Emma's mom looked up from her cutlet. "Where did they send you?"

"El Camino Rojo."

Her mother dropped her fork. The clatter echoed from the kitchen to the family room. "Roger, can't you do something?"

"It's a job, Sharon."

"That doesn't mean — "

"It's a job." He scooped up the last few peas and dredged the side of his fork through a pool of melted butter.

Emma shivered. She couldn't reconcile the images of her gentle father and the asshole in the hallway who threw a punch over an elbow's worth of space.

An elbow. The dumbest body part to start a fight over.

El Camino Rojo was in the heart of the east side, where most of the gangbangers lived. Its residents didn't expect, or want, white people knocking on their doors.

Emma glanced at her mom, whose lips were clamped shut. She wasn't going to say it, even though they were all thinking it. "Dad, don't they have Spanish-speaking people they can send?"

"They sent me, Em."

She bowed her head. It was the same work ethic he'd instilled in her, the one that allowed her to do stupid homework assignments that had no bearing on real life. *If you accept a challenge*, he said, *you accept everything about it, good or bad.*

"How about your day?" he asked. "Did anything interesting happen at school?"

Before today, she might have answered honestly. But knowing he had to go into the heart of East Malo Verde tomorrow, she couldn't do it. "No," she said. "Not a thing."

• • •

After dinner, she went up to her room. At the far end of the hallway, it had a view overlooking the street. She filled it with books and stuffed animals and rarely put away the pile of folded laundry her mom left on the foot of her bed. A small desk sat beneath the window, holding her ancient desktop computer, a hand-me-down from SeedCorp. She spied on the neighbors with zero shame and even less impunity, having personally tested her desk's visibility from street level.

Emma turned on her computer, listening to the hard drive grind like a bike chain without oil. Her English paper was on *The Great Gatsby* and the green light across the bay, the one Gatsby watched from his yard and turned into a symbol of Daisy. To Emma, a glowing green light indicated only one thing: a phantom. Every kid who watched re-runs of *Scooby-Doo* knew that. The phantoms were always the product of an old caretaker, left alone with an abandoned amusement park and a gallon of phosphorescent paint.

She scooted out the tiny desk chair, sized for an eight-year-old, and held her fingers over the keyboard. Since second grade, when she'd won an essay contest about why she loved her parents (they killed spiders), her teachers had pushed her to read more and write more. In fourth grade, she won first place in the school book fair, but fell to a disappointing third place in fifth grade. She'd been trying to catch up ever since.

Words never came to her in casual conversation or on the phone, but when she sat down to type, something happened. All the words she didn't know she knew formed a cyclone in her head, whirling wide and low and slow. If she pulled out the right ones, the cyclone narrowed and whirled faster, and all she had to do was type fast enough to keep up.

She took a deep breath. *Green light, dream, phantom, bay, curse.* Then the landline rang and her cyclone's nascent whirl flattened into a death spiral.

A few seconds later, Emma heard a knock on her door. Her dad poked his head into the room and held out the cordless. "Phone's for you," he said, eyes red and bleary.

"Thanks, Dad. You can fall asleep in front of the TV now."

"Way ahead of you," he said, closing the door behind him.

Emma put the phone between her shoulder and her ear. "Hello?"

"Hey," Via said. "Are you writing your English paper?"

"I'm trying."

"What is yours going to say?"

"I don't know. I'm staring at the blank screen of death."

"I have five pages about how the American Dream is bullshit. I'm so fucked."

"And that made you think of me?"

"Not in a lesbian way or anything. I just wanted to get your opinion."

Emma thought about her dad. Until the census job came through, he'd been days away from applying to work in fast-food restaurants. Now, he was going door-to-door in hostile territory for minimum wage. "I think you're right. The American Dream is probably bullshit. But I don't think that's what you should turn in."

"I knew it. Goddamn. I can't absorb another B in this class."

"Didn't your dad come here from Ethiopia? That's the American Dream."

"It was until he decided he didn't want a wife and kid anymore. No one ever told that asshole to be careful what you wish for. My mom wants to have his citizenship revoked."

"Can she do that?"

"Shit, I don't know. AP Government's not until next year." Via sighed. "The last time I turned in a paper with a negative slant, Evans gave me a B-. Our antiquated school system isn't equipped to handle pessimism as an alternate worldview."

"Maybe they should. Look what it did for Nick Carraway."

"What do you mean?"

Emma pushed the blinds apart to look out at the dark street below. A busted-ass Corolla sat two feet from the curb across the street. Next door, two of the four solar lights lining the front walkway had gone out. "Look at Nick and then look at Gatsby. The one who floats through the book, all passive and pessimistic, survives. The one who stakes everything on a belief in love ends up dead. Think about what that means."

"I'm too tired to think. What does it mean?"

"If you care too much, this world kills you."

"Dibs. I call dibs. That's my angle."

"You can have it. But I'm charging for the next one."

"You don't have the balls. Thanks, Em."

When Via hung up, Emma returned to the blank page. *The green light*, she thought, trying to recapture the serpentine swirl of words that had slipped away when the phone rang. *But why green?* If she combined Mendelian genetics and Ziploc bags, green was the product of yellow and blue: one dominant, one recessive, creating the hybrid child. If the green light symbolized Gatsby's hope, what two things had produced it?

Before Gatsby could hope, he had to want something. It had to be as big and blue as the sky. It had to pulse like the blood in his veins, also blue, deep and dark beneath the surface of his skin. But if you wanted something that big, you had to realize you might not get it. And if you did get it, you had to fear you might lose it. Yellow was the color of fear — in her dad's favorite westerns, the cowboys always called the bad guy a "yellow-bellied coward."

That was it.

The blue was desire, and the yellow was fear. Together, they created a hybrid offspring, the phantom green light of hope. Her heart beat faster at the thought. She could make this work.

The cyclone picked up speed as she began pulling out words. She set her fingers to the keyboard and began to type.

CHAPTER SIX

Friday, March 28

THE NEXT MORNING, EMMA TOSSED her backpack onto the front seat of her mom's Buick. She liked the car in spite of its age and robust dork factor. The stereo increased or decreased volume at a whim and sometimes the power windows didn't work, but its smooth ride camouflaged her jerky turns, allowing her to pass her driver's test on the first try. Every morning, rain or shine, she and her mom piled in for the eight-mile trip to school.

"Seatbelt," her mom said, clicking the garage door opener.

Emma yawned as grey morning light filled the empty garage. Her dad's truck was already gone. Her mom sighed as she adjusted the side and rearview mirrors. "Your father's been in the car again. What time did you go to sleep last night?"

"One-thirty." Between the Gatsby paper and the metric buttload of irregular verbs she had to memorize for the French quiz, it was the best she could manage. She leaned her head against the cold window as her mom pulled out of the driveway.

"Do they sell coffee at school?" her mom asked.

"Coffee's gross."

"You won't say that in college."

"College won't change the chemical composition of coffee, Mom. It'll still be gross."

"There's a dollar in my purse. What can you buy at the cafeteria for a dollar?"

"Hope."

"Price has come down, then." Stuck behind a slow-moving Subaru in the fast lane, her mom zagged to the right and stepped on the gas. The most frequent words out of her mom's mouth as she'd taught Emma to drive were *Don't ever do this*, offered as she executed illegal U-turns and passes over the double-yellow line.

One year younger than Emma's dad, her mom had dropped out of college when he graduated. In their high school prom picture, she had the most elaborate hairdo Emma had ever seen: long golden strands piled on her head in perfect hot-roller curls.

Emma thought it was weird what her mom did and did not have patience for.

"I'll be at Christy's this morning," her mom said, pulling into North Malo Verde High's drop-off area. Their neighbor ran a daycare out of her home and her mom did the bookkeeping. It didn't pay much, but Christy gave them a cut of all the thank-you gifts parents dropped off, everything from fruit baskets to homemade soap. "Will you be out at the usual time?"

"Barring a catastrophe of epic proportions."

"Naturally." Her mom smiled. "Have a good day, sweetie."

Emma waved as her mom sped back to Carver Boulevard. High-school students weren't supposed to wave, but it made her mom happy and Emma was so far off the radar of cool that it really didn't matter.

As soon as the Buick rounded the corner, she turned to face her school — the ugliest ever built, in her opinion. The rich kids' school across town had graceful arches, terra-cotta tiles, and pointed rooflines. They got a flat cement box with a rough-rock exterior.

She stepped up to the gate, monitored by a yard duty. The district couldn't afford metal detectors or actual security guards, so volunteer parents staffed the entrances. They wore yellow nylon jackets and patrolled with walkie-talkies. If they spotted anything suspicious, they radioed one of the four assistant principals whose job it was to look mean and scare kids straight. Last year, one had been fired for smoking weed confiscated from a student.

Emma hurried to the junior locker bay, which sat perpendicular to the third hallway in the school's rectangular main building. She dropped her backpack and bent to divest it of three binders, four books, a pencil case, and a sack lunch. *I'll be a hunchback by graduation*, she thought. *Just like Richard III.*

When she stood up, she saw a broad expanse of green T-shirt that said I WISH MY LAWN WAS EMO SO IT WOULD CUT ITSELF. Startled, she banged her hand on the locker door. "Ow. You scared me."

Dan smiled at her. Despite his size, he was a year younger, a sophomore who had somehow gotten into AP Chemistry. In seven months, she'd never seen him wear a sweater or long pants. "You're jumpy," he said, leaning against the locker bay. "Are you nervous about something?"

"Usually."

"Like what?"

"Life."

"Life?"

"That about sums it up," she said.

"You need to relax."

"Tell it to the judge."

"How about your PO?"

Emma blinked. Eudora Welty was no help in deciphering the meaning of PO in this particular context. "I don't know what that means."

"Parole officer."

"Oh." Her hand clenched around her combination lock. Rachel would use a well-timed hair flip to pause the conversation and regain control. But Emma's hair was only shoulder length to start with, and she didn't trust herself not to bang her own head into the locker door.

"So," Dan said, shifting his weight.

Sweat pooled in the center of her bra. Think of something, she ordered herself. How's the weather? What about that chemistry test? How shitty are these combination locks? Why doesn't anyone get the dead bugs out of the fluorescent lights in the hallways?

"Hey," Dan said. "Can I borrow some paper?" He bent his head, looking at her through lashes thicker than hers. It made her angry that he probably rolled out of bed with perfectly tousled hair and never washed his face outside of the shower.

She pulled the pink binder out of her bag, opened the rings, and grabbed a hunk of paper.

"Dude," he said. "It's world history, not *War and Peace.*"

"I have a lot of paper."

He smiled and she saw his crooked right front tooth, tilted up and over the left one. "What am I going to do when you go to college?"

"Stop being a cheapskate and spend a dollar to get your own paper?"

"Do you know where you want to go?"

"USC."

"I can't picture you in LA."

"Why not?" She regretted it as soon as she said it. She'd just invited him to give her a laundry list of her personal failings: She wasn't ninety-eight pounds, she didn't have blonde hair, she didn't have fake boobs, she didn't have a flashy car, and she'd never been in an episode of *The Vampire Diaries.* She'd never even seen *The Vampire Diaries.*

"You're too nice for LA."

"You don't know that. Two seconds ago, I was angry at you for having perfect hair."

"That's nothing. My older brother lives there and I can tell you, it's full of assholes."

She raised an eyebrow.

"Yeah, he's one of them." Dan shrugged. "So what made you want to go there?"

She looked at her boots. The two-year-old suede was shiny at the toes. When it wore through, the whole world would know she wore Daffy Duck socks. If she told him the real reason she'd decided on USC, he'd think it was stupid. *Just say you don't know,* she thought.

"Don't say you don't know," he said.

Just say you like their football team.

"And don't say you like their football team."

"Goddamn it." Emma sighed. "I'll be late for class."

He pulled his phone from his pocket and held it out to her. "We have time. See?"

"I need to study."

"It's fine if you don't want to tell me. But I'm just gonna keep asking."

"Do you go 'in' the 'out' door, too?"

"Sometimes."

"Your social skills could use some work."

"That's what they tell me."

"Who's 'they'?"

"My PO."

"You don't actually have one of those, do you?"

He flashed a lopsided smile, the kind only a boy with curly hair could smile. Then he tucked the paper under his arm and walked away. "See you in chemistry," he called.

As he walked away, she watched his legs — they turned out slightly — and wondered why he'd decided to play water polo. She hated the water. The only stroke she could do with any precision was the backstroke because it didn't involve getting her face wet. Suddenly, he turned around. When he saw her staring, he cupped his hands around his mouth. "I thought you had to study!"

With burning cheeks, she picked up her backpack and slammed her locker with more force than intended.

• • •

"Alors, tout le monde. Etes-vous préparés pour le quiz?"

"Non," the class chimed.

"Une minute?" Monsieur Jordan asked, his finger hovering over the projector's "on" button.

"Oui," the class chimed.

"Alors, une minute."

Emma pulled out her notes for one last cram session. Her third-year French class (with all of twelve students) was composed of mostly Mexican girls. Native Spanish speakers weren't allowed to take Spanish for credit, so almost all of them took French instead. Behind her, Juan Sanchez made a hissing noise. "Eh, did you hear what happened last night?"

She knew he couldn't be talking to her, so she looked back at her notes for the conditional conjugation of *dormir.*

On her right, Griselda Gutierrez snapped the gum she wasn't supposed to be chewing. "Hector almost got his ass killed is what I heard," she said. Griselda always wore red lipstick and cut-off T-shirts with Mickey Mouse on them. She looked better with her hair in a ponytail, but she hardly ever wore it that way.

"Two *chingado Sureños.* Fucking scraps followed him and waited for him at his sister's house. Shot up his car and everything. He ran out the back."

"Damn, that car was tight. It had rims."

"Mi hermano talked to Hector after it happened. He said starting now, no one except the NF crosses Sobrante Street. Fuck those *ratas* and the *eme.*"

Emma held her breath. Sobrante Street was the unofficial border of East Malo Verde, the dividing line between billboards in English and billboards in Spanish. Her father would have to cross it to get to El Camino Rojo. Whatever the NF was, she knew her dad wasn't a part of it. Who was this Hector, and why did Juan think he could control who went anywhere in East Malo Verde?

"*Alors, tout le monde,*" Monsieur Jordan said. He stepped back in front of the overhead projector. "*Pas de livres, pas de notes.*" After they'd all put their books on the floor, he flicked the projector's "on" switch and ten questions appeared. Three were easy fill-in-the-blank, and seven were irregular verbs they had to conjugate in the *conditionnel.*

Emma jotted down her answers quickly. While she was double-checking them, Griselda leaned over and hissed at her. "Psst. What's number two?"

With a quick glance at Monsieur Jordan's roving eye, Emma shrugged. "Don't know," she whispered.

"What about number three? Is it *nous voudriez*? Or *nous voudrais*?"

Emma glanced down as Monsieur Jordan's eyes canvassed her side of the room.

"Hey, did you hear me?"

"*Oui.*"

"So which one? The first or the second?"

"Second," she whispered, through clenched teeth.

Griselda nodded and wrote the answer on her quiz.

Emma tilted her head to hide a smile. The correct answer was *nous voudrions.*

• • •

The Buick was already waiting at the curb when Emma stepped past the gate. "Hi, Mom," she said, tossing her backpack onto the floor.

"Good day?" A smudge darkened her mom's temple, like she'd rubbed her eye and smeared her makeup without realizing it.

"Average."

"Mine, too."

Her mom turned onto Carver Boulevard. Two stoplights down, they passed a vacant strip mall. "Used to be an Alpha-Beta," her mom said, following Emma's gaze. "Then a Lucky's, then an Albertsons, then a dollar store." She shook her head. "How the dollar store goes out of business in this town is beyond me."

It wasn't just the dollar store. The video rental place, dry cleaner's, insurance agent, and Baker's Square were gone, too. One of the storefronts had graffiti all over the boarded windows, with XIV NORTE featured prominently. None of the tags said NF.

"Where's Mattie?" Emma asked.

"Going home with Kayla."

"Which one is Kayla?"

"She lives on Maple, near the fire station."

Emma frowned. "I thought that was Kyla."

"Which one dyed her hair purple?"

"That's Kyla."

"I swear," her mom muttered. "There were three Madisons at daycare today. It's like there are only five names left in the entire world."

When they got home, her mom turned on the TV and made a pitcher of iced tea. She dumped a handful of tortilla chips into a bowl and the two of them leaned over it, foreheads almost touching, dipping chips into a jar of homemade salsa she'd brought back from Christy's. "This is good," Emma said, holding a hand over her mouth as she crunched. "What's the green stuff?"

"Cilantro."

Emma scooped out a sodden leaf with her fingernail and put it on her tongue. It burst to life in her mouth, a combination of sunlight and grass and dew. "This is what a four-leaf clover should taste like," she said.

"Lots of people hate it." Her mom dug a chip into the pile of tomatoes and jalapeno. "Your father does."

"Why?"

"He doesn't like how it overpowers everything else."

On TV, the local news station ran an update over a talk show's closing credits. An anchor in a sleeveless blue dress said, "We have breaking news from East Malo Verde this afternoon. A man has been shot and killed in front of the El Toro Carniceria on Guadalupe Street. The victim has been identified as a *Sureño* gang member. Gang task force agents believe this incident is retaliation for last night's attack on a prominent *Norteño* gang member. The man's name has not been released."

The video feed rolled a clip of a bearded Mexican man wearing sunglasses and a flannel shirt, black braid dangling over his shoulder. Carlos Vasquez, Malo Verde Gang Task Force, the subtitle said. "We really need residents to tell us when they see something or hear something," Vasquez said. "In many cases, they're not comfortable doing that in case the gang retaliates against them. That's why incidents like this happen, and will continue to happen, until we can convince people it's okay to talk to us. We can't help unless we know what they know."

Emma looked at her mom, whose gaze drifted out the window to the roses in the backyard. "Mom," she said softly. "I heard someone at school talk about that shooting."

"You don't know what you heard."

"I'm not stupid. I know what they were talking about."

"You're not to have anything to do with this."

"But that man just said people need to come forward."

"He didn't mean you."

"Dad's in East Malo Verde. What if I could help?"

"I printed out the paperwork for a transfer. It'll be over soon." Her mom put the iced tea pitcher back in the fridge, her hand grasping the door's narrow handle long after it shut. "I don't want you involved in this."

I already am, Emma thought. She remembered what the Mexican boy had said to Tim in the hallway: *Maybe I'll be behind you. Maybe we all will.* "Mom, what's the NF?"

"I don't know," her mom said, her voice pulled tight as a guitar string.

The pretty anchor smiled. "We'll keep you updated as we learn more. Join us at six tonight for an exclusive interview with the state's Secretary of Education about the recent tuition increase for California's public colleges and universities. Tuition now tops $6,000 per semester at even the lowest-priced CSUs, making higher education out of reach for many. We'll talk to students and get their reactions."

Emma squeezed her fingers and shattered the chip in her hand. White corn shards slid across the floor.

"Pick those up," her mom said.

• • •

Later that night, she turned on her computer, brushing her teeth for the eternity it took the thing to boot up. When it was done clanking like the ghost of Jacob Marley, she closed the bedroom door behind her. Just in case, she opened a Word file as well as a browser tab.

In the browser, she searched for "East Malo Verde NF." The first result was a news piece from the *Sacramento Bee*, about *Nuestra Familia* gang members from Malo Verde who'd been sentenced to life in prison after their indictment on drug charges. She read the entire story, noting the names of Malo Verde sub-gangs also referenced: South Sobrante, East Palomar. The FBI had taken seven years to bring down the four gang members mentioned in the story.

Emma sat back in shock. Seven years.

The Empire State Building had been built in one year and forty-five days.

A knock on the door startled her. She clicked back to her Word doc, an old English essay on *Hamlet*. "Come in," she said.

Her mom opened the door. Dressed in a blue bathrobe, she'd tied her hair back and washed her face. The skin beneath her eyes shone with some sort of face cream that smelled like milk and honey. "Still working?"

"For a little bit."

"You know we've cut back a lot lately." Her mom stood behind her and placed warm hands on Emma's shoulders. "It's not what I wanted for you and Mattie."

"It's okay."

"But I saved up a little money." Her mom's hands gathered up her hair and began finger-combing it, teasing the tangled strands straight. She kept her right hand turned so the pointy diamond's clasps wouldn't catch on Emma's hair. "Enough for a dress."

Emma bent her head. Her cheeks turned the color of cherries. She couldn't tell her mom that no one of the opposite sex wanted to be seen with her, at the prom or anywhere else. Hell, Dan hadn't even returned her pencil after the chem test.

She swallowed and felt the saliva stick in her throat. "Thanks, Mom."

"Don't stay up too late." Her mom bent and kissed her on the forehead, then closed the door behind her on her way out.

Emma let out her breath in a whoosh.

I'm such an asshole, she thought. *Again.*

CHAPTER SEVEN

Sunday, March 30

HER MOM POURED A CUP and a half of milk into the waffle mix and whisked with strokes that would put a swimmer to shame. Emma watched with a feeling of deep inadequacy. The one time she'd tried to mash potatoes ended ten seconds later, with her arm feeling like it was on fire.

"Are we ready?" her mom asked.

Mattie swiped her fingers under the kitchen faucet and flicked them over the open waffle iron. Water droplets hopped like a tap dancer on hot coals. "Ready."

Her mom held up the mixing bowl and poured some of its contents into the waffle iron. She tilted the bowl to shorten the stream and keep it from splashing on the counter. Emma wondered if all moms could do that, or just hers. "Go get your father. Tell him to wash up."

Mattie skittered to the sliding glass door just as the phone rang. "It's telemarketers," she said. "Don't answer it."

"It's probably for you," Emma said as she picked it up. "Hello?"

"Hey, Emma, it's Rachel."

"Hi. What's that noise?"

"It's the microwave. I'm making dinner."

"Hot Pockets?"

"Chicken nuggets. Hey, do you want to come with me to youth group tonight? It's at eight."

Emma bit her lip. By that time, she usually had her Daffy Duck pajamas on. Plus, she had to start reading *Lonesome Dove* for her book report. "I was just going to read tonight."

"There are lots of guys from other schools. I thought you might be interested."

Emma wondered what Rachel wanted more: a couple she and Tim could double-date with, or not to be the only one who picked up a date at church. "I don't think so."

"Come on, Emma. Just try. You might actually have fun. I thought that's what you wanted."

"It is." She remembered the toothy smiles of the Mexican kids in the courtyard. "Wait for me in the parking lot, okay?"

Her dad and Mattie came in from the backyard, each carrying four red blooms. "Ingrid Bergman is early," he said. "Look at that color." The crimson blossoms matched the SeedCorp logo embroidered on his white polo shirt.

"I have to go. See you tonight." When Emma hung up with Rachel, she turned to her mom. "I need the car later. Is that okay?"

"Where are you going?" Her mom lifted the lid of the waffle iron and forked out a perfectly browned waffle.

"Rachel invited me to her youth group."

Her dad filled the iced-tea pitcher with water. "What church does she go to?"

"That's not a vase," her mom said. "What if I wanted to use that?"

"First Baptist," Emma said.

"I couldn't find a real vase."

Mattie reached for a waffle. "I want sprinkles on mine. Do we have any?"

"You can't have sprinkles for dinner," her mom said. "Em, I'll draw you a map after dinner." Every time Emma went somewhere new, she left with a hand-drawn map that kept her far away from streets like El Camino Rojo and Sobrante Street. *You can't be too careful*, her mom said. *People in this town get shot at the mall.* "The car has plenty of gas. And don't forget to park under a street light."

• • •

First Baptist was in South Malo Verde, the oldest and nicest neighborhood in town, full of sprawling brick houses and trees with sidewalk-buckling roots. The church was on a corner, with a lit marquee in front that said DON'T TELL GOD HOW BIG YOUR STORM IS, TELL THE STORM HOW BIG YOUR GOD IS.

When she pulled into the parking lot, she saw a back door propped open with a folding chair. Rachel's Kia was there, penned between two white pickup trucks. She parked as close as she could to it, even though there was no streetlight above the space she chose. Rachel was nowhere to be seen.

Emma looked toward the rectangular doorway. The night's inky darkness surrounded the one yolk-like source of light. She took a deep breath and walked toward it.

Inside, she found herself in a gymnasium with a polished hardwood floor and a basketball hoop at each end. *Shit*, she thought. Was "youth group" code for intramural sports? Rachel should have known better than to invite her *anywhere* to play basketball, especially on a weekend.

On the other side of the room, a few guys bounced a ball back and forth. A few more leaned against stacks of folding chairs. They were mostly white, except for a few Filipinos and one Asian guy.

"Em, there you are!" She turned to see Rachel's gleaming eyes and pink cheeks. Instead of her usual T-shirt and jeans, Rachel wore a fluffy floral skirt and white tank top.

"I looked for you in the parking lot."

"I was in the bathroom. Come on, let me introduce you to my friends here." She led Emma across the gym to a group of girls standing in the corner. "Emma, this is Tina, Madison, and Carmen."

"Hi," Emma said. "I'll probably forget your names."

"Do you go to school with Rachel?" Madison asked. Her hair was three or four different colors from root to tip, ranging from dark brown to white blonde.

Emma nodded. "We met in middle school."

"So you were there?" Tall and thin, Tina had blunt-cut bangs and skin with the same blue undertone as one-percent milk. "When Tim punched out that guy?"

"Yeah, except he didn't actually punch anyone out."

"He was going to," Rachel said. "He was defending me."

"He was defending him*self*. And you never told us if he got suspended."

"Suspended?" Carmen asked. "Doesn't that mean he can't go to prom?"

"My dad's looking into it."

"Who's your dad?"

"A lawyer. The kind you don't want to piss off."

Emma bit her lip. Rachel's dad was a patent lawyer.

"Hey, have you guys seen Tim?" Rachel asked, turning her head to scan the room. "I want to say hi."

"What about me?" Emma asked.

"I'll introduce you to Owen. Come on."

Once again, Emma followed Rachel across the gym. She tapped her finger against her chin, wondering how much of her healing zit was still visible. "Who's Owen?"

"You'll see." Rachel stopped in front of a boy standing alone in the far corner, barely taller than Emma. He had pale grey eyes, an overbite, and shaggy brown hair, thinner and less curly than Dan's. He wore a long-sleeved black thermal under a navy T-shirt. "Hi, Owen."

"Who are you?" he said.

"See?" Rachel turned to Emma. "He has a weird sense of humor, just like you."

"Owen, this is Emma. Why don't you guys talk while I go say hi to Tim? I'll be back in a few minutes."

Emma stared, wondering why Rachel had chosen Owen. His eyes were bright but cold, and she couldn't picture him with a smile. "Sorry you got stuck being my babysitter."

"Happens all the time."

"Why?"

"I don't know, but it's good practice for the day someone trusts me with something worth stealing."

Emma watched Rachel cross the floor, to the group of guys gathered in the far corner. Tim stood in the back of the pack, wearing a cowboy hat. The hat made the contrast between his bronze skin and pale hair vanish, which was the part of his appearance that bothered her. Suddenly, she understood Rachel's attraction. "I don't trust anyone," she said.

"You've never been here before."

Across the basketball court, Rachel stood with her weight on one leg, hip jutted out. When she laughed, she reached out and put a hand on Tim's bare arm. "Safe to say I'm not coming back, either."

"Why not?"

"The sign outside creeped me out." Emma turned back to Owen. His lashes were long like Dan's, but they didn't have glossy silver tips. It seemed like every guy on the planet had better lashes than she did. "Why do you come here?"

"Good place to find out what I'm up against."

"I don't want to know."

"You should always want to know." He followed Emma's gaze and sighed. "Stop looking over there. She's not coming back."

"I know."

The door at the far end of the gym opened and a pudgy man wearing glasses and pleated shorts emerged. His dark hair was cut short over his ears and forehead, but it curled down the back of his neck — a mullet. Looking at it made her want to get a pair of scissors and cut it off.

"Okay, everyone!" he said. "Welcome! Come on over so we can get started."

Owen pushed himself off the wall and shuffled toward the pudgy man, hands in his pockets. Emma followed. Nothing about the night made sense. Rachel's dad wasn't a flesh-eating lawyer. Tim threw a punch to defend himself, not Rachel. Wasn't it against the general idea to tell so many lies in a church?

"Huddle in so we can pray." The youth minister held out his arms as if he could embrace everyone present. The kids around her bowed their heads and Emma followed suit, studying the cleanliness of everyone's shoes. Not surprisingly, hers and Owen's were the worst.

"Dear Lord," the youth minister said, "we thank you for your many blessings. Thank you for opening the hearts and minds of our youth, thank you for providing a place where they can come and learn about your holy grace. Help us in our walk with you, Lord. We all need you in our lives — "

Someone said, "Amen."

" — and I know it's hard for these kids to believe in you in a world that tells them you don't exist. But you do, and we're going to help them see it. All things are possible through you, Lord Jesus. May your peace and blessing be upon us as we worship and praise you in your almighty father's name. Amen."

"Amen," the crowd repeated.

"Amen," Emma said. She wondered what would happen if she asked God to let her ace the chemistry test. The paper with her answers on it was already in Mr. Lopez's possession. Maybe she had to ask before the test? *It can't work like that*, she thought. There was no way God was just an office manager, rubber-stamping prayer requests like Michael Scott on *The Office*.

After the "amen," everyone floated back to their familiar orbits. Owen trudged back into his corner, one leg crossed in front of the other. She felt his eyes on her and turned her back to protect her face from his grey-eyed scrutiny.

"Hey," Rachel said, jostling her elbow. "You okay?"

"I guess so."

"Did you like Owen?"

"He tells the truth."

"Why don't you go talk to him again?"

Emma looked at her friend. "Tell me why you really invited me here."

"It's a church, Emma. There's no motive except to be a better person."

I don't believe you, she thought. "I have to go. I'll see you at school." She reached into her pocket for the car keys.

"Emma, wait." Rachel reached out and touched her arm. "Remember when you said you wished everything was over? I just wanted you to see there's more to life than school." Her cheeks bloomed, making her freckles invisible. "Via has art. I have church. What do you have?"

"My family." She walked to the door, still feeling a prickle between her shoulder blades. *Owen*, she thought. With her lips clamped shut, she held her breath and hoped Rachel wouldn't ask her to come back.

In the parking lot, she heaved herself into the Buick's driver's seat. She slid the key into the ignition, but an uncomfortable thought held her hand in place. Maybe Rachel was right. Maybe her life was empty. Maybe she'd never write a story worth reading because she never did anything worth writing down. Maybe she was the only one looking backward when everyone else was looking forward.

Emma pulled the key from the ignition. "Shit," she said. "Shit, shit, shit."

• • •

Forty minutes later, when the side door to the parking lot opened, she watched the flood of participants emerge in the rearview mirror. Owen bypassed the parking lot entirely and walked across the church's front lawn on foot. She spotted Tina and Madison as they got into their cars and drove away. Carmen stood on the curb and waited for someone to come pick her up.

A couple of Tim's friends got into the same pickup truck, which meant one of them was over eighteen or they didn't care if they broke the law. She turned in her seat and saw the youth pastor pull back the folding chair that propped the door open.

Where is she? Emma thought. The parking lot was almost empty — only four cars left, plus the Buick.

Then the door opened again, and two shadowy figures emerged, one with a waterfall of red hair. Emma slouched in her seat and watched them in the side mirror. The taller figure, Tim, bent down and kissed Rachel. Rachel's fingers came up around his arms, squeezing his biceps.

The blood rushed to Emma's face. What was she supposed to do now? If she waited until they were done, Rachel would know she'd been seen. If she left now, Rachel would recognize the car and think Emma had stayed to spy on her.

Emma slid lower in the seat and rested her face on the door, at eye level with the rearview mirror. Tim put his hands on Rachel's shoulders. One finger slipped under the strap of her tank top and slid it off.

"Stop," Rachel said, giggling and pretending to swat his

hand away. She left the strap of her tank top where it fell. His hand caressed her bare shoulder. Rachel tilted her head and Tim buried his face in her neck.

Emma's stomach began to tingle. She wondered what it felt like to have a boy touch her shoulder, to push off part of her clothing. What if she tasted like sweat? What if it tickled? She closed her eyes for a moment and imagined Dan's long fingers tracing her collarbone. The tingle in her stomach turned into something sharper and deeper, warming her from the inside out. *It doesn't tickle*, she thought.

In the rearview mirror, she saw Rachel's mouth fall open in a gasp. When Tim lifted his head, their mouths came together, heads bobbing back and forth. Rachel stepped back against the wall and Tim pressed the length of his body against hers.

The heat in her belly was starting to make her uncomfortable. She shifted in her seat, wanting to hide her face even though no one was looking at it. She took a deep breath, in through her nose and out through her mouth. When she exhaled, she heard another car start its engine.

She peeked her head above the door frame to see who it was. The car was on her right, further from Rachel and Tim. White and rounded, it was some expensive car she'd seen in a commercial the other night. The driver had parked under a street light so she got a clear glimpse of him as he reversed out of the space.

Short blond hair, glasses, freckles — Emma recognized him instantly.

Rachel's dad.

CHAPTER EIGHT

Monday, March 31

ELVIRA STARED LONGINGLY AT THE empty badminton court next to them. Rafael was absent, and Juan sat on the bench, taking turns in an awkward threesome with John Betts and Raymond Choi. "What a waste of make-up."

Emma glanced at her partner's face, with its drawn-on eyebrows and lashes thick as a tarantula's leg. "Did you do something different?"

"No. That's why it's a waste."

The class had progressed from a singles tournament to a doubles tournament. Emma hastily accepted Elvira's offer of partnership, and they now faced their first opponents: Marion Bates and Yesenia Santos.

Across the net, Marion shouted the score and served the birdie like she was spiking a volleyball. Marion was five-eleven, the center for the girls' JV basketball team. The birdie whistled down at Emma and she swung. Her racket tipped it, but it fell to the floor well short of the net. As she trotted to retrieve it, Marion pulled her phone from her sweatshirt pocket, her fingers flying to send a text.

"Incoming," Emma said, tossing the birdie back over the net for another serve.

"I should have known he wouldn't be here," Elvira said. "His brother's a *Sureño*."

A nervous stab tickled Emma's stomach. "What does that have to do with it?"

"One of their shot callers got hit the other night. Maybe it was his brother."

The carniceria, Emma thought. *The body on the pavement.* All she'd seen on the news was an upturned hand, fingers limp, lying on blood-spattered asphalt. Below the wrist, she'd seen a tattoo — SUR on one wrist and 13 on the other.

"Four-two service," Marion called as she delivered another air strike in their direction.

Elvira leaned forward, racket down. The birdie bounced off its strings and back over the net. "When things get like this, you never know."

"Like what?"

"Like a war."

Yesenia turned her racket sideways and lobbed the birdie back over the net. Elvira backed up two steps and lobbed it back.

"Is that really what it's like out there?" Emma asked.

"Worse. In a war, they fight on a battlefield."

My dad's out there, she thought. *And there's nothing I can do to help him.*

Yesenia raced up and spiked the birdie. Emma and Elvira watched it fall to the floor with a rubber-tipped thunk.

"Come on, you guys," Yesenia said. "You're not even trying."

•••

The ranchero music commenced at 12:01 p.m. Across the courtyard, four members of the debate club stood behind a hot dog cart, each in a blue blazer and yellow tie. HOT DOG, WE'RE GOING TO STATE, their banner read. Via sank her teeth into one of their offerings and a glop of mustard plummeted onto her jeans. "Mother*fucker*," she swore, mopping up the mess with a napkin. "Two dollars for a hot dog and all I get is indigestion and laundry. Tell me you're having something better than lips and assholes for lunch."

"I had a candy bar last period," Rachel said.

On Rachel's neck, beneath the edge of a fluffy scarf, Emma spotted the feathered purple edge of a hickey. Memories burst like fireworks in her mind: Rachel and Tim, his face buried in her neck, his hips pressing her up against the wall. She tore open her lunch bag and sank her teeth into her thin turkey sandwich.

"So," Rachel said, adjusting the neck of her scarf. "How did you like Owen?"

"Owen?" Via asked. "Who's Owen?"

"I introduced him to Emma at youth group last night."

"What the hell? Are you one of *them* now?"

"I'm just me," Emma said. "And I left early."

"You should have stayed," Rachel said. "Everyone wondered where you were."

No one wondered, Emma thought. She looked across the table toward the group of Mexican kids standing near the speakers. The boy with the mole stood next to a different girl today. This girl had a partially shaved head, with wild red streaks woven through the black. Most of them were laughing, dancing, or scrolling on their phones. They didn't look like kids whose siblings or parents were in a war zone. *Please let Dad be okay*, she thought. *Please let Elvira be wrong.*

Emma reached for whatever was left in her bag — apple slices and a plastic container of peanut butter — and dipped the biggest slice.

"Oh, my God," Via groaned. "Can your mom adopt me?"

"Dad's holding out for a boy."

"What a coincidence. Mine, too."

Rachel sat up straight. "Why did you look at me when you said that?"

"Because our dads are fucking deadbeats and Emma's dad actually lives with her. I forgot what that's like."

"Me too," Rachel said, eyes drifting to the prom ticket table.

Emma put down her apple slice. "Your dad's not a deadbeat. You said last night you talked to him about Tim."

"I take it he got suspended?" Via said, licking ketchup from her thumbnail.

Rachel nodded. "My dad's going to fix it."

"What can he do?"

"Write a letter or something. Lawyers always have a way."

"At least your dad responds when you ask for something. Mine doesn't know I'm alive." Via pointed at Emma's plastic container. "What kind of peanut butter is that?"

"The cheapest." Emma shoved another apple slice in her mouth to keep from having to say anything else. All she could see was Rachel's head tilted back and her mouth hanging open, while her dad turned on his car and drove away. *He was there and you didn't even know*, she thought. *You didn't even look for him, or for me.*

The words were there, aching to tumble out of her mouth. They rushed up from her gut, gaining speed and strength as they went. "I have to study," she mumbled, reaching into her backpack for a book. It didn't matter which one she pulled out. All that mattered was that she kept her mouth shut for the rest of lunch.

"Hey, what's our chem homework?" Via asked.

"Would it kill you to write this stuff down?"

"That's why I have you." Via grinned. No matter how much coffee she drank, her teeth gleamed titanium white against her brown skin.

Emma sighed. "Chapter 13.4 to 13.6, problem set two."

The courtyard's loudspeakers hissed and popped as the student DJ changed tracks. A band of mariachi singers began to yodel in piercing falsettos. Some of the Mexican kids in the courtyard began to imitate the singers, shrieking like air raid sirens. Others posed for the girls snapping pictures on their phones, tilting their heads back and splaying their fingers in gang signs Emma couldn't read.

Suddenly, she understood what Elvira had been trying to tell her. The pushing in the hallways, the gang signs in the courtyard . . . sometimes you didn't need a gun to fight. She glanced back at the boy posing for a photo and sketched his sign in the margin of her chemistry book. She turned the page before Rachel or Via could ask why.

• • •

That afternoon, she did her pre-calculus homework first. It didn't take long to realize she and composite functions were never, ever going to get along. She stared at the first problem in the set:

$$\textit{Find } (f \circ g)(x) \textit{ and the domain of } f \circ g\!:$$
$$f(x) = (x\text{-}1)/(x\text{+}3), \; g(x) = (x\text{+}1)/(x\text{-}3)$$

"Seriously?" she growled, glaring at the vomitous mass of letters and numbers. She still had to go over her French vocabulary, do her chemistry problem set, and keep reading McMurtry. There wasn't time to understand something so opaque it was literally spelled *fog*. She only had time to guess, collect partial credit, and move on.

An hour and a half later, she'd wiped out the pre-calculus and French and stopped to massage her pounding temples. Logarithms, masculine versus feminine nouns, indefinite article contractions, functions, exponents, graphs, irregular verbs . . .if each new piece of information had actual physical weight, her brain would drop like an overloaded cargo elevator, squish her eyes out through their sockets, shatter the canals between her ears, nose, and throat, and impale itself on her spine.

Her stomach growled and she looked at her watch. It was 6:22 p.m., almost half an hour past the time when her dad usually came home. "Mom," she called. "What's for dinner?"

Her mom stepped into the dining room doorway, patting her hands dry with a red dish towel. "Tuna chip casserole. I'll serve up as soon as I hear the truck. You can keep working."

"I don't want to keep working," she said as she opened her chemistry book to *Chapter 13, Acids and Bases*. What did any of it matter when she wasn't going to be a science major? If an apple fell from a tree, she didn't care what invisible forces controlled the direction and speed of the apple's fall. She cared how fast she could pick it up and eat it.

Her sixth-grade teacher had had a poster on the wall, pitting the word "history" against "herstory." But complaining about the word itself was as useful as banging your head against a brick wall and then asking who put the wall there. *Sometimes,* she thought, *grown-ups' entire lives were designed to keep them from doing anything real.*

Emma looked at her chemistry book and realized it was herstory in sheep's clothing. She slammed it shut and headed for the kitchen as her mom pulled the casserole from the oven.

A yellowed three-by-five recipe card sat on the counter, written in Great-Grandma Jennings's loopy cursive. Emma knew for a fact that Great-Grandma Jennings didn't know anything about covalent bonds, but there were seven scarves and two sweaters she'd knitted tucked away in the cedar chest upstairs, intact seventy-five years after she made them. And whether Emma liked it or not (*not*), people still used her tuna casserole recipe decades after she wrote it down. That had to count for something.

The rapid fire of her sister's feet pounded the stairs. "I finally heard the truck!" she said. "I'm starving."

"Don't say you're starving if it's not true." Her mom carried the casserole to the table and setting it on a raffia potholder. "Let your father serve up first."

"Gladly," Emma said, shrinking from the steaming pile of mush. When she heard her dad's footsteps in the hall, she turned to tell him how glad she was that he would eat her portion for her. "Dad, thank goodness you're — "

She stopped. His shirt was wrinkled and untucked. The top two buttons were gone, their white threads caterpilling blindly into the air. The neck of both his shirt and undershirt snaked sideways, stretched until they sagged. A smear of something dark slid across his sleeve.

"Roger," her mom said.

"Dish up," he said softly, retreating into the half-bath near the garage. Emma heard the door shut and the faucet turn on full blast.

Mattie wrapped her arms around her sides. "Mom."

"Don't talk." Emma's mom pulled out her chair. "Sit."

"But what —"

"I said sit."

Emma's fingers gripped the back of her chair. No matter how many shifts he'd worked at SeedCorp, he always came home with his shirt tucked in and a wink for each of them. Of course, something could have happened to his truck. But the smear on his sleeve wasn't grease, and it hadn't gotten on his hands or face. She didn't know anything about cars, but there had to be a reason mechanics wore coveralls.

Her mom piled his plate with three scoops of casserole, two spoons of baked carrots, and two spoons of salad. "I told you to sit," she said.

Emma sank into her chair and slid her palms beneath her thighs. She imagined her dad breaking up a mugging or helping someone who got hurt. There were plenty of reasonable explanations for that reddish smear on his sleeve.

She met Mattie's eyes across the table and nodded in silent encouragement. *It'll be all right*, she wanted to say. *It always is.*

Emma kept her eyes on the scoop of cooling tuna chip casserole. A few minutes ago, having to smell warm tuna had been the worst thing about this night.

Finally, they heard the faucet shut off, followed by a squeak from the circular towel ring mounted on the wall. The door handle turned, and her dad's rubber-soled shoes padded onto the tile. He'd rolled up both shirt sleeves, making the rust-colored smear invisible. He sat down at the table and picked up his fork. Her mom followed suit, and then Mattie.

Emma stared at the casserole. She wanted to eat it because everyone else was eating it, but tuna casserole made her stomach revolt under the best of circumstances. She speared a carrot slice, but it got stuck in her throat and she had to hold back a cough. She didn't want to make a noise or do anything that would associate her with this moment in their collective memory.

"Roger," her mom said, holding her knife like a scalpel.

"It's nothing."

"What happened?"

"I told you, it's nothing." He chewed slowly, the way Emma had when her braces were tightened. "I knocked on a few doors at a time, then moved the truck."

"On El Camino Rojo," Emma said.

He nodded. Black and white stubble dotted his cheeks and chin, as if a child had drawn on a beard and only partially erased it. "I had my badge," he said, patting his chest. "I show it to people so they know it's safe to open their doors. But I guess not everyone feels that way."

Emma saw Mattie open her mouth and kicked her under the table.

"A man came up to me and said I looked like a cop. He told me to go away. Everyone there was getting too nervous." He scooped a forkful of salad. One leaf, stacked with cheese cubes, fell off the fork and splattered back onto the plate.

Emma pushed the tuna chip casserole to the corner of her plate. When they interviewed cops on the news, they always behaved a certain way, using words like "victims" instead of "people," "suspects" instead of "murderers." Their voices were loud and they looked over the reporter's shoulder while they talked. Nothing moved them. Her dad spoke gently and always looked you in the eye.

No one could think he was a cop.

She waited for him to finish the story, but he didn't say anything about how the buttons from his shirt came off. A sick, cold feeling spread through her chest, far worse than the kind of stress she felt over a test or paper. That kind of stress had an end point that gave it shape and made it manageable. She could shove it in a box, put a lid on it, and tape it shut. This feeling had no shape or limit, like a pre-calculus graph that ran forever, always approaching an axis but never actually touching it.

Her mom took a bite of casserole and chewed methodically. After she swallowed, she said, "Did you turn in the paperwork I gave you?"

"After the first round of inquiries. Not now."

"You didn't even ask?"

Her dad bent his head and Emma saw his fragile white scalp beneath the grey hair. Suddenly, a world of evil opened up before her. Her dad was *human*. The man who had picked her up from the sandbox when she was three, held her on his shoulders, and danced her around until she felt like she was flying.

The man who had put her in some sort of baby sling and carted her up onto the roof of their first house, where Mom snapped a picture of them from the front lawn. The man who had taught her how to do everything she was afraid of, from riding a bike to bumping a volleyball. He was the one who made her feel like fearless could be normal. If that wasn't true, if he was fallible, then everything she thought was real life had only been luck.

"I can't," he said.

"Why not?" Mattie asked.

He turned his head to look at her. The smile on his lips was thin and scared. "We need this. I can't complain after only a few days."

"But it's dangerous."

"Yes." He nodded. "Lots of things are."

"I want you to ask for a transfer," her mom said.

"Sharon."

"Roger."

He scooted his chair back and carried his plate to the kitchen island. He used the red plastic tongs to put two handfuls of salad on his plate. "The girls want to talk about something else."

Her mom leaned back in her chair and crossed her arms over her chest. She wouldn't be any help.

Emma breathed in deeply. "Dad, do you want my casserole?"

His dark eyes looked straight into hers. "I'd like that."

She scraped her scoop onto his plate and tried to think of something else to say. "We started reading a new book in English class. We're done with Gatsby."

"Oh?"

"*Of Mice and Men.*"

"Where does that one take place?"

"Here, I think. The books got passed out today. I'll start reading tomorrow."

"What do you have in the meantime?"

"*Lonesome Dove*, still."

"You're not done yet?"

"Dad, it's like eight hundred pages."

"You read fast."

"I have other classes."

Everything she said was pointless. No one wanted to hear it, including her father. But she couldn't let him sit there, contemplating a world that had turned ugly in a day. She thought of Scheherazade, who had spun beautiful stories because her life depended on it. Those stories had saved her — not a weapon or the ability to flee. It was her brain and her voice. With every word, Scheherazade had created a brick. She mortared those bricks into place around her, to the point where no one could hurt her. Knives couldn't pierce it, and poison couldn't seep through it.

I can do that, too, Emma thought.

She babbled about school as if her father's life depended on it, until her mom stood up to clear the table. When she took his plate, her dad went straight upstairs and made no noise. Long after the dishes were dry, her mom stood at the kitchen sink, staring at the rose bushes in the backyard, her pale hands pruning in the soapy water.

CHAPTER NINE

Tuesday, April 1

EMMA TURNED THE COMBINATION LOCK slowly, afraid she'd miscount. She'd already washed her hair with body wash instead of shampoo and put on two different socks.

Most mornings, her dad sat at the kitchen table and read the paper while she and Mattie poured their cereal. Mattie teased him that nobody got actual papers anymore, and he said he didn't see how anyone could read anything on a two-inch screen. But that morning the table was empty, except for a note tucked under her placemat:

Em, everything is going to be fine.
See you tonite.
Love, DAD.

That was how he always signed off, with rounded block capitals, partially eroded like the rocks of Stonehenge. Her locker clicked open and she closed her eyes, leaning her forehead against the cool metal. Girls in Afghanistan worried about being murdered on the way to school. This was nothing. *You're lucky*, she told herself. *You are so goddamn lucky.*

"So," she heard. "We're getting our chem tests back today."

Emma jumped, banging her head against the locker. "Shit. You scared me."

"I always scare you. It's my thing." Dan tilted his head. "I think you're the only person I've ever managed to sneak up on. I feel pretty good about that. You aren't mad, are you?" His hair looked wet at the tips, gleaming under the fluorescent lights.

"I aim to please."

"Really?"

"No."

"It's better that way." He pressed one black flip-flop against the locker beneath hers and leaned forward, stretching his calf muscle. There was a freckle on his big toe, just beneath the knuckle fold. It was perfectly circular, like a drop of black ink. "How'd you do on the test?"

"I don't know."

He peeked into her locker. "Why do you have so much stuff? What is all this?"

A magnetic pencil holder hung on the inside of the door. She'd tucked a picture of herself and Rachel and Via into the top, and a picture of her family under the bottom. The photos had been screened to avoid squinty eyes, red eyes, yellow teeth, double chins, unflattering profile shots, or any pose where her legs looked fat. "Books. I have lots."

He pointed at the photo. "Are those your parents?"

Her fingers tugged it from the pencil holder's magnetic grip. "We were at the Boardwalk."

He took it from her, holding it as close to the edges as possible. She and her family stood in front of the carousel. For the first time ever, she'd successfully completed the ring toss: a precision-timing maneuver that involved grabbing metal rings from a chute and heaving them at a small hole in the wall.

With her sunglasses low over her sweaty nose, she stood sandwiched between Mattie and her parents. Her knees looked like biscuit dough, but her hair was in a cute ponytail and, for once, she looked happy.

"You look happy," Dan said. "Most days you look depressed."

"Have you ever been to the Boardwalk?"

"Once, when I was a kid."

"You never went back?"

Dan shrugged.

"But they have funnel cake."

"You say the weirdest things sometimes."

"Who doesn't want funnel cake?" She snatched the photo from his grasp.

"Don't be mad. You still haven't told me why you're so set on going to USC."

"It's like funnel cake. You won't get it."

"I swear I'll get it. If I don't, I'll just keep my mouth shut."

"Well, that makes for a great conversation."

"I'm serious." He leaned forward, blocking access to her books. She looked into his eyes, the same color as her mom's martini olives.

A freshman with an enormous backpack shoved past her, scraping her arm. "I need my books," she said.

"We have time."

"I like to get to class early."

"Only nerds go to class this early."

"What do you think I am?"

"I'm talking pocket protector nerd. Library on a Friday night kind of nerd."

"I have to go," she said, reaching around him.

"No, you don't."

"I do."

"Stay." He put his hand on her arm. Through her thin sweater, she felt an instant rush of warmth radiating from his skin. "Talk to me."

"Why?"

"Because talking to you isn't like talking to anyone else in the whole world."

His hand rested on her forearm. Emma let her fingers slide down the fuzzy spine of her grocery bag book cover. But as her arm fell to her side, so did his. *Put it back*, she wanted to say.

"So, are you going to tell me?"

"What?"

"USC."

Emma sighed. Telling him would only embarrass her more. But maybe if she did, he'd put his hand on her arm again. An arm was almost a hand. If there was some way to parlay an arm-touch into a hand-hold, she'd be in new territory. *Rachel* territory. What was pride compared to that? "Fine," she said. "Have you ever heard that '80s song, 'A Little Respect'? They play it on Kool 105 during the all-request lunch hour. My mom requests it, like, every day.”

“I don't know.” The right corner of his lip curled toward his cheek. “How does it go?”

“Nice try. The point is, I heard it years ago in the car, when my mom was taking me to the library. She said it was her favorite when she was younger. But I couldn't figure out what this one part in the lyrics said. So when I got to the library, I looked up the name of the group. The DJ called them Erasure, but that name didn't match any CDs the library had. It only matched the title of a book.”

“What was the book?”

“*Erasure.* Do you have any idea how the library works at all?”

Dan smiled. “Not really, no.”

“It was by a guy called Percival Everett. So I read it. And when I did, I knew what I wanted to do and where I wanted to go to school.”

“Does Percival Everett go there?”

“He teaches there. I want him to teach me how to write.”

“You know how to write.”

She shook her head. “Not stupid essays for class. I want to write something real. I think I could. I just don't know how.”

“Have you tried?”

A tinny bell rang in each of the school's six hallways. Normally, she'd be in her seat in Mr. Parker's class by now. Her heart began to pound as she reached for a book. “We're going to be late.”

“That's just the first bell. There's two, you know.”

“I know how the bell system works.”

“I'm teasing you, Em.”

"Okay, no joke, I really have to go now. See you in chemistry," she said, slamming her locker and speed-walking down the hall. When she arrived in history class, pink-cheeked and out of breath, she slipped her backpack off her shoulder. It took her at least a minute to realize what had just happened.

Dan had shortened her name.

Em.

No one but her parents ever called her that. She'd never heard what it sounded like from the lips of someone not related to her. It sounded like home.

• • •

"The Monroe Doctrine," Mr. Parker said, writing the words on the chalkboard and underlining them twice, "supported the idea of manifest destiny. President James Monroe, the so-called War Hawks in Congress, and a majority of the American people all believed it was America's destiny to rule everything between Kentucky and the Pacific. It didn't matter that there were Native Americans already living there, or Spanish settlements in Florida and the Southwest." He paused. "In a lot of ways, we've never changed."

Mr. Parker was tall and thin, with short dark hair and wire-rimmed glasses. His defining characteristic was the big silver buckle on the belt he used to hold up his black jeans. He'd been in the army before becoming a teacher, and on rainy days when he didn't feel like lecturing, he told them stories about Afghanistan and the desert and how far shrapnel flew when a mortar round detonated in your camp.

Rachel sat in front of her, long red ponytail coiled onto Emma's writing surface. She brushed it gently out of the way so she could turn over her paper. Rachel put her right arm to the back of her neck, pretending to scratch an itch, and dropped a folded piece of paper onto Emma's desk. Her lack of a cell phone forced her friends to go old-school in their methods of intra-class communication. Emma unfolded the note slowly.

Saw you with Dan at the lockers. Do you think he's going to ask you to prom?

Emma bit her lip. As much as she might wish otherwise, it was comic-book improbable, like digging a treasure chest of Spanish gold out of the backyard.

A second piece of paper flew over her shoulder onto the desk, followed by a sharp poke in the spine from Via's pen.

A sophomore? Really?

Emma shoved both notes beneath her binder. Let them ask her face-to-face. There were more important things to do now, like write down why Monroe, a guy who'd lived through the American Revolution, thought it was okay to bully people who were just trying to survive in a wilderness. She watched the classroom clock tick its way to 9:00 a.m. Her friends would pounce as soon as Mr. Parker set down his chalk — the signal his lecture was over.

Via struck first, as soon as the chalk hit the silver rail beneath the board. "Hey, you didn't answer my note."

"Mine either," Rachel said, turning around. "What happened with Dan?"

"We talked."

Rachel rolled her eyes. "It's never just talking when there are prom tickets on sale."

"What's so interesting about that underage beanpole?" Via asked. "And what does he see in you? I'm kind of stumped, to be honest."

Emma flung her backpack over her shoulder. "Sometimes I lend him paper. That's it."

"So he's just using you. I guess that makes sense."

"People only date someone in a younger class when they can't get anyone in their own to notice them. You just need to try harder." Rachel led the way out of the classroom, pulling her ponytail out from under backpack and draping it across her shoulder. "What about Owen?"

"What about him?"

"No," Via said. "You can't hook up with someone you met in a church."

Rachel sighed. "Why are you so hung up on this? A lot of nice, normal people go to church."

"It doesn't matter," Emma said. "I'm not hooking up with anyone."

"But you want to." Rachel lowered her eyes. A guy wearing a Stanford T-shirt squeezed past her in the hall and she turned sideways to watch him go.

"I saw Dan touch your arm." Via wrapped thin fingers around the padded straps of her backpack. "Second base is only a few inches away."

"I wouldn't know. I think I'm still in the batter's box," Emma said

Via snorted. "You don't even know what to do with a bat."

"Are we still talking about sports?"

"Never answer a question with a question," Rachel said. "My dad says lawyers only do that when they need to distract the jury."

"Distract them from what?"

"The truth."

"What truth?"

"You're not listening."

"Look," Via said. "I've gone out with guys and Rachel's gone out with guys. You've never even come close. We're just trying to figure out what's different."

Emma looked at the fluorescent light hanging above them in the hallway. Two cords suspended it from the grey ceiling. It swayed from side to side when the door at the end of the hallway opened, but the sway didn't mean it was going to fall down. "Maybe I'm what's different."

She pushed past a JV football player and put a few feet of distance between herself and her friends. If they were going to give her a scarlet "S" for consorting with a sophomore, she at least wanted a chance to earn it.

• • •

When she got to chemistry class, she unzipped her backpack and took out her binder and book. Dan had said they were getting their tests back today. How did he know? Was it a bad sign they were coming back so quickly? She crossed her left leg over her right and tapped her toe against the empty seat in front of her.

A minute later, Dan shuffled into class behind Rena Hao, the shortest girl in the junior class. "Hey," he said, sliding his long body into a desk built for short people. His left leg sprawled into the aisle and Emma wondered what he'd do if he got stuck in the middle seat on a plane.

Another boy on the water polo team stepped over Dan's legs as he marched to the back of the class, punching Dan on the shoulder as he passed. "Dick," Dan said.

"Are those guys on the team really your friends?" she said.

"Sure."

"Do they ever say things that sound like a joke, but they actually mean the mean thing that's underneath the joke?"

Dan's eyes flickered across the classroom, to Via and Rachel's empty desks. "Being friends with a girl is the hardest thing in the world to do."

She pictured him hanging out with an ex-girlfriend, going to coffee shops and superhero movies, finishing each other's sentences and popcorn. "How do you know?"

"I have sisters."

As quickly as it formed, the vision of a popcorn-stealing ex-girlfriend dissolved. She smiled with the relief of not having to compete with the memory of someone who liked coffee and Zack Snyder. Her eyes floated down his leg to the omnipresent black flip-flops. "Has anyone ever told you that you have really hairy toes?"

"Don't you?" He leaned forward and reached for her foot.

"No!" The thought of him sliding off her black flats and seeing unpolished toenails, dry skin, and monstrous calluses was too mortifying to contemplate. She swung both feet into the aisle on her left, out of his reach.

"Cheater."

"I prefer 'conscientious adopter of non-traditional rules.'"

He laughed and shook his head. "You're gonna kick my ass."

"You're out of your mind."

"Put your money where your mouth is?" He sat up straight and held out his hand. "If I win, you have to come to my water polo match on Saturday."

"Okay. But if I win, you have to come to the library with me on a Friday night."

His face froze and so did the blood in her veins.

"I'm sorry, you don't have to do that. I take it back."

"Why? You're not gonna win."

Emma blinked. "You're taking the bet?"

He held out his hand. "Shake n' bake, West."

She placed her palm against his and shook. "Shake n' bake."

As their hands clasped across the aisle, Via and Rachel's shadows broke the silhouette of light in the doorframe. "Oh please," Via said. "This is how communicable disease is spread."

Emma slipped her hand out of Dan's grasp and slid down in her seat. *Is not*, she thought, flashing back to Mr. MacDonald's seventh-grade science class.

Dan shook his head. "I've heard that tone before. I hope you have a big shovel."

"Thanks," she said as Mr. Lopez barreled into the room. "Thanks a lot."

Mr. Lopez clutched a stack of paper under his arm and she wondered if it was possible to get a paper cut through a polo shirt. "Sorry I'm late. There was a glitch in my grading software."

Yeah, Emma thought. *It gave you an error message when the entire class failed.*

Mr. Lopez drew his bushy brows together and took a breath. He opened his mouth, shaped a word, and then gave up. He shook his head and stared at the floor. "I'm disappointed in you guys. We went over this stuff for weeks. I don't know if it's burnout or the prom or what, but you have to do better." He hefted the stack of paper and walked up and down the narrow aisles, dropping off tests and mouthing each student's name as he did. "West," he grunted, floating her four stapled pages back to her.

She snatched them up to make sure her eyes hadn't deceived her. A-.

"MacLee-odd." Mr. Lopez mispronounced Dan's name and dropped his paper without ceremony. Dan grabbed it up faster than she had.

"All right," he said, spinning in his seat to face her. "On the count of three."

Emma nodded.

"One, two, three."

She held up her test and peeked around it. He held up a stone-cold B+.

"Highlander," his water polo teammate hissed. "What'd you get?"

Dan turned his test sideways to show him. "Shit, man, you kicked my ass," the boy said.

"And she kicked mine," Dan said, pointing at Emma.

Emma grinned. She couldn't help it. She'd only scored higher than Dan on three quizzes the whole year. One on balancing chemical equations, one on orbital diagrams, and one on wave mechanics. On everything else, he smoked her like a salmon. Something in the universe was on her side after all. She was going to get an A in chemistry, she was going to go see Dan's water polo match, and friends or not, she was going to go to the prom.

CHAPTER TEN

Tuesday, April 1

"**H**EY, EM," MATTIE SAID. "WHAT does 'forsooth' mean?" The two of them sat at the dining room table, working on homework before dinner. Emma had *Lonesome Dove* open in front of her, while Mattie struggled with *Romeo and Juliet*. At the end of the table sat today's offering from Martin Rodriguez: a stuffed bunny with a blue ribbon around its neck.

"It doesn't mean anything. It's like saying 'for real.'"

"Then why do they say it?" Mattie tossed down the paperback. "This sucks."

Emma picked up the book. "Is this where you were?" When Mattie nodded, she skimmed the scene. "Okay, right here, this is Juliet's dad asking where she is."

"Wait," Mattie said, scooting her chair next to Emma's. As Mattie leaned over her shoulder, Emma smelled something heavy and tropical—their coconut conditioner. She didn't understand why it clung to Mattie's hair but deserted hers five minutes after she hung up her wet shower towel. If there weren't baby pictures to prove it, she would think either she or Mattie was adopted. "Okay, now," Mattie said.

Emma ran her finger along the text as she translated. "Juliet's dad asks if she's gone to see Father Laurence. He says church will do her good because she's been misbehaving lately. Then Juliet comes back, and says she's sorry for acting up. She says she'll behave from here on out."

Mattie frowned. "But she's lying."

"How do you know?"

"She already took the sleeping potion from Friar Laurence. She doesn't care what her dad wants her to do."

"See, you understand more than you think."

"Why can't they just say what they mean?"

"Because Shakespeare had to sell tickets." Emma pointed at the rabbit. "What did you name it?"

"Bunnicula."

Emma smiled. "That's a good name."

In six weeks, Mattie would graduate eighth grade. Next year, they'd be at the same school. She hoped her classification as a socially toxic nerd wouldn't destroy Mattie's popularity. In middle school, smart kids were tolerated because you never knew who the next doctor, lawyer, sheriff, or president might be. By high school, most of that hope and goodwill had been erased.

She turned back to *Lonesome Dove*, wishing the characters were a bit more lonesome to cut down on the number of pages she had to read. When she heard her dad's truck pull into the driveway, she dog-eared her page and slammed the book shut.

"What's for dinner?" her dad asked as he opened the front door. "I'm starving."

"I saw cauliflower," Mattie said. "And Mom says don't say 'starving.'"

"Cauliflower. Yuck."

Emma glanced at a measuring cup of orange liquid sitting on the counter. "With cheese."

"That's more like it." He gripped the doorframe and used his toe to squeeze off his left shoe, then his right. "I'm going to wash up."

"Don't take long," her mom said. "The food's nice and hot." She pulled a glass baking dish from the oven. Four chicken breasts, covered with bread crumbs, hissed and sizzled as she set the dish on a trivet.

While her mom served up, Emma watched the dark-skinned news reporter on TV stand on a street corner, crime scene tape spun like a spiderweb behind him. When the video rolled, a Mexican woman sobbed and pointed to a chain-link fence surrounding a yard with dead grass and a garden hose so old it looked like a shed snakeskin.

The mug shot of a Mexican boy flashed onto the screen, his hair gelled stiffer than meringue. Tattoos covered his neck, branching toward his chest with the thick stems and fine arcs of Old English calligraphy. His black eyes were empty. Whatever he had been arrested for, he felt no regret.

The boy's name was Jesus. Emma didn't understand why Mexican mothers named their boys after the son of God. All it did was set them up for failure.

In the background, she heard her dad's footsteps pound down the stairs. His eyes went straight to the chain-link yard on TV. He sucked in his breath and balled his fists. Emma felt the movement in her bones, shearing through the muscle and tissue like a shock wave. He knew that lawn, that house, that corner, and he knew they meant danger. "Dad," she whispered.

"Turn it off," her mom snapped. "Now."

Emma reached for the remote and pressed the big green POWER button.

"Eat," her mom said. As they sat down, Emma's stomach growled, drowning in enzymes produced by hunger and fear. The cheese on her cauliflower rolled down the stalk and pooled against the chicken breast.

They slurred their way through grace, unable to adjust the rhythm to get it over with any faster. When it was over, her dad tucked his paper napkin into the collar of his dress shirt. He forked a piece of cauliflower and a drop of stoplight-yellow cheese splattered onto his sleeve.

"Roger," her mom sighed.

She stared at him, performing a silent count to five. Then she went to the sink, held a corner of the sponge under a dribble from the tap, and dabbed at the stain. Her dad sat, motionless, while she worked.

Emma looked away. Her mom hated stains. She hated scratches on the hardwood floor. She hated juice glasses being put on the right side of the top dishwasher shelf instead of the left.

"So," her dad said. "What did you guys do in school today?"

I fell in love, Emma thought. "I got an A- on my chem test."

"I knew you could do it." He raised his hand to give her a high five. More words crept up from the pit of her stomach, temporarily suspended in the blackness behind her throat. They were all there, jumbled like Scrabble tiles, but she couldn't sort them out in time. *Boy, test, Dan, pool, car.* She coughed and reached for her milk.

"How about you, Matt?"

"We did Act IV, Scene 1 of *Romeo and Juliet* in class."

"Was it fun?"

"No."

"I never really understood Shakespeare."

"Forsooth," Mattie said.

Emma tried to think of another antiquated word or phrase to answer with, but the only thing that popped into her mind was, *Yea, though I walk through the valley of the shadow of death.* She kept her mouth shut.

Mattie reached for the dish of peas. "How was work, Dad?"

"Fine." He shoveled a forkful of chicken into his mouth.

Her mom sliced her chicken breast into three rows, four bites each. "Did you ask for a transfer?"

"Mshgm."

"Don't talk with your mouth full," Mattie said. "Even I know that."

"He knows it, too." Her mom set her knife against the plate and the diamond in her ring caught the light, flashing blue and orange and silver, every color co-existing in one simple shape.

Emma felt the mood begin to slide into something unstable, a house on stilts on a cliff in the rain. She did the only thing she could think of to prop it up. "I might need the car on Saturday."

"For what?" her mom asked.

"School stuff."

"What school stuff?"

"A friend asked me to go to the water polo match."

"Rachel?"

"No." She knew she was going about this all wrong. Her mom had already offered money for a prom dress, which meant she was okay with the idea of there being someone to go with. But what if she insisted on meeting Dan first? What if Dan somehow didn't meet expectations? "Via has a crush on this guy on the water polo team. She wants to see a game, but her mom won't let her go unless she brings one of the girls with her."

"Water polo?" her father asked. "When I was in high school, we only had football, basketball, and softball."

Mattie smiled. "Back in the ice age?"

"Yeah, after we carved the football out of stone."

Emma reached for her glass. "So it's cool if I go?"

"I suppose," her mom said. "It's just at school?"

"Yeah."

"Well, don't forget to call if you'll be later than noon. Via has a phone?"

"Everyone has a phone, Mom." Emma looked down at her chicken breast. Some of the bread crumbs lodged in a small depression had turned charcoal black. She cut into the chicken and ate all the parts with carbonized crumbs, wondering if that's what it felt like to swallow her own soul.

• • •

After dinner, Emma took *Lonesome Dove* to the ancient hide-a-bed sofa in the living room. She was only three hundred pages into the book, with a ten-page paper due next Friday. Percival Everett would be disappointed in her if she resorted to Wikipedia or SparkNotes. That meant averaging almost two hundred pages a night for the next few nights.

Seventy pages later, she heard a car pull into the driveway. She glanced out the narrow window next to the front door and saw a blue Kia kill its headlights. There was no sound from the family room except the familiar good-cop-bad-cop interrogation of a detective show, which meant her mom was probably asleep already.

Emma slipped out the door, closing it gently behind her. The porch light's motion detector clicked on as soon as she stepped onto the doormat.

"Rachel?" she said, walking out onto the driveway. "Is that you?"

Her friend opened the car door. Still clothed in the yellow polo and khaki shorts of the Falafel Hut, she shook her hair out of its ponytail. "Sorry I didn't call first. I thought you might not answer after earlier."

"I would answer."

"I wanted to apologize for what happened earlier, when Via said she didn't know what Dan saw in you, or that you'd get communicable diseases from holding his hand." Rachel picked up a strand of hair and wound it around her index finger. Her perfect skin reflected milk-white in the moonlight. "I don't think she knows how rude she was."

"Via," Emma repeated. "Right."

She looked up at her bedroom window, above the garage. Her door was open, and she saw the hall light flick on. Mattie must be headed to bed. Mattie, who had trouble with Shakespeare because people couldn't just say what they meant.

She took a deep breath and looked straight into Rachel's eyes. "Why don't you ever date anyone except right before a dance?"

"I don't know what you're talking about."

"You do. We all do."

Rachel looked toward the street, her hands pressing against the body of her car.

"You could date anyone, any time you wanted. I might finally have a chance to date one person. In three years, that's all I've ever had."

Rachel looked past Emma's shoulder to the front door. "Is there a question in there somewhere?"

"You have everything that matters in high school."

"And you have everything that matters in real life," Rachel snapped, flinging open the car door. "I was just trying to be nice."

Say it, Emma thought. *Tell her what her dad saw in that parking lot.*

Rachel turned the key in the ignition and Emma felt her throat close up. Even if she told Rachel what she'd seen, it would somehow end up being her fault. Rachel would still drive away and be angry tomorrow.

Emma let her go.

Rachel rolled through the stop sign at the end of the block, brake lights flashing like Morse code. A breeze shook the elm tree's new leaves above her. In the moonlight, Emma saw a dozen hairline cracks in the driveway, spreading toward the lawn with long, spidery roots.

CHAPTER ELEVEN

MARIACHI TRUMPETS WAILED through the courtyard speakers, punctuated by the thump of an accordion. Three groups of students were painting Cinco de Mayo murals on the glass wall of the southeast corridor. Every year, the student body voted on a winner and the principal awarded prize ribbons during a lunchtime ceremony.

The MEChA club had the window closest to Emma's table. Ana Gonzales, a girl Emma recognized from freshman year typing class, stood on a ladder outlining an enormous Mexican flag waving behind an Aztec head in profile. She had a piece of paper folded in her back pocket and pulled it out every few minutes to make sure she was drawing it right.

Emma turned to look at the other panels. One had an Aztec pyramid and a man holding an unconscious woman in his arms. She'd seen this motif on Mexican boys' T-shirts before. The unconscious woman was always beautiful, with dark, tumbling hair and enormous breasts about to fall out of her top. Most of the time she was dressed like a cavewoman, in tattered animal skins or rags.

The last group was also sketching out the Mexican flag. They were slower than the other groups, so it was impossible to tell what else they had planned. She hoped they had more than a flag up their sleeves if they wanted to beat Ana's group.

Emma pushed back her sleeve to look at her watch. There were still fifteen minutes left in morning break. On the bench beside her, Rachel crammed for a Spanish quiz. She hadn't said a word to Emma all morning. Via either didn't notice or preferred not to comment. Emma sighed and looked back to Ana's Aztec pyramid. She wondered if Ana had ever seen the real thing. Mexico was so close — not like Sweden or Scotland or any of the other places in her family tree.

"Via, do you ever want to go to Africa?"

Via put down her midmorning snack, a corn dog from the cafeteria's express window. "Why do people say 'Africa' instead of the name of a country? Africa is a big fucking place."

"Ethiopia, then. Don't you want to see where your dad came from?"

"Hell, no."

"Why not?"

"Before my parents split up, I remember my dad taking a rug out onto the balcony five times a day." Via dredged her corn dog in a combination of ketchup, mustard, and hot sauce. "I thought he was doing yoga."

Rachel looked up from her notes, a finger holding her place on the page. "What does that have to do with it?"

"He also kept a machete under the driver's seat of the car." Via put the corn dog down and looked out at the courtyard. Thick black lashes scraped her high cheekbones as she blinked. "I can't go somewhere people pray five times a day to a god who lets so many bad things happen that you can't leave the house without a machete."

"What kind of bad things?" Emma asked.

Via held up her right index finger. Emma and Rachel leaned forward to see the small white line carved across her fingerprint. "If I ever go missing, that's how you'll find me."

Emma couldn't imagine a place where people hacked at each other with sharpened blades to get what they wanted. "What happened?"

"My dad happened. Can we change the fucking subject?" Via picked up her corn dog and pointed it at Rachel. "What happened to your jailbird boyfriend?"

"Suspended," Rachel said. "My dad's still working on it."

"Rewriting school rules for your personal convenience?"

Rachel held up a hank of hair and nearly crossed her eyes inspecting it for split ends. "Lawyers don't actually have to *do* anything. They just have to threaten to do it."

"Can he get an injunction to keep sophomores out of the prom? Or outlaw hand-holding on campus?"

"We weren't holding hands," Emma said. "We were shaking to seal a bet."

"Who won?"

"He did. I have to go to his water polo match on Saturday."

Via paused in mid-bite. "Are you fucking kidding me? You made me go to the afternoon showing of that Sundance documentary because you couldn't get out of bed for the matinee."

"I made you go to the afternoon showing because it was a Sundance documentary."

"So you'll change your routine for a guy, but not for your best friend?"

That was just a movie, Emma wanted to say. *This is my life.* Freshman year, when Via had crowed over her date with Will Decker, Emma had drowned her admittedly faint hopes of doing the same and gnashed out a smile as Via described their fevered groping in a dark movie theater. When Will dumped Via, Emma had hugged her and called Will an asshole even though he probably wasn't. She never talked to him again and didn't look at another boy for six months. "How would you know what I changed for you?"

"Maybe you do belong in a church." Via flung her backpack over her shoulder and picked up her half-eaten corn dog. "You sure think you're holier-than-thou."

Emma watched her storm off, feeling the same numbness as when Rachel had driven away last night. She knew she should feel something. A thesaurus's worth of emotions flew through her head (shame, anger, regret, resentment), but none of them touched her heart. A grotesque gulp of laughter crawled its way out of her throat.

"I don't know what's so funny," Rachel said. "In less than twenty-four hours, you've managed to alienate your only friends."

"Is that what we are?" A fierce longing swept through her for the days when she and Greg Rudisil had played together in the fields of their elementary school, running all recess until they were sweaty and breathless. When they got tired, they laid down in the grass and let bees walk on their arms to see who could stand it the longest. In five school years, first through fifth grade, neither one of them had ever been stung.

• • •

She and Elvira were scheduled to play Vu Thi Tran and Mindy Prescott that morning. Elvira waited for her inside the girls' locker room, hands curled at eye level to inspect her nails. She had fresh gel polish put on every weekend at her cousin's salon. This week's color was black with hot pink polka dots.

"Thanks for waiting," Emma said. "You're the first friendly face I've seen today."

The smile failed to reach Elvira's eyes. "No problem, *chica*."

"Are you ready to watch Rafael break a sweat?"

Rafael was still Elvira's favorite subject. Emma found these conversations informative but depressing. From the sound of things, Elvira had already been to third base. Emma couldn't fathom a world in which she had to deal with both homework and sex. She waited for Elvira's glossy-lipped smile, usually so quick to flash at the mere mention of Rafael's name, but it didn't come. "Are you okay?"

"No." Elvira gathered her hair into a ponytail and lassoed it with an elastic she kept around her wrist. "Something bad's about to happen."

They stepped out from the shadows of the locker room. To their left lay the math portables. To their right, the practice football field. Elvira's eyes went straight to the field. Emma followed the direction of her gaze and pointed. "What's going on out there?"

"*Cállate!*" Elvira grabbed her wrist and pulled it down, watching over her shoulder until Grace Esparza had passed behind them. "Rocio Alvarez and my cousin are going to fight."

"What? How do you know?"

"Just go to the gym without me. Tell Mrs. Patterson I'm absent today."

"If there's really going to be a fight, someone could get hurt. You have to tell someone."

"I can't." Elvira shook her head, swaying the four golden hoops in her ear. "You can't, either."

"Why not?"

"It's for *la familia*." Elvira's skin had gone so pale that the line of her foundation was visible between her chin and jawbone.

"You're really scared."

"I know what Rocio can do."

Emma glanced over her shoulder at the locker room. Mrs. Patterson would be in her office. She'd stop the fight before Elvira's cousin got hurt. Elvira would calm down and they could play badminton like it was any other day. "We have to tell someone."

Elvira's clammy fingers gripped her wrist. "If they don't fight now, they'll do it after school, when there's no one to stop it. Do you know what happens when no one stops a fight?"

Once, in elementary school, she'd caught a glimpse of Matt South wailing on a younger kid named Eddie. Teachers had broken it up a few seconds later, but not before two thick streams of blood stained Eddie's T-shirt. "No," she said.

"Someone wins."

"Why does the gang make girls fight for them?"

"*Chica*, no one makes them."

A red ant crawled on the pavement beside Emma's foot. She watched its antennae strobe as it sensed the obstacle in its path. The man who'd threatened her dad might have been a gang member, too, another soldier in the war. She remembered what Owen had said about his reasons for going to church. She needed to see this. She needed to know what she was up against.

"I'll stay with you," she said. "But we can't go past the tennis courts."

CHAPTER TWELVE

Wednesday, April 2

A COLD WIND STRETCHED THE slack in the tennis nets. Emma's palms began to sweat as fear unfurled within her like an anemone. Each tendril, barbed with the possibility of the unknown, stung her where the flesh was already raw and tender. A week ago, she never would have cared about Elvira's cousin and she never would have walked out of class to watch a fight.

At the end of the tennis court, Elvira put her toes on the line delineating fair balls from foul. Her feet looked small in their canvas sneakers, baggy sweats ballooning over the tongues. "This is what you said, right?"

Emma nodded. "I still don't understand why anyone would do this."

"What?"

"Fight for a gang."

"They're her family."

"You're her family. The one that doesn't ask her to get beat up."

"A real family doesn't have to ask." Elvira looked sideways at Emma. "When my cousin was two, my uncle got fired from his job. They moved in with my *abuelita*, but she kicked him out for stealing from her. He lived on the street with nothing until a *Norteño* gave him a place to live. He raised his daughter with them. He would have died without them."

Emma thought of the homeless people on the sidewalk near the YMCA, where her mom used to take her for swimming lessons. They had shopping carts draped with garbage bags and cardboard signs. They didn't look happy, but they weren't gang members and they didn't hurt anyone. "He wouldn't have died. People wouldn't just let him die."

"What people?"

"The people who run shelters. And churches."

Elvira grasped the pole that marked the edge of the tennis court. "If you're poor and Mexican, those people just want you to disappear."

Emma looked away. "I don't see anyone. Maybe they changed their minds."

"There," Elvira said, pointing. Six people strode onto the field from the direction of the parking lot. Two boys and four girls, all dressed in black pants and some form of red shirt — a tee, a tank, a flannel. They walked six wide, arms swinging at their sides. "Monica's in the middle."

Monica was the same height as Elvira, minus twenty pounds. She wore her hair in a braided bun, shining with a layer of gel so thick Emma could see the comb marks in it.

"They're going to get caught."

Elvira shook her head. "We're in the gym, Schneider's class is in the pool, Vega's is on the basketball court, Hunt's is on the softball field, and Garcia's is on the real football field."

"Look," Emma said, nudging Elvira with her elbow. Another group marched out from the gate behind the math portables. This group had four members, one girl and three boys, dressed in the same baggy black pants, but with blue shirts. One of them had a bandanna tied around his forehead.

"*Sureños*," Elvira said.

The girl, Rocio, was taller than Monica and heavier by a good fifty pounds. She wore black lipstick and a shelf of gold chains around her neck. The green calligraphy of a tattoo snaked above their tangled skeins. The tattoo scared Emma. Anyone who let a needle pierce her neck that many times must have a high threshold for pain.

Elvira gripped the fence pole until her knuckles lit up. The two groups met in the center of the field and arranged themselves into curved lines, their fighter at the apex. Emma blinked, trying to remember where she'd seen that shape before.

Cell division, she thought. *Mitosis. Anaphase.* It was freshman-year biology, enacted before her like a ballet. But instead of continuing to separate, the two lines moved closer together. When they were close enough to touch, they stopped. The fighters circled each other, eyes narrowed and arms held out from their sides.

Then the girl named Rocio bowed her head and plowed into Monica's stomach. Monica planted her feet, wound her hands in Rocio's hair, and pulled.

Rocio shrieked, but the *Sureños* urged her on. She barreled forward and pushed Monica off her feet. As they fell, Monica pulled up her knee and slammed it into Rocio's nose. Rocio's carbon-dark lips split in a shriek of pain. A stream of blood poured down her face.

Quick to press her advantage, Monica launched her right fist into the side of Rocio's head. Rocio absorbed the blow and rolled to the side, wrapping her arms over her skull. Disappointed clicks echoed in the mouths of Rocio's supporters.

The clicks seemed to rouse her. Rocio unfolded her arms and raised her head, wiping her bloody nose onto a flannel sleeve. *"Pinche norputa,"* she hissed. "I'll fucking kill you."

"Go ahead and try, sewer rat." Monica smiled and rolled to her feet. "I fuck up scraps like you every day."

Emma glanced over her shoulder. On a normal day, she'd be playing badminton in the gym. The world could tear itself to pieces, and unless it happened in one of six classrooms, she'd never know. She wondered if that's how Piggy and Ralph had felt when they stepped out of the fuselage into dense, hot jungle.

Rocio grunted and charged, windmilling her right fist into Monica's stomach. Monica wheezed and dropped to her knees.

Rocio pounced, jumping on top of Monica and pummeling her head with both fists. Monica turned from side to side, trying to wriggle out from under the hail of blows. Her heels dug into the ground, trying to get enough leverage to dislodge Rocio. It didn't work. Rocio's fists swung faster, hitting their target with greater force each time. The blood from her broken nose dripped onto Monica's arms.

Monica's kicks grew weaker, then stopped altogether.

"Fuck." A tear carried glistening specks of eyeliner down Elvira's cheek. "I have to help her." Her hands curled into fists and she rocked forward on the balls of her feet. "They're going to kill her."

"No!" Emma said, reaching for her arm. "Don't go."

Monica tried to roll her upper body, but Rocio was too heavy to shake. Suddenly, Monica's hand shot out and latched onto Rocio's chains. Monica jerked Rocio down to her eye level and rolled. They lay next to each other, entwined like lovers, until Monica slammed her forehead into Rocio's.

Monica's friends clapped and hissed. She scrambled to her feet, blood pouring from a cut over her eye. She held out her arms for balance as she kicked Rocio in the stomach, the ribs, and the neck.

Rocio groaned and moved her hands toward her face. Monica launched a boot into her wrist. It flopped against the ground, useless. Four kicks later, Rocio's head slumped sideways, dark blood still oozing from her nose. Monica spit on Rocio's body and contorted her fingers into a gang sign, held high above her head. Then she picked up the tail of her shirt and wiped the blood from her face.

There were more insults and curses, all in Spanish. Two of Rocio's companions bent to pick her up, draping her arms over their shoulders. Her nose was a pulpy mess, and a lump bulged above one closed eye. Monica's friends taunted them as they retreated in the direction of the math portables. Rocio's limp toes scraped the ground as they hustled her out of sight.

Emma closed her eyes to block out the image of Rocio's battered face. All that blood used to be blue when it was in her veins. Now it was red, staining her skin, her clothes, and the ground itself. Weren't those the colors the gangs fought over?

They're the same thing, Emma thought. *They'll turn each other inside out before they realize it.*

"We should get out of here." Elvira wiped the tears from her cheeks and led Emma back to the locker room, where they shut themselves in adjoining bathroom stalls and perched on top of the toilets to avoid detection. Emma rested her head against the cold metal, covered in etchings that preserved the names and lackluster wit of girls who thought a toilet stall was a good place to leave their mark on the world.

After a few minutes of silence, she realized there was something she had to ask. She tapped her fingernail against the partition. "Why didn't the others help her?"

Elvira sniffed. "I don't know."

"Is it against the rules?"

"Maybe."

"Then that isn't family."

Half an hour later, when they snuck out of the stalls amid the rush of girls returning from the gym, Emma thought of something else. The women in the gangs fought like their lives depended on it. What did the men fight like? She thought of her dad, asking questions those men didn't want to answer, and ran back into the stall to throw up her breakfast.

• • •

That night, her mom made tostadas for dinner. It was one of her "easy" meals — no baking, no simmering, nothing but grating cheese and chopping up veggies. Her dad preferred casseroles or meat, with salad and vegetables on the side, but she and Mattie liked the easy stuff better: tacos, hot dogs, BLTs. Emma had no idea what her mom's favorite foods were.

As soon as they said grace, Emma bit into her tostada. The shell cracked in half, dumping lettuce and diced tomatoes onto her plate. Most of their food came from the dollar store these days, and cracked tostada shells were just one of the casualties.

"Damn it," her mom said softly.

"It's fine, Mom."

"It's not fine."

"Anyone want hot sauce?" Her dad tilted the bottle, sloshing the thin red liquid inside.

Monica's knee slamming into Rocio's nose.

Emma shivered.

"I'll have some," Mattie said.

"You never have hot sauce," her mom said.

"I'm trying new things. Martin puts hot sauce on everything."

"I don't think you'll like it."

"Mom, please."

Her sister took the bottle from her dad's hand and unscrewed the cap. She shook it over her tostada and a few drops of red splashed against the sour cream and lettuce.

Rocio's fists pummeling Monica's head.

Emma put down her tostada.

"Em? Everything all right?" Veins, forked like lightning, traced the whites of her dad's eyes. It was the same pattern as the cracks in the driveway she noticed last night.

"I'm full," she said.

"But that's only your first one."

She couldn't tell them that her stomach was still raw from throwing up earlier, that the smell of the moldy grout and unflushed toilet in the far locker room stall wouldn't leave her nostrils. "I'm not hungry."

"But you love tostadas," her mom said.

Monica's foot connecting with Rocio's stomach.

"Dad, how do you fix cement?"

"Depends what needs to be fixed."

"Those little cracks . . . the ones that spread out like split ends. How do you fix them?"

Her dad patted his mouth with his napkin. "You can't, not really. I guess you'd have to repave it. Why do you ask?"

"Once you start looking, they're everywhere."

• • •

After dinner, Emma went straight to her room. She sat cross-legged on the floor, *Lonesome Dove* open on her lap. She read one paragraph and reached onto the bed for her stuffed beagle, Wellington. She stroked his head with her left hand, turning pages with her right.

Ten minutes later, the phone rang. Her dad's footsteps shuffled down the hallway, ending with a knock on her door. "Come in," she said.

Bleary-eyed, woken from a nap, he clutched a blanket to his chest and held out the portable phone. "Don't talk too long. It's already after nine."

"I won't." He smiled at her and closed the door gently behind him. "Hello?"

"Hey, are you studying?" Via asked. "You weren't online."

"I'm reading *Lonesome Dove*."

"Guess what. The black man dies and the last word is whore."

"You could have prefaced that with a spoiler alert."

"Like you actually care what happens? It's a book."

"After you stormed off earlier, I wasn't sure you were ever going to talk to me again."

"Don't be stupid."

"What made you pick up the phone?"

"I need the pre-calc homework."

Emma tightened her grip on Wellington. *Of course*, she thought. She slid open her desk drawer and reached for a small spiral-bound notepad. The first three pages were filled with hundreds of tiny hash marks, front and back. Emma added one more and reached for her backpack.

The completed problem set had the chapter and section number written at the top of the page. Her eyes unfocused and the numbers swam before her eyes. Reading them wrong, even a little, would be so easy.

"Are you there?" Via asked. "Hello?"

"Yeah." She blinked and the numbers solidified on the page. Her dad would never give someone the wrong information just to teach them a lesson. He would never hang up the phone because he didn't feel like walking all the way to her room to tell her she had a call. *I can't do it*, she thought. "Chapter 12. Problems 1-3, 5, 9, and 12."

"Thanks."

"My dad wants me to get off the phone now."

"By all means, obey the patriarchal structure that gives an old white male control over your life," Via said, and hung up.

Emma carried the portable phone back to its charging cradle in the spare-room-turned-office. Her dad was asleep in a chair, his grey hair blending with the dusty slipcover. His mouth hung open in a snore, as if he were screaming in space and she couldn't hear the sound.

Unwanted images flashed before her eyes of blood and bone, calligraphy and chains. Red, white, green, and gold — all the colors of the Mexican flag.

CHAPTER THIRTEEN

Thursday, April 3

"THE MISSOURI COMPROMISE," MR. PARKER said, "was an attempt to regulate the spread of slavery as America headed west in pursuit of Manifest Destiny. The goal was to balance the number of slave states with the number of free states. Now, how many of you have siblings?"

Emma raised her hand, along with most of the class.

Rachel and Via did not.

"Then you're familiar with the kind of moaning and groaning that happens when one sibling thinks the other is getting a bigger piece of the pie."

It's not just siblings, Emma thought. Via had barely said a word as Emma stumbled into her seat before class. She'd mumbled "hi," but never looked up from her phone. Emma had only seen her scalp, cocoa brown beneath a horizontal flurry of black curls.

"So how do you think they solved the problem?" Mr. Parker put down his piece of chalk and brushed his hands together, releasing a white cloud of dust. "Give me your best guess."

"Flipped a coin," said Dominic Abrego.

Mr. Parker hung his thumbs on an enormous silver belt buckle with a turquoise stone embedded in the center. "Anyone else want to pretend they care about passing this class?"

"They didn't solve it," said Via. "They went to war."

Emma tightened her grip on her pen. *What do you want from me?* she thought.

"Not yet they didn't. This time, to keep things even, they split Massachusetts in two, creating the new free state of Maine. That created one new free state to balance the new slave state of Missouri."

"Bullshit," Emma mumbled.

"What was that?" Mr. Parker asked. "Speak up, West."

Emma looked up and felt the blood rush to her cheeks. "Nothing."

Mr. Parker tilted his head, looking at her down the bridge of his nose. "I'm pretty sure I heard you say something. I think you should tell the class what it was."

Some sort of fan or vent clicked on, shaking the ceiling tiles. Emma cleared her throat and took a deep breath. "They called it the Missouri Compromise, but what did the slave states compromise on? They got everything they wanted."

"Go on," Mr. Parker said.

She looked up at him anxiously. "That's as far as I got."

"Then it's time to go further. You have a theory, West. Let's hear your evidence."

"Well." Her cheeks felt heavy and bright. "There were a set number of people in Massachusetts, whether they called it one state or two. But Missouri was going to be full of people who could all own slaves. More slaves meant more population and more representation in Congress. The free states didn't get any more people."

Via's hand shot up behind her, rustling the nylon of her jacket. "Let's not forget that slaves were only counted as three-fifths of a person. People always forget that."

"No," Emma said. "They don't."

Mr. Parker raised an eyebrow and she bent her head, breaking eye contact. The whole thing should have been called the Missouri Clusterfuck. No one got what they really wanted and all they did was push back the deadline for a war.

"Moving on," he said, picking up a piece of chalk.

• • •

In chemistry, Dan greeted her with a wink, the flimsy rope straps of his natural-fiber backpack looped over the chair. "Hey. You look tired."

She dropped her backpack and slid into the orange plastic seat. Someone else's long hair was caught on the silver bracket that held the seat to the metal frame. "Not an ideal conversation starter, but I'll take it."

"Why?"

"I have low self-esteem."

"No, I meant why you were tired."

"I stayed up late reading for history class."

"You've heard of SparkNotes, right?"

"That's a cop-out."

"Speaking of cop-outs, are you still coming on Saturday? No excuse about washing your hair or a *Real Housewives* marathon or a second cousin's wedding?"

"I don't even know any of my second cousins." She smiled. "I'll be in the bleachers by the pool."

"Keep an eye on the line judge. They like to cheat and give points to the other team."

"I'll keep him honest." Emma held up two fingers. "Scout's honor."

"That's not scout's honor. That means you're a Wudan swordsman."

Emma held up all four fingers and separated them in the middle. "How about this?"

"You don't know anything about anything, do you?" His eyes flickered over her face, like she was a painting with brushstrokes that held a hidden meaning. "That's what I like about you."

Before she could reply, Mr. Lopez hustled into the room, his aggressively pleated khakis rustling like Edith Wharton's bustle. The next forty minutes vanished in a flurry of furrowed brows and disappointed sighs as he tried to explain shifting equilibrium and Le Chatelier's Principle and Emma realized her A- wasn't going to save her on the final.

After class, Dan took off down the hallway in the opposite direction. She watched his backpack bounce on his shoulders and realized he didn't have anything in it.

As if he knew she was watching, he raised his hand and waved without turning around. As if she knew he'd feel it, she waved back.

• • •

The clubs had all finished their Cinco de Mayo murals in the courtyard. Student council reps had passed out voting slips in first period, and the winner would be announced tomorrow at lunch. They were supposed to circle the name of the painting they liked best: Aztec Glory, Mexican Pride, or Viva la Raza. Emma pulled her ballot out of her backpack and circled Aztec Glory, hoping that was the title of Ana Gonzales's window.

For once, the speakers weren't blasting ranchero music. Hip-hop rumbled like an earthquake through the courtyard. Emma felt it in her veins, fighting with the natural rhythm of her heart as she unpacked her lunch. Today, she had peanut butter and honey on wheat bread, green grapes, a brownie, and a foil-wrapped can of iced tea. Via was nowhere to be found.

"She can't stand the sight of us," Rachel said, tearing open a bag of chocolate candy.

"Us? I'm pretty sure you mean me."

"In Spanish, I told her my dad's almost done with his letter to the principal. She didn't say another word to me." Rachel dug a piece of candy out of the bag. A constellation of glittering specks in her nail polish caught the light, throwing rainbows on her neck. "Has Dan asked you to the prom yet?"

Emma shook her head. "I'm going to his water polo match on Saturday."

"He'll ask you then. He just doesn't want to do it when everyone else is around."

"It's okay if he doesn't."

Rachel lifted one perfectly arched eyebrow. It was weird how much attention Rachel paid to her eyebrows: plucking them, darkening them with a chubby brown pencil, then shellacking them with sealer. "You need to have more confidence in yourself."

Emma glared at her. Someone with perfect skin, perfect teeth, a flat stomach, and concave thighs shouldn't be allowed to say those words to anyone. "Sure, but why stop there? While you're at it, why not ask all those people with Parkinson's to just stop shaking all the time?"

Rachel tilted her head, studying Emma like a stain on her favorite sweater. "You're different these days."

"I don't feel different."

"You are." Her glittery nails dove into the bag of chocolate again. "I think you need to remember how you used to be."

"How's that?"

Rachel shrugged. "Nice. Happy. Grateful."

Emma looked at one of her grapes, brown and sunken at the stem. If you only ever looked at it from the bottom, it was the most perfect specimen possible. "I'm just me. And I've always been this way."

"That's too bad." Rachel turned her head toward the Cinco de Mayo windows. She circled "Viva la Raza" and folded her voting slip in half.

• • •

Emma held up her hand to shield her eyes from the glow of the late afternoon sun. She watched other students pour out of school, unencumbered by thirty-pound backpacks and the resentment of their supposed friends.

Griselda Gutierrez opened the door of a low rider blasting ranchero music and slid into the passenger seat. She wasn't carrying a single book. "But we have French homework," Emma muttered.

Ten minutes later, her mom's Buick pulled up with Mattie sprawled in the back seat. Emma heaved her backpack onto the floor and three tiny frown lines appeared on her mom's forehead. "Careful," she said. "You'll leave a dent."

"Like the one in my shoulder?"

"Bad day?"

"Yes."

"Is there anything you want for dinner?" This was her mom's favorite peace offering—the equivalent of a hug or pat on the back. Today, she would rather have had the hug.

"Let me think about it."

"Tell her you want macaroni and cheese," Mattie said.

"Let your sister decide."

They drove home through Malo Verde's north side, full of subdivisions with names like "Overlook at Sunbright by Rush Builders IV." No matter how white-bread the names were, they all butted up against El Jalisco Road or La Grenada Boulevard.

At the stoplight on El Jalisco, her mom pulled up beside a Cutlass with an airbrushed woman on its side, a shirtless *bandolera* with bullet belts covering her enormous breasts. She sat with one leg crooked, holding a pistol over her crotch. Emma wondered if any little girls had to ride in that car and, if so, how long it took for them to wish they didn't.

"Last call," her mom said as they turned into their subdivision. "Anything you want to stop and get?"

Emma wanted the frozen chicken patties that made excellent sandwiches when paired with dill pickles and mayonnaise, but the box was over four dollars for four patties. Her dad always ate two, which meant they needed two boxes for one dinner. "I can't think of anything."

Mattie shook her head. "You should have said mac and cheese."

• • •

When her stomach let loose a growl that rivaled a guard dog's, she realized Mattie was right. She set down her pencil and rubbed her eyes. Somehow, she'd blasted past her French homework, read the first five chapters in *Of Mice and Men*, and finished half of the pre-calc problem set. But now the sun had dipped below the fence line in the backyard and the table wasn't even set yet.

"Mom," she called, "what time is it?"

"Quarter to six." Something on the stove sizzled. It smelled warm and dry, like cumin.

"What's for dinner?"

"Tamale pie and Spanish rice. I'll dish up as soon as your father's home."

Cornbread, ground beef, kidney beans, and olives topped with sour cream, cheese, and salsa. Emma's mouth watered. She went back to her math problems, expecting to be interrupted at any second. But she finished one problem after another after another, until she was on the verge of actually understanding vector cross products. Her stomach growled again. She licked her lips, which had gone Gobi Desert dry, and went into the kitchen to snitch a pinch of cheese to hold her until dinner.

The first layer of night had already shaded the back yard in grey. She looked at the microwave clock: 6:33 p.m. "Mom, I'm starving." She reached for the paper towel holding a haystack of grated cheese. "Why isn't Dad home yet?"

"Don't touch that," her mom said without turning around. "And you're not starving."

"Did Dad call to say he'd be late?"

"No."

Emma stopped her hand in mid-air, fingertips hovering over the grated cheddar. Her dad always called when he was going to be late. Unwanted thoughts burst like fireworks behind her eyes: El Camino Rojo, the boy named Jesus, the chain-link fence. "Mom, do you think —"

"No." She clutched a wooden spoon in her hand, dragging it aimlessly through the congealed contents of the saucepan.

Emma blinked. Her mom never stirred with diagonal strokes. She scraped the edge of the pan with wide circles that left no particle unstirred. It was how she'd taught them to make gravy and alfredo sauce — wax on, wax off, always moving, always circling, like a shark.

Emma pulled her hand away from the cheese.

What if the man who'd threatened her dad did it again? Or, even worse, what if there was more to the story? Maybe her mom was scared because she knew things her dad had only confessed behind a closed door. But if that were the case, wouldn't her mom have insisted on a transfer? She wouldn't have let him walk back into danger, would she?

At the stove, her mom pushed her sleeves up past her elbows. Two white scars swooshed in parallel just above the right elbow. Emma wondered what had put them there.

Eight days ago, she'd have assumed her dad was giving someone a ride home or stuck in traffic. Not now. The sharp edge of fear replaced the blunt edge of hunger in her belly. "Mom," she whispered. "What do we do?"

"He'll be here soon, Em."

"What if he's not?"

"He will be."

"How long—"

"Em, please." Her mom's knuckles shone star-bright where they clutched the wooden spoon. "Just be patient."

But the last thing she wanted to be was what they called people in hospitals. She leaned against the counter and stared at the oven clock.

Dogs barked.

Lawnmowers fired up.

Horns honked.

Her stomach growled. Her mom's stomach growled.

Windows opened and closed.

Doors opened and closed.

There was no sign of her father.

At 7:32 p.m., Mattie padded downstairs, her bare feet sticking to the hardwood floor. "Where's Dad? Are we ever going to eat?"

Her mom let go of the wooden spoon. Shiny patches of skin stood out on her forehead and on either side of her nose. "Your father's late. It'll just be a f—few more minutes."

"He always calls." Mattie yawned and flung herself onto the couch. "Why didn't he call?"

"I don't know." Her mom spun around and reached into the cabinet for a stack of plates. The seams of her blouse under her arms had darkened in the shape of half-moons. Emma wondered how long it would be before Mattie realized what they were scared of.

She bent her head and pictured an antique television set, the kind with rounded edges and rabbit ears capped with rubber pellets. It had two dials on the front with black hash marks representing channels. The screen was a field of snow. She imagined climbing inside it, barely finding enough space between the black zigs and white zags to breathe. As long as she stayed inside it, nothing could be real.

In third grade, she'd learned that Hebrews never spoke the name of God. In *Rumpelstiltskin*, the dwarf's name was his power and once the princess knew it, he was done for. If you went into the bathroom and stared at the mirror and said "Bloody Mary" three times, a ghost would appear. Bad things happened when you said the names of things you shouldn't. She wouldn't be the first to say it, not out loud.

From the corner of her eye, she caught the change of the oven clock's readout. 7:59 p.m.

A minute later, the microwave's clock followed suit.

"Mom," she said. "The clocks don't match."

"I know, baby." Her mom's voice was thick and raw, as if she'd been crying silently the whole time.

Emma covered her face with her hands. This was how families ended up on the news, begging the police to find their father, brother, sister, mother, daughter, son. It started with something as simple as a missed dinner. Time progressed on a sliding scale of doom that grew darker with every half hour.

Cop shows made it clear that missing people couldn't be reported for forty-eight hours. But when you did report them, everyone hustled like a chicken with its head cut off, spouting figures about how the first few hours are the most important. If that were true, why did you have to sit on your hands for the first forty-eight? The real first few hours were long gone.

Mattie padded across the floor, slipping her arms around their mom's waist. "Something's wrong, isn't it?"

"I think so, baby," her mom said, pulling Mattie to her chest. The two of them sniffed and sighed and tried to pretend they weren't crying.

Emma kept her face in her hands, breathing the smell of graphite and sweat. Her mom hadn't cried when her dad fell off the ladder at a vacation cabin while trying to dislodge a wasp's nest. Or when he was knocked unconscious after a runner slid into him at second base during a SeedCorp softball game. If anything, she'd seemed angry, as if he could have prevented these events and spared her the difficulty of caring for him. But there wasn't any anger in her now. Without it, she seemed lost, like an electric car drifting to a stop after it lost its charge.

If her dad came home in twenty minutes and said he had a flat tire, they could all feel stupid and smile as their bones shook with relief. But if he didn't, Emma knew she'd have to face the truth: The only reason they were still in this godforsaken town was because of her.

CHAPTER FOURTEEN

Thursday, April 3

THE PHONE BOOK LAY BURIED under a pile of notepaper, the kind her mom made by cutting up botched photocopies. Emma's hand shook as she pulled it from the drawer. Her mom stood by the phone, an old-school model mounted on the wall with a twirly cord connecting it to the handset. She held it in front of her, its rectangular number pads glowing alien green in the darkness. "Give me the number," her mom said.

Emma turned page after page, but her hot tears blurred all the tiny black type. "Mom, I can't see."

"Go back to the beginning."

In the front of the book, white pages with blood-red borders marked the city's official phone numbers. She looked at the numbers for poison control, the national runaway switchboard, and the suicide prevention line. There were also numbers listed for the FBI, the US Marshals, and the Secret Service. "I don't know which one."

Mattie sniffed. "W — what about 911?"

"No," her mom said.

Emma flipped to the very first page. To the right of the obscenely large 911, she found a list of numbers labeled Non-Emergency Calls, including the police and county sheriff.

"Read it," her mom said.

Emma put her finger on the paper to guide her and opened her mouth to speak.

The phone beeped out an alarm, one angry pulse after another.

"Goddamn it." Her mom pressed the clear plastic button that reset the circuit. "Again."

Emma chose the number for the police. She didn't know what the sheriffs did, other than put signs on street corners to beg for re-election. "831-555-8714."

The phone rang three times before a male voice answered with, "MVPD, how may I direct your call?"

Mattie choked on a sob and ran into the hallway.

"Matt, wait." Emma gave chase as her sister stumbled toward the living room and knocked over a big ceramic vase sitting on the floor. Emma kicked the shards out of the way and opened her arms. Her sister fell into them, just like in a Polaroid they'd snapped when Emma was six and Mattie three. "It's going to be okay. Don't be scared."

"I am," Mattie sobbed. "I'm scared, Em."

"We'll fix it, whatever went wrong."

"How? We're just kids."

"I'll figure it out."

In the kitchen, her mom hung up the phone and then followed them into the hallway. Black mascara trailed from both of her lower lash lines. She stepped over the shattered bits of vase and wrapped both of them in her arms. Emma smelled a faint floral perfume, underscored with sweat. She closed her eyes and imagined her dad there, too, surrounding all of them with his arms, a concentric circle of love that belonged only to them.

• • •

They fell asleep in the living room because it was closest to the door. Mattie and her mom slumped on the couch, while Emma curled into her dad's recliner, face pressed against the headrest. Her mom clutched the portable phone as she dozed. The desk sergeant had said he'd call the local hospitals and radio all officers on patrol to ask about accidents, incidents, or crashes. That was before ten.

It was after three.

Emma fought the crescent of nausea rising from her belly. If her dad could come home, he would have. Sleep was impossible until she knew why.

In the corner of the room stood a giant faux palm. Its nylon leaves were shrouded in a skin of dust, cemented by months of temperature cycling. Emma imagined the tree gasping for air.

She got up and took one crinkled leaf between her fingers, gouging it with a fingernail the way she would a scratch-off lotto ticket. The part underneath her scratch was still bright, but now it looked diseased next to the uniform grey of the rest of the leaves.

She stumbled back to the recliner and pulled her thighs to her chest. Everything felt wrong, even the color of the light. It was orange, tinted once by the streetlight outside and once by her mom's fabric window blinds — but a strange, computerized orange with a hint of blue behind it, as if orange had gone extinct thirty years ago and an artist was trying to render the color from memory. Her nose began to run and she sniffed quietly to keep from waking her mom and Mattie. But when she tilted her head onto the recliner's headrest, she heard something.

Leaves.

Moving leaves.

But which ones? There were bushes under the living room's front window, a mandarin tree in the corner of the front yard, and a pot of small pink roses next to the door. There were also lots of animals in the neighborhood: cats, birds, squirrels.

She held her breath.

The crackling sounded again, louder this time. *Not a cat*, she thought. *Not a cat, not a cat, not a cat, not a cat, not a cat.* "Mom, wake up."

Her mom's eyes flew open, fingers still clenching the phone. They pressed several of the buttons, making them glow a ghostly green. "What is it?"

"Something's outside."

Her mom hurled the phone to the floor and jumped up from the couch without a care for Mattie, asleep on her shoulder. Her hands shook as they fumbled with the stiff door lock, the one she kept asking Emma's dad to grease.

She threw it open hard enough to dent the wall with the doorknob. A mushroom cloud of paint flakes and drywall exploded into the air.

"Roger!" she shrieked, flinging herself toward the bushes.

Emma pitched herself out of the recliner and crawled on hands and knees to the door. Mattie scrambled after her, peering over her shoulder when she stopped dead in the doorway.

Her father lay in the bushes. She didn't recognize his face because it was hardly a face at all. His glasses were gone, his right eye swollen shut. Dozens of tiny red marks and lines speckled his cheeks. A dark clump of purpled skin and dried blood peaked where his nose should be. Blood trailed out of his mouth on both sides. Red handprints dotted his torn undershirt like a prehistoric cave painting. His button-down was gone.

"Mattie," her mom ordered. "Get the First Aid kit and bring it upstairs. *Run.*" Her sister's feet clapped down the tile entryway. "Emma, get under his right arm."

Emma squatted beside him and reached for his arm gently. "Faster," her mom snapped, flinging his left arm over her shoulder. His head lolled onto her shoulder, staining it red instantly. Emma didn't look at his face; if she did, all the strength would leave her knees. "I love you, Daddy," she whispered.

They swayed inside just as the neighbor's porch light came on. Her mom kicked the door shut behind them. With one arm, she reached out and locked the doorknob and the deadbolt.

Her dad's breathing was shallow and snagged, like a net on a harbor buoy. "Go," her mom said. "Hurry."

They lumbered toward the stairs like contestants in a three-legged race. Twined together, they moved one step at a time to the landing, then the hallway, then her parents' bedroom, where Mattie stood clutching a white box with a red cross. Something wet trailed down Emma's left arm. The sour smell of sweat and blood made her throat convulse and she clamped her lips shut.

"Go toward the bed," her mom said. Instantly, Mattie reached to pull back the bedspread. "Leave it. Em, put your arm behind his shoulders. Hold him up."

For a moment, Emma bore all his weight as her mom reached for his feet. Once she had them, they lifted him onto the bed as gently as they could. His dangling hand painted a poppy-red smear across the spread. Emma picked it up and held it, squeezing it until she felt the beat of his pulse.

"The First Aid kit," Mattie said.

"Set it next to me." Her mom lifted one of his feet and untied his shoe. "In the bathroom, Em, get tweezers and my contact lens solution. The saline, not the cleaner."

Emma blinked. "Mom, the police —"

"Emma, please."

"They need to see this, don't they?"

Her mom looked up, the muscles of her jawbone quivering. Her hands gripped her dad's bare ankles, the vertical lines of his socks still imprinted on his skin. "I asked you to do something."

"You're hurting him."

Her mom's deep golden eyes never blinked. "So are you."

Emma let go of his hand. She would get the saline and then call the police and there wasn't anything her mom could do about it. "Don't worry," she whispered in Mattie's ear as she handed off the saline bottle. "I know what to do."

• • •

The squad car arrived forty minutes later. Mattie had followed her downstairs, unable to watch their mother tweeze dirt and broken glass out of their father's face. Emma stood in the doorway, fingers choking the brass handle, as two officers stepped up to the porch.

"It's my dad," she said, wiping away a tear and waving them inside. She locked the door behind them and laced her cold fingers with Mattie's. Together, they led the way, squeezing each other's hands as hard as they dared. The policemen jingled as they walked, the click and clatter of their gear echoing against the tile entryway.

For the first time, Emma noticed the smears and stains of blood on the walls and carpet. It was on her hands, too, in her nails and in the crevices of her fingerprints. "Don't step in the blood," she said, blinking as more tears flooded the corners of her eyes. "My mom will get mad."

The officers didn't respond.

At the top of the stairs, she pointed at the double doors of her parents' bedroom. One of the officers crooked a knuckle and rapped. "Mr. and Mrs. —" He paused, reaching into his pocket.

"West," Emma said. "Our name is West."

"Mr. and Mrs. West?"

The second policeman leaned over the bannister, following the trail of blood with his eyes. "Jesus," he said. Silent tears fell from Mattie's eyes to her bare feet.

Her mom slipped out from behind the double doors. Beneath the skylight, her skin looked dull and dead, smeared with blood and stretched thin over cheekbones and chin. She waved the policemen inside and they obeyed, handcuffs slapping against their hips as they moved. "Girls, to your rooms."

Emma stepped forward. "Mom, I want to —"

"No."

"Don't they need to talk to us?"

"Just do your chores and go to bed."

"Mom, I can't."

"Please." There were streaks in her hair, dark ones, in the shape of blood-stained fingers. "Emma, please."

"We have to go, Em," Mattie said, pulling on her arm.

All the words jumbled up inside her, in the wrong order, wrong tense, wrong case. They wouldn't form a cyclone, like they normally did, so it was too hard to sort them out. She let Mattie pull her the rest of the way down the hall.

"Thank you," her mom said softly.

Emma ignored her. She turned into the bathroom and stuck her hands under the faucet, watching her father's blood swirl down the drain. The water ran for minutes until it was clear. When she finally turned it off, she dried her hands and cracked the bathroom door. As expected, she couldn't hear much from her parents' bedroom. Her mom had shut the door, and the muted mutterings she detected were no help at all.

She crept out of the bathroom, lining up her footsteps with the right side of the hall. The squeaky floorboard was smack in the middle. As long as she avoided it, her mom would never hear her. She scuttled sideways past Mattie's door to the spare bedroom.

Once inside, she grasped the sliding closet door in both hands, easing it half a foot down the center of its track. A whiff of potpourri from inside the closet overwhelmed her, something fruity and warm, like berries on a picnic table. She held her breath and slid the door closed behind her. If she closed her eyes and concentrated, with her ear to the closet's back wall, she could make out most of what the policemen were saying. Some of it was about the attack, and some of it was about the theft of her dad's pickup truck.

She forced everything but the words themselves out of her mind — no connotations, only denotations. To cement them in her memory, she pretended to write them out, holding her imaginary pencil in a death grip. The officers talked fast, but so did Mr. Parker. She had a lot of practice using abbreviations to get everything down in time.

When her parents' door opened, Emma held her breath. Would her mom notice the smell of potpourri . . . what if it had drifted from the office into the hallway? But her mom didn't seem to notice anything as she walked the officers downstairs. She closed and locked the front door behind them, then sank against it and began to cry. Emma heard one fist strike the door, rattling the locking mechanism in the handle.

She pressed one hand to her mouth and reached out into the darkness with the other, as if she could comfort her mother. She put her head on her knees and bit her lip hard enough to keep her own sobs from becoming audible. Blood dripped from her lip onto her knees, staining her legs with what she'd just washed off her hands. When she heard her mom's bedroom door close one more time, she padded back to her room and slid into bed, letting her red knees stain the covers.

CHAPTER FIFTEEN

Friday, April 4

THE KNOCK ON HER DOOR came after first light. Her mom paused for two beats, then turned the knob. "Em," she said. "Time to get up." A breath of heather-colored shadow clung to her mom's eyelids and black mascara raccooned the skin around her eyes. She looked old and thin and brittle. Emma felt the opposite — thick and spongy, like a limb atrophied without circulation.

She blinked to separate her tear-crusted lashes. The world looked like a watercolor painting, all color dissolving in the flood of liquid pooling over her irises. "Is it Dad?"

Her mom shook her head. "It's time to go to school."

School. The word didn't even register. Only three hours ago, a police car had been parked in their driveway. Men with nightsticks and guns had been inside their house.

"Everything has to stay normal," her mom said. "I'll drive you in an hour."

"I want to stay home today."

"You can't fall behind."

"It's just one day."

"We leave in an hour."

It was impossible. She couldn't think about the *conditionnel* or the molecular architecture of liquids. The things she learned in school only mattered as long as nothing else mattered more. Yesterday, nothing had mattered more. Today, nothing mattered less.

Emma tossed back the covers and saw dried streaks of blood on her legs. She raised a hand to her broken lip and touched the scab, long and oval like a spaceship. Someone would ask her about it and she wouldn't know what to say. In the shower, she tried to think of a convincing lie as she let the hot water pummel her. The pressure made fireworks explode behind her eyelids, bursts of deep red and green that she saw long after she turned off the water.

When Emma left the bathroom, hair wet and skin scalded, she stumbled on something in the hallway. Rubbing her eyes, she bent down to see what it was — a towel spread out on the carpet. She peeled it back and saw a pale red stain spread out like a flower, fragrant with the smell of a chemical floor cleaner.

• • •

When her mom pulled into the school's cul-de-sac, Emma folded her hands in her lap. If she refused to get out, maybe her mom would just take her home. She'd already mapped out her bargaining chips: cleaning house, scrubbing toilets, changing sheets, doing laundry, buying aspirin, and telling the insurance company someone stole the truck.

A Honda Civic pulled up behind them, with Mexican flags flying from plastic rods attached to the windows. She clutched the straps of her backpack and looked at the Cinco de Mayo murals. *I see the Mexican flag more than I see mine*, she thought.

"Em," her mom said.

"I don't want to go."

"Please."

"I want to see him."

"Not yet."

"I won't bother him. I just want to see him."

A tear splashed onto her mom's arm, spotting the rolled cuff of her blouse. She folded the cuff one more time to hide it. "It's just one day. Can you do that for me?"

The Civic zoomed off and a Dodge Charger took its place. Socorro Ramos got out, dressed in her cheerleading uniform. The short, knife-pleated skirt flounced as she shut the door. Her legs were long and thin, straight as a ruler from calf to thigh. She carried one thin spiral-bound notebook in her arms.

Her mom turned her head, signaling the end of the conversation. Emma picked up the left strap of her backpack and got out of the car.

• • •

The combination lock's ridges grated her fingers as she turned it. Every inch of skin on her body hurt. It had gone from a shield to a sieve, full of holes that let everything through. The metal of the locker felt colder, the corner sharper, the books inside it heavier.

As she put back her French book, she realized she had no lunch and no money. Could she survive the day with no food so she wouldn't have to ask for help?

Asking for help meant giving a reason. Giving a reason meant telling the truth or telling a lie. She didn't want to do either. She could explain everything, but not until she'd seen her dad smile again. Not until she closed her eyes and didn't smell his blood.

Emma slammed her locker shut and shuffled down the hall, counting black streaks on the linoleum as she walked. One, shaped like the tail of a comet. Two, brushed thin like a smear of ink from a leaky pen. Three, shorter than her pinky finger. Four, five, and six, all thick and straight like the tip of a highlighter. She let out her breath after six and slipped into her seat in the far row of Mr. Parker's classroom.

Via arrived a few minutes before the bell, turning her back to Emma as she scooted sideways through the aisle. Emma's gut wrung itself like a wet sweater. How could anyone give a shit about the prom or the weather or whatever else Via was mad about when there were people who would beat a gentle man and leave him for dead? The prom was a stupid dance in a stupid room for a few stupid hours.

Rachel arrived fifteen seconds before the bell, smiling without showing her teeth. Emma pulled the scab on her lips between her teeth and bit it as hard as she could.

After the tardy bell, Mr. Parker hitched up his jeans and wrote the title of the lecture on the board: *Manifest Destiny, Part Deux.* "Today we're going to talk about Texas, which shows us the flip side of any expansionist policy. Any guesses on where this is going?"

While he waited for an answer, he rested his thumbs on his silver belt buckle. Emma looked at his glasses, rimmed with silver wire. She wondered how much he could see without them. Her dad was nearly blind without his. Tears seared her corneas as she thought of him stumbling for miles across town, crawling if he had to, squinting at blurry street signs without his glasses to find his way back to them. She curled her right hand into a fist, nails digging into the lifeline of her palm.

"No takers?" Mr. Parker said, glancing from side to side. "The Mexican government had given land grants to Americans who settled in Texas. But their system worked a little too well, and in 1830, the Mexican president forbade any more American settlers to come into Texas. It didn't work, though. The Americans ignored this law, and it really started frustrating the Mexican government."

They know how it feels, she thought. *They didn't like it, either.* Last night, in the closet, she heard the policemen reading parts of her father's mumbled statement back to him for confirmation. "El Camino Rojo?" they'd said. "You're sure that's where you were?" Slowly, painfully, her dad told them about his assignment as a census worker.

"Eventually," Mr. Parker continued, "the settlers saw no way to safeguard their religious and economic interests but to revolt. The most well-known battle of their fight for independence happened in San Antonio, Texas. Does anybody know what it's called?"

"The Alamo," she said, and Mr. Parker nodded.

All she knew about the Alamo was that it had to do with Davy Crockett and a massacre. She remembered a song her dad used to hum: "Davy Crockett, king of the wild frontier." She'd never heard the whole song, but guessed it didn't mention the part where the hero died in a massacre.

Mr. Parker adjusted his glasses and turned back to the chalkboard. "The Mexican army besieged the Alamo, a church that had been converted into a fort. There were more than two hundred people inside, including women and children. After thirteen days, the Mexican army attacked. They had about 1,500 soldiers, so it wasn't much of a fight. Of all the Alamo's defenders, about two made it out alive."

"Whoa," Daniel Rocha said.

Via raised her hand. "What about the women and children?"

Mr. Parker crossed his arms over his chest. "Most survived, but they almost didn't. See, the Texans tried to destroy all the cannons and gunpowder to keep the Mexican army from getting them. The guy whose job it was to blow the gunpowder got shot before he could do it. If he had, the whole place would have gone up in flames, women and children included. So, ironically, it was a Mexican sharpshooter who saved the women and children."

"Whoa," Daniel Rocha said again.

"When Texan settlers heard," Mr. Parker continued, "they got angry. I mean, really angry. It brought a lot of new recruits to the Texan army."

Emma thought of the Mexican flags painted on the courtyard windows and the blood that stained her father's face. Of the Scottish after the English killed William Wallace. Of the French after the English burned Joan of Arc. *Sometimes,* she thought, *anger makes you strong.*

• • •

It happened between English and chemistry. On the way to class, she caught a glimpse of a man in a yellow windbreaker. The short silver hair, the weathered skin on the back of the neck — it was him. Even the stance was right, with thin legs clad in unfashionably pale denim. Her heart seized in her chest, stutter-stepping like a JV hurdler.

"Dad!" she cried, running toward him. "Dad!"

The man turned around. He held a walkie-talkie in his hand, with an assistant principal's badge clipped to the pocket of his windbreaker. Dark hair sprouted from his bulbous nose.

He held the walkie-talkie at chest level, waiting to relay her problem or request. "You okay? You need something?"

As a little girl, if an adult had asked what she needed, there was every expectation that the adult could help. Tell a fireman you were lost and he'd take you home. Tell a yard duty you fell off the monkey bars and she took you to the nurse's office to get patched up. There wasn't a single thing this man could do to help her.

"Do you need something?" he asked again.

"No," she whispered. Then she turned and ran, pushing through the crowd. She rounded the corner, shoved past a girl in a blue sweatshirt, and flung herself through the bathroom door. Three more steps, one more push, and she was safe behind the metal walls of a toilet stall.

She dropped her backpack on the damp green tile and leaned her forehead against the metal. Rust-etched tracks of ancient graffiti bit into her skin as she rolled her head back and forth. She needed to see her dad, to talk to him, to hear his voice. Until she did, she'd keep imagining the worst.

She brought her cold palms to her temples and pressed as hard as she could, wondering how hard she'd have to squeeze before something shattered.

If she hurt herself, she wouldn't have to go to class. She wouldn't have to explain anything to Via and Rachel and Dan. She could go to the nurse's office, and maybe even get sent home. In her backpack, she carried a pair of nail clippers. It would be so easy to pull them out and dig into her skin with those sharpened metal edges. It didn't have to be a lot. Just enough to draw blood, to convince the school nurse to keep her out of class. Pain she could control had to be better than pain she couldn't.

But it still wouldn't help her dad. Nothing she could do, not with nail clippers and not with a machete, would help him get better. And that was all she wanted.

"Goddamn it," she said, grabbing a handful of one-ply toilet paper to blow her nose. She wadded up two more handfuls and put them in her backpack for later.

• • •

"What happened to your lip?" Elvira asked, pointing one stubby finger at her scab.

"I couldn't sleep."

They stood together outside the locker room, but Emma couldn't bring herself to start moving toward the gym. She wondered who had invented the game of badminton, and why that person had had nothing more important in his life than the desire to hit a bunch of glued-together feathers over a net.

"So you tore off half your lip?"

Emma touched the scab with her fingertip. Ridged and crusty, it felt like the surface of an alien landscape. She wiggled her finger and felt it begin to detach. "I can't go in there today. I'm sorry."

"Wanna go sit behind the math portables? I have pictures of the soccer team on my phone. They're not wearing shirts. That always cheers me up."

Emma stretched her torn lip into a smile. She nodded and felt the first spark of life inside her since yesterday. They jogged past the tennis court like they were heading to the practice field, and then dashed left, taking cover behind the first in a strip of brown portables. Elvira tapped her barrel-roll bangs to make sure they were intact. "Your bangs are perfect," Emma said. "Thanks for staying with me."

Elvira nodded. "You stayed with me when I needed someone. I won't forget that."

"How is she? Your cousin?"

"My aunt threw her out, so she's staying with us. Last night, she was yelling at my mom to bring her some tamales. I guess that means she's all right." Elvira sank to her knees and shifted sideways, leaning against the portable. "So tell me what happened, 'cause you look like shit, *chica.*"

Emma sank to her knees and stayed there. "It's my dad," she said, reaching out to pull individual blades of grass from the earth. "He was in East Malo Verde for work and he didn't come home last night. We were so scared we called the police."

She wanted those hours to blur in her mind, the way chemistry formulas did after she studied for too long, but they were still hyper-vivid, like the Lo-Fi filter on her old phone's photo app. "We didn't know where he was until he crawled home. Someone hurt him. Whoever it was almost beat him to death."

Elvira gasped. "Oh my God, are you serious? Is he okay?"

"I don't know. My mom made me come to school instead of staying with him. Why would she do that?"

"She doesn't want you to worry."

A flare of anger lit the darkness inside her. "How the fuck am I not going to worry?"

"I don't know," Elvira said softly. "I'd worry, too."

"I called the police afterward. She didn't want me to."

"Why not?"

"It makes trouble."

"Where in East Malo Verde was he?"

"El Camino Rojo."

"Shit." Elvira shook her head, velvet eyes gleaming with tears of her own. "I didn't know your dad worked there. I'd have told you everything if I did."

"What do you mean, everything?"

"Your mom was right not to call the police. Even they stay away from El Camino Rojo."

"Why?"

"The *Norteños* have an agreement with them."

"But they're the police. It's their job to help."

"*Chica*, who do you think the police hire? And who do they send to the east side?" Elvira shook her head. "Mexicans who grew up there."

Emma bent her head to her knees. She knew her dad was walking into a war zone and she'd never said anything to warn him. She'd never said anything about what Elvira told her or what she'd seen between Monica and Rocio. Instead, she let her mom warn her away with a whispered hush.

"This is all my fault," she said, leaning her head on Elvira's shoulder. "I should have told him."

"Would it have made a difference?"

Emma thought of the way he'd walk into cold, dark parking lots to retrieve their car, bringing it to the curb to pick them up. If it was raining, he never took the umbrella. He left it with them, even if they were waiting under an awning. Once, he'd gone alone to the Christmas tree lot during a rare sleet storm because Mattie was having a slumber party that night. But none of Mattie's friends' moms had braved the sleet. She and Emma had spent the night alone, in sleeping bags, beneath the fragrant pine.

"No," she said.

"Then it wasn't your fault." Elvira laced their fingers together in a fierce, protective grip. "It'll be okay. You'll see."

Emma breathed in the sharp aerosol scent of Elvira's hairspray. They sat together, unmoving, until the bell rang.

CHAPTER SIXTEEN

Friday, April 4

AFTER SHE SAID GOODBYE TO Elvira, she'd gone to the lunch table like usual. Via and Rachel were already there, backpacks open and binders flat against the table. Rachel wore an oversized sweatshirt with shorts that barely showed beneath the sweatshirt's hem. Her legs were blue with cold. "You weren't in chemistry," she said.

Emma took a deep breath. "I need to tell you guys something."

This time, she held her voice steady. She pretended she was telling a story, like Scheherazade. Like breathing or walking, storytelling was just about putting one action into motion over and over again: *Noun, verb, adverb. Subject, object, predicate.*

Via and Rachel listened to the story, put their arms around her, and asked if there was anything she needed. When she asked for a tissue, Rachel handed her one from her pocket. But when she asked to borrow money to buy a hamburger in the cafeteria, Rachel lowered her head and waited for Via to make the first offer. "Here," Via said, shoving a five-dollar bill into Emma's hand and giving Rachel a dirty look. "Buy anything you want."

While she stood in line at the cafeteria express window, a student council member announced the winners of the window-painting contest. Ana's group, the one that painted the Aztec head, took the top prize. Afterward, the DJ resumed the ranchero music and she carried her cardboard tray back to the table. Rachel checked her texts, holding the phone underneath the table top, as if that made it invisible.

Two hours later, Emma stood on the bottom step of the school's entrance, waiting for her mom's car to round the corner. A white mid-size sedan had turned off Carver Boulevard, but she couldn't tell if it was the right one. She stood on her tiptoes and leaned forward to get a better look.

A tap on her shoulder shot her off the ground. She spun, hands balled at her sides. "Look at you," Dan said, imitating her stance. "You look like you're ready to fight someone." Then the smile fell away and his green eyes darkened to the color of summer grass. "*Are* you going to fight someone?"

"Don't be ridiculous."

"Then why the shadowboxing? Bad day?"

Emma struggled to wrap the word "bad" around her day. It was too small. She blinked and scanned the school's front lawn. Girls in sleeveless short-skirted cheerleader uniforms chattered about dates or movies or parties. The words she had to find were different. *Father, missing, blood, beaten.* They were magnets. When she tried to put them next to each other, they repelled.

Dan reached out for her arm and then stopped before his fingertips touched her, as if she might object. "This is serious, isn't it? Is this why you weren't in class today?"

Emma nodded. "Did someone else give you paper?"

He held up his hand. A chemical equation bled blue ink across his palm. "You know you're the only one who gives me paper."

"Something bad happened to my family."

"Can you talk about it?"

Emma shook her head.

"Will I see you tomorrow? At the water polo match?"

"I want to," she said. "But I can't."

He nodded and looked at the ground. She caught a glimpse of his part, soft and pink beneath his thick brown hair. "Em, you've never been like this before."

"How do you know?"

"I sit down next to you in class every single day. I know what you look like when you're happy, when you're stressed, when you're sad. But not this."

She turned her head, not wanting to think about what might be revealed by a close scrutiny of her face right now: red eyes, dark circles, the scab on her torn lip, snot threatening to trickle out of her right nostril. "I have to go."

"Em, I want to see you."

She looked up at him, feeling tears pool in her eyes. *Why?* she wanted to say.

He grasped her hand and pulled it toward him. With his other hand, he pulled a blue pen from his pocket, bit off the cap, and licked the tip. He pressed it onto her skin, scrawling a series of numbers. "Call me. I'm here if you want someone to talk to."

Emma's face crumpled with a sob she couldn't hold back.

"No crying!" he said, moving his hands to her shoulders. "If you wipe your eyes with your hand, you'll erase my number. So you can't cry. Okay?"

"Okay." She bit her lip and the scab caught against her teeth.

"I'm serious. I don't have a Sharpie, so that needs to last."

Out of the corner of her eye, she saw her mom pull up at the curb. "I have to go," she said, sliding away from him. "I'm sorry." She walked to the door of her mom's car and turned around.

Dan hadn't moved. *No tears,* he mouthed.

She pursed her lips in a weak smile, then threw herself into the car. "I want to see Dad."

•••

The bedroom door squeaked when she pushed it open. A plastic nightlight sagged in the outlet on her dad's side of the bed, its eggshell light flickering over an oval patch of carpet. She looked at the windows, covered by the expensive blinds her mom had ordered when things were still good. Thin and silky, they honeycombed into layers that blocked all light and sound.

"Dad? Are you awake?"

"Em?"

Her mom had propped him up on two enormous pillows, stripped of their shams to avoid accidental bloodstains. His left eye was swollen shut, the lid bulging and crinkling at the same time, like a plum rotting in the sun. Dozens of raisin-colored scabs speckled his cheeks.

"Do you need anything?"

"No," he whispered. "Just you."

Crusted blood traced brackish runes on the pink skin of his lips. Five butterfly bandages held the right side of his brow together. His nose looked like his eye, swollen and purple and custardy. Near the neck of his white T-shirt, she saw streaks that looked like fog.

She pricked herself with words like *angry* and *sad* and *revenge*, but the needles didn't pierce the skin of her soul. Instead, she felt only relief. He could have died, but he'd been saved because she and Mom and Mattie loved him so much. Something had taken their love into account and brought him home alive. *Thank you*, she prayed. *I don't know who you are, but thank you.*

Her dad's lips twitched in the beginnings of a smile. He lifted his right hand a few inches and patted the bed beside him. "I missed you," she said, sitting down beside him.

"I'm sorry," he whispered.

For what felt like the hundredth time that day, her eyes burned with tears. All he'd done was go to work and try to support them, to help send her to college. She was the one to blame for everything. "You don't have anything to be sorry for."

He blinked his good eye several times. He was about to cry, too. "Mom gave us TV dinners," she blurted. "Mine was still frozen in the middle. It was Salisbury steak."

His lips twitched again, another smile, medium rare. "School." The scabs on his lips kept him from enunciating, turning every word into a growl. His right eye, the good one, was red all the way around the iris.

"I forgot my lunch. I had to eat a hamburger from the cafeteria."

"Good?"

"The bun was soggy. And they didn't have pickle relish."

"Not good."

She smiled. Her dad was a hamburger aficionado. Every year, she asked him to make them for her birthday and every year, rain or shine, he fired up the grill.

"Homework?"

"Lots."

"What kind?"

"Math, French, history, English, chemistry." She paused. She didn't want him to think she was complaining. "Mostly easy stuff."

He nodded. Starting in first grade, he'd inspected each of her report cards. If it measured up, he took her to the bookstore and told her she could have any book she wanted. She took him to the cleaners, always selecting huge coffee-table editions: a picture book about dinosaurs, an encyclopedia of world events, a glossy animal taxonomy, a compendium of presidents or kings. He paid cash for her selection, then took her for an ice cream cone. When they got home, the first thing he did was inscribe her new book with the date and a note of congratulations:

To Emma, for doing well in the third grade.
I am very proud of you.
Love, DAD

She knew kids whose fathers gave them a cookie or let them stay up late to watch a movie when they brought home a good report card. Her father soared over them. And because he did, so did she. "Dad, thanks for always buying me books."

He covered her hand with his. She laced their fingers together and squeezed. Despite the blood-red white of his eye, the warmth was still there: the softness, the gentleness, the goodness. It was still *him*.

She felt a wave of sadness for Via and Rachel. This moment would never exist for them. Some parents never understood how much their children needed to believe in them.

"School," he said. "What else?"

"We're reading *Of Mice and Men* in English class."

He made a brief grunt, signifying approval.

"Did you ever read that one?"

He tried to shake his head.

"Do you want to?"

"Yes."

"I'll read it to you." She dashed down the hall to dig the book out of her backpack. When she brought it back, she got through all of three paragraphs before he fell asleep. She read to him for at least an hour more, hoping the sound of her voice would keep him soothed and asleep, where he could heal and live in dreams that had nothing to do with the present.

• • •

Emma waited until her mom had gone to bed to turn on her computer. It groaned and wheezed, but did as she asked. She opened three browser tabs, one for each of the local news stations: Fox, CBS, and NBC. In the search box for each, she typed "El Camino Rojo, Malo Verde."

She found multiple reports for the incident earlier in the week, the one at the house her dad had recognized. Police had arrested the suspect, Jesus Javier Reyes, and charged him with stabbing Simon Castillo eleven times. At the bottom of the page, someone had updated the story yesterday, two days after the stabbing: *The suspect was released after the weapon in question disappeared from police custody.*

She clicked a few other stories, all about shootings or drive-bys in East Malo Verde. Each mentioned the escalating tension between *Sureños* and *Norteños*. An MVPD sting carried out earlier in the year had sent several high-ranking *Norteños* to Pelican Bay and San Quentin. The *Sureños* jumped at the chance to fill the void in the power structure, leading to a per capita homicide rate on the east side equal to that of Detroit. The articles all ended the same way: "Police have no suspects and have made no arrests."

Elvira was right.

Emma closed the browser and shut down her computer. If crimes in East Malo Verde didn't produce arrests, who filled the cells in the county jail a mile down the road? Why wasn't there a class in school that explained these things? Instead, they taught her how to calculate the volume of a sphere and what a red "A" on someone's dress meant.

If she'd stayed home today, she could have helped her mom paint over their blood-smeared walls or spray carpet cleaner over the stains in the hallway. But her mom believed the things she'd learn in school were more important. Were they? If she committed a crime and got locked up, she could earn her degree for free. If she obeyed the law, it would be called college instead and she'd emerge with thirty to sixty grand of student debt.

The world was a fucked up place.

CHAPTER SEVENTEEN

Saturday, April 5

SUNLIGHT STREAMED THROUGH THE TOP of her window. Emma felt the heat on her face and tossed back the comforter. It seemed just a second ago she'd gone to sleep, but when she opened her eyes, the clock on her nightstand read 12:30 p.m.

Dan's water polo match would be over by now.

She pushed her pillow out of the way and brought her hand to her eyes. The faded blue digits he'd written on it were still there. Yesterday was a blur of blood and tears, but she remembered the look in his eyes when she'd said she couldn't come to his match. She jotted his number on a piece of paper before stumbling to the shower.

When the water was as hot as it could get, she tilted her face and let the water hit her cheeks and eyelids. The word made her cringe. The water wasn't *hitting* her at all. It didn't inflict any pain. It didn't break any bones or blood vessels or even leave a mark. She promised herself that when she wrote a story, she'd never use the word "hit" to describe one gentle thing falling against another.

• • •

Downstairs, she found her mom and Mattie in the family room. Mattie slumped in a wicker chair, arms crossed on her chest. Her blonde hair looked greasy at the roots and she still wore last night's pajamas, fleece pants with hearts on them and a baggy pink T-shirt. On TV, a woman in a low-cut dress drizzled olive oil into a skillet.

"How's Dad?" Emma asked.

Her mom tried to smile. Even that faint movement accentuated the parentheses around her mouth. The lines beside her eyes seemed deeper and darker, too, like some part of that terrible night had crept beneath her skin. "He's resting."

"Is he feeling better?"

"He liked you reading to him last night."

"I want to read something to Dad, too," Mattie said, "but we're still on *Romeo and Juliet*."

"There's cereal." Her mom pointed to the kitchen island, where a plate and bowl lay untouched. "Or raisin bread for toast in the freezer."

"I hate raisins."

Something else had occurred to her in the shower, after evaluating the real-life consequences of the word "hit." She looked out the kitchen window, to the roses along the back fence. The full sun caused some of them to droop, the top of their stems arched like a cane. "We should take Dad to a doctor."

Her mom got up and headed for the kitchen. "Toast?"

"I don't want any."

"One slice or two?" She pulled out the loaf of raisin bread and slid two slices into the toaster oven.

"What if he has internal bleeding or brain swelling?"

Her mom reached into the fridge for the yellow tub of store-brand margarine. The label shouted at them: *Heart healthy! Zero grams trans fat! New look! Better value!* "He doesn't."

"How do you know?"

The toaster button popped and her mom skidded both slices onto a plate with her fingernail. "He can't go to the hospital," she said, spreading margarine on the toast with a knife. "We don't have any insurance."

"But I have a card in my backpack."

Her mom scraped the knife against the margarine container. "We tried to pay, at first. But they wanted $1,800 a month to insure all of us. And then $1,950. And then $2,200. We could insure all of us, or we could eat."

Her mom handed her the plate and she watched the margarine melt into glistening puddles. She thought sodas from the school's vending machine were expensive. She couldn't imagine spending $1,800 a month on an insurance bill. What if they didn't have insurance for her dad's stolen truck, either?

Emma blinked. There was so much more to be afraid of than she'd ever known. "Mom, who let things get like this?"

"Like what?"

"So bad they can't be fixed."

Her mom looked at the basket beneath the phone, full of unopened bills. "I don't know."

Emma took a bite of the toast. A raisin caught in her throat and she coughed to dislodge it.

The woman on TV crushed garlic and spread it over a baguette. "Mmm," she said. "This is going to taste great."

• • •

At 5:30 p.m., her mom asked her to help get dinner ready. Normally, this was one of her least favorite chores, second only to taking out the trash. Today, she was happy to have an excuse to put down *Of Mice and Men*. It wasn't helping her mood, what with Carlson wanting to kill Candy's dog and Curley beating the shit out of Lennie. Plus, there was only one woman in the whole book, and she was an empty plot device, a literary blow-up doll. What was she supposed to learn from that?

"What about Dad?" she asked.

"We'll go upstairs to eat with him."

Mattie turned from the TV. "Really?"

"He won't eat much, but we can still have a normal dinner together. Something easy."

"Soup and sandwiches," Emma said. She dove into the kitchen and scanned the pantry's offerings: chicken noodle, cream of chicken, and tomato soup, all store brand. She reached for the tomato, dumped it in a saucepan, and held the can under the faucet.

"Wait." Her mom put a hand on her wrist, the circular stone in her wedding ring flashing in the window's light. "Use milk."

Emma smiled. Her mom never let them do that; milk ran out too quickly in their household. She poured a can of two-percent milk and turned on the burner while Mattie and her mom sliced up cold cuts left over from Christy's. They arranged the sandwiches on a silver platter, an old wedding present, and Emma poured the soup into mugs. A mug seemed easier since it wouldn't require her dad to handle a utensil.

She and Mattie brought everything upstairs in two trips. Her dad was awake and smiling, sitting up further than yesterday. He wore a clean white shirt and although the swelling around his left eye hadn't changed, his right eye seemed a little less bloodshot. "Ready for dinner, Dad?" she asked, setting a glass of water on the nightstand for him.

"I'm always ready." His voice sounded like rocks in a blender and she tried not to look at the bruises on his throat.

"Emma chose the soup," her mom said, spreading a napkin over his lap.

"It smells good."

"It's tomato," Mattie said. "With milk."

"Milk." There were three visible cuts where his lip had split, each with a brick of a scab on top. "What's the occasion?"

Mattie smiled. "You are."

Emma reached for one of the sandwiches, a salami on white. "Wait," her dad said, as she lifted the sandwich to her lips. "Say grace."

She put the sandwich on a napkin and folded her hands. It was her responsibility to start since she was the one who'd forgotten. "Come, Lord Jesus, be our guest," she began.

Her mom and Mattie chimed in and her dad mumbled along a half-second behind. "Let these gifts to us be blessed. Amen."

"Amen," he said.

"I made sure the soup's not too hot, Dad. You don't have to blow on it."

"Thank you, Em." He tilted the rim toward his lips. Emma heard a slurp, and then he grimaced. Some of the soup dribbled down his chin onto the white shirt.

Her mom sighed, tossed her sandwich down, and ran into the bathroom. She came back with a handful of toilet paper and blotted the stain. "There's tomato paste in that. It needs soap or it'll stain." She scrunched the toilet paper into her hand and left the room.

"Dad, it's my fault," Emma said. "Maybe I made it too hot."

His right eye drooped as he looked at the blotchy orange specks on his shirt. "Not your fault."

"Do you want a spoon? Would that help?"

"I don't know, Em."

"We can try. I'll be right back." She put down her sandwich and ran downstairs. Her mom stood at the sink, pumping dish soap onto a sponge. "I need to get a spoon for Dad," she said, reaching into the silverware drawer.

Her mom squeezed the sponge until it bled suds. "Tomato, Emma? Really?"

Emma narrowed her eyes. "You saw me open the can of soup. Why didn't you say anything if you didn't want me to make tomato?"

"What were you thinking?"

"It's not Dad's fault."

"Then whose fault is it?"

"The person who did this."

Her mom stared out the window above the sink. "I should have picked up more clients. You could have gotten a job, too. What about the place Rachel works?"

"Mom, can we just finish dinner?"

"I'm already finished," her mom said softly.

Emma clutched her dad's spoon in her hand. "I'm going back upstairs. Soup is gross when it's cold."

• • •

Half an hour later, Emma brought the dirty dishes back downstairs. Her mom stood in the same place, except now it was dark and Emma knew she couldn't see anything except the neighbor's back porch light. "Mom, I brought the dishes."

Her mother turned, tear tracks glowing crystalline on her pale cheeks. "Put them in the sink."

"Mom, sit down. I'll do the dishes."

"Things are going to change, Em. You know that, right?"

"You mean money?"

"I mean lots of things."

Emma stood next to her mom and put the dishes in the sink. The mesh grate over the drain had a piece of tomato skin caught in it. She grabbed at it with her fingernail and it shredded over the wire mesh.

"Just leave it, Em, please."

Emma stared at the lacerated fruit skin. "Being a grown-up is like bleeding to death one drop at a time, isn't it?"

"Sometimes more than one," her mom whispered.

Emma heard Mattie's footsteps on the stairs behind her and lowered her voice. "I don't have to go to college, Mom. I can't pay for it. Neither can you."

Mattie jumped the last step to the floor, her bare feet padding back to the blanket she'd spread out earlier. She sat cross-legged and reached for a year-old magazine. "I'm the one who doesn't need to go to college," she said calmly. "You can give Em my portion."

Her mom gripped the edge of the sink and lowered her head. "Goddamn it, you're both going to college and that's the end of it."

"Mom, it's not like I'm — "

Her mother reached into the sink for one of the dirty soup mugs and threw it onto the floor. "Don't ever let me hear you say that again! If you two don't go to college — " A heavy sigh rattled her chest. "Why else would we be doing all this?"

"Mom," Mattie said, picking ceramic shards out of the folds of her blanket. "Violence is not the answer. You don't need to go to college to learn that."

• • •

Calling Dan was out of the question. She'd have to leave her room to get the portable phone and there was no way she'd emerge from her cocoon of sanity until she had to. She'd escaped upstairs after helping Mattie clean up the broken mug, mumbling an excuse about extra reading.

It wasn't far from the truth. She was within striking distance of finishing *Lonesome Dove*. But instead of reaching for her book, she turned on her computer instead. She'd never seen her mom or Mattie do anything like that before. There were only two people in the world who might understand, and it wasn't likely either one of them would want to talk to her. Still, she had to try.

When she signed into chat, she saw one familiar name.

BookGirl14: Hey, are you there?

Redhead_Rachel: Yeah. What's going on? How's your dad?

BookGirl14: I'm not sure. Things are all weird right now.

Redhead_Rachel: Weird how?

BookGirl14: My mom freaked out. Mattie's acting weird.

Redhead_Rachel: My mom freaked out after she left my dad. She got mad at me for talking about him.

BookGirl14: Why?

Redhead_Rachel: She thinks I don't need him just because she doesn't. She'd kill me if she knew I still see him sometimes.

BookGirl14: I saw him. That night I came to youth group.

Redhead_Rachel: He wasn't there that night.

BookGirl14: He was waiting for you in his car.

Redhead_Rachel: You must have seen the wrong car. His letter worked, did I tell you? He threatened to sue the school, so the principal said Tim and I can go to prom.

BookGirl14: I'm glad you got what you wanted.

Redhead_Rachel: Don't worry, it'll be your turn soon.

BookGirl14: That won't help my dad.

Redhead_Rachel: You won't skip any more class, will you? Via and I are worried.

BookGirl14: She called you for the homework, didn't she?

Redhead_Rachel: Come to youth group tomorrow night. It'll help.

BookGirl14: I just want to be with my dad.

Redhead_Rachel: You could pray for him.

BookGirl14: I'd do that here if I thought it would work.

She didn't understand how Rachel could have so much faith in something no one could prove. Especially after freshman-year geometry and all they'd gone through to learn how to prove that the angle between a chord and the tangent at an intersection point equals half the central angle subtended by the chord. *Maybe,* she thought, *school had a few important lessons after all.* They just weren't the ones in the books.

CHAPTER EIGHTEEN

Monday, April 7

MRS. EVANS LEANED AGAINST THE podium, brandishing the blue legal-sized bulletin issued by the office every morning. Most teachers pinned the bulletin to a corkboard, but Mrs. Evans believed it of vital importance they know which holidays were coming up and whether the varsity tennis team won against Hollister.

"Good morning, class," she said, eyes on the bulletin. "Today is April 7. If you are in MEChA, you have a meeting at lunch in room 1512. The girls' varsity tennis team won its match against Live Oak on Saturday, but the boys' varsity and both JV teams lost. The water polo team lost to Carmel in straight sets on Saturday, too."

Emma kicked the seat in front of her. She wondered if Dan was also the type to slam locker doors or kick things to vent his anger. Since he never wore real shoes, she doubted it. Maybe he was like her, and kept it all on the inside.

"The guidance counselors found two scholarships up for grabs," Mrs. Evans continued. "The Italian Brotherhood of St. Anthony will give a $500 scholarship to a graduating senior with Italian ancestry. If your parents or grandparents were born in Italy, you are eligible to apply."

Emma thought of the names her mom spent hours poring over: Townsend. Sevier. Evans. Kendall. Hamilton. She was surprised her mom even liked marinara sauce.

"The second scholarship is offered by the Mexican-American Alliance of the Bay Area. The scholarship will be awarded to two students of Hispanic origin who have demonstrated outstanding leadership skills over the past two years. If you're interested in either of these, pick up an application from Betty in the counseling office."

Emma sighed. No one wanted to give any money to the meek, pudgy descendant of a bunch of Pilgrims. She scratched a line through the day's date, written with unfounded optimism at the top of the page.

•••

After English, she went to her locker to swap *Of Mice and Men* with her chemistry book. The first thing she saw when she opened her locker was the Boardwalk photo. Her dad smiled broadly, his grey T-shirt and pale jeans blending together in a fog-like smear. She'd told him those were the worst jeans ever, the "dad" version of "mom jeans" that he should be embarrassed to ever be seen in. Now she felt guilty for having thought the criticism was worth a single breath.

She wondered what he was doing now. Was he still sleeping? Eating breakfast? Maybe today was the day he'd finally be able to open his left eye. His right eye was so red she wondered what he could see out of it. Her mom still hadn't called the optometrist to get him another pair of glasses. *Goddamn it,* she thought. *Hitting a man with glasses was one of those things even kids' cartoons told you not to do.* She leaned her forehead against the locker, hoping the cold metal would cool her anger.

A familiar pair of black flip-flops shuffled up beside her. "What's up?"

"Doc," she said softly.

"Nice. You can't go wrong with a Bugs Bunny reference." Dan bent his head to look into her eyes. "How are you? You were really freaked out on Friday."

"I'm okay."

"How are things with your family?"

"Bad."

"Can you tell me about it?"

"I want to."

"Em, you look like you're about to cry."

"They hit a man with glasses." Her dad didn't even have those fancy shatterproof lenses or twistable frames. He had old, brittle lenses that would have shattered the minute they hit the ground, kaleidoscoping into a shower of star-shaped shards. Shards shaped exactly like the nicks and divots dotting his cheeks.

"Oh my God," she whispered.

Dan reached for her hand. "Em, what's wrong?"

"I know what they did." A rush of heat flushed her cheeks.

Suddenly, her knees shook and she wasn't sure how much longer they'd hold her. How could one human being do that to another?

"Okay, let's get you out of here." Dan pulled her away from the locker and shut it behind her. "Come on."

She closed her eyes and leaned into him. His flannel shirt smelled of detergent, a chemical-based clean meant to replicate an ocean breeze. It was new to her — her mom only used unscented. He picked up her backpack and slung it over his shoulder. Then, with one arm around her, he piloted her down the hallway.

Emma kept her eyes shut. She trusted him not to trip her or push her into the boys' bathroom. Even if he did, it didn't matter. She would just stay there until someone made her leave.

"Step," Dan said.

She obeyed and sunlight fell upon her. Like a vampire, she turned away.

"Okay, one more."

She lifted her foot and felt for the ground with her toe.

"There you go. It's flat now. Keep moving."

A bell clanged in the courtyard. She knew she was supposed to be somewhere, that she'd told Rachel she wouldn't skip any more class. Rachel would understand, wouldn't she? She had to, once she knew.

A few steps later, Dan's arm tightened around her shoulder. "Okay, here we go."

She heard a doorknob turn and raised her foot to step over a threshold. When the door closed behind them, she let her eyelids flutter up slowly. They were in a dark room that smelled like sweat and metal.

"Where are we?"

"It's a room. In the music studio. For practicing."

As her eyes adjusted, the ceiling and walls began to give off a faint glow. She made out the edges of pale perforated tiles. "Is it soundproof?"

"It's for jazz band."

"Are you in jazz band?"

"No."

He reached for the light switch. "Don't," she said. "Not yet."

"Here, you should sit down." He pulled a chair toward her. "Can you see that?"

She nodded, but he reached for her hand anyway and placed it on the chair back. He pulled a second chair over and sat in it backwards, propping his arms on top. "What happened to you back there?"

She put her hands on her temples, as if she could squeeze out the image forever. "I figured something out that I wish I didn't know."

"What was it?" He stretched his long legs out toward her. If he brought them together, they would touch hers.

"Why are you doing this?"

"You know why."

"Tell me anyway."

He rested his chin on his forearms. "Because you're beautiful."

She pulled her chin into her neck, the way her mother had told her never to do in pictures. "What?"

His eyes stared straight into hers. "You heard me."

I heard you, but I don't believe you, she thought. But as she looked at him, she recognized something in the loose curl of his lips and the warm light in his eyes. She shook her head, confused. "When?"

"The first day of class. You came in with Rachel. Her hair was in a lumpy braid and yours was smooth. She asked if she could borrow a pencil."

"I don't remember."

"You pulled your backpack toward your chest and reached into the pocket to give her a pencil. You didn't even wait until you sat down."

On the first day of school, she'd worn a floral T-shirt and jeans with brown suede boots. She'd wanted to use her mom's hot rollers but didn't wake up in time. "Is that why you asked me for paper?"

"I wanted to see if you'd treat me the same."

She shook her head. The images and facts in her brain were all mixed up, aligned around poles that had suddenly reversed. Maybe the Earth's axis had slipped, and the resulting orbit wobble disturbed the stars, the sky, the tide, the moon, the waves. Maybe in this brave new world, she *was* beautiful.

She looked back at Dan. His eyebrows were thicker than hers, longer, with a less pronounced arch. Where his left brow originated, over the inner corner of his eye, the hairs stood straight up instead of curving toward his ear.

They were nothing alike.

He was long and lanky and she was short and stocky. He had perfect vision, and she was probably going to have to get glasses. He walked like a basketball player, all grace and slouch, and she shuffled like a sloth. How could there be something in her that made him want to be around her? Even her parents, genetically obligated to believe in her higher-than-average redemptive qualities, praised her brain and her heart, but never her face. Somehow, Dan saw something else.

"Something happened to my dad," she said.

"Is he sick?"

"Some bad people hurt him."

"Why?"

"He was a census worker."

"Why would anyone hurt a census worker?"

She looked down at her hands and then back at his face. His eyes hadn't moved. They weren't looking at the floor or the wall. They were looking at her.

She took a deep breath and told him everything, hoping all the poison had come out in the telling. "I wanted to come on Saturday," she finished. "But we didn't even know if he'd be okay. I'm sorry I didn't call."

"You don't have to be sorry." Dan reached out with his right hand, resting it against the plump part of her cheek.

"Not even for fighting with my mom?"

"Not even that. You should hear me and my dad. We fight all the time, over stupid stuff, like who put the milk container back without any milk in it."

"Was it you?"

Dan nodded. "I was too lazy to take out the recycling."

"You probably deserved it, then."

"I did, didn't I?"

He pulled her chair next to his and settled her head under his chin. She nestled her face in his flannel shirt, closed her eyes, and listened to the footsteps in the hall without any desire to re-emerge among them.

•••

Mattie drummed her nails against the white tile countertop and flipped the pages in their homemade cookbook, compiled from family recipes dating all the way back to Great-Grandma Jennings. "What's scrapple?"

Emma shrugged.

"Read the recipe," her mom said, using plastic tongs to toss a cabbage salad.

"Is Dad coming down to dinner, or are we eating upstairs again?"

"He's sleeping."

"Should we wait until he wakes up?"

Her mom slapped an unopened package of ramen noodles against the kitchen island, breaking the noodle chunk. The recipe called for toasted almonds, but they couldn't afford the package of almond slivers, so her mom substituted crushed ramen. She slammed it five more times, then crunched it between her fingers.

"I think it's dead," Emma said.

Her mom's eyes glowed, lit by a sudden amber flare of anger. "Would you like to make dinner, then?"

"That's crunchy," Mattie said. "Are you sure Dad can eat it?"

Emma shifted her weight, bumping her knee against the edge of the kitchen island. "We don't even know if he's getting better. We should take him to the hospital."

"There weren't always hospitals. People survived."

Emma thought back to Mr. Spelman's sixth-grade class, when they studied ancient Rome. He showed them an artist's rendering of suburban apartment buildings, as well as an infirmary and leper colony. "Yes, there were."

"Emma."

"There were hospitals in ancient Rome. I remember it from sixth grade."

"You know what I meant."

"No, I know what you said." She wanted the words to pick at the skin of her mom's coldness, opening a scab to let some of the warmth beneath seep out. She hadn't hugged either of them since calling the police on Thursday night.

"Do you have a house to clean? People to feed? A sick person to care for?"

"Dad's not sick," Mattie said. Her fingertips curled over the edge of the island. "Is he?"

Emma looked at the salad bowl. Its geometric border was composed entirely of red blobs and orange triangles arranged to look like roosters. As she stared at them, she realized you could turn those shapes into anything if you tried hard enough. "Mom, you need to call the car insurance company. And the optometrist."

Her mom held the salad tongs in mid-air. She stared at Emma for a moment, then stabbed the tongs into the salad and left the room.

"Em," Mattie said. "Why did you do that?"

She picked up the tongs and scooped out a portion for Mattie. "Eat," she said. "Don't let it get soggy."

• • •

When her sister had eaten and gone upstairs, Emma dug the phone book out of the drawer and looked up the number for their car insurance agent. She remembered his name from the card her mom gave her to keep in her wallet: Michael Cavarossi. She found his agency's number and dialed.

The automated system picked up after the second ring. "Thank you for calling Cavarossi Insurance. Press '1' to continue in English."

Emma's knuckles tightened around the plastic phone. *Why is my own goddamn language an option?* She held the phone away from her ear and jammed her finger against the key.

"Thank you for your selection. Please note that our business hours are from 9 a.m. to 4 p.m., Monday through Thursday, and 10 a.m. to 3 p.m. on Fridays. If you are calling outside of regular business hours, please stay on the line to leave a message or call back during our regular business hours. *Gracias por su selección. Por favor, note que nuestro horario es de 9 a.m. —*"

At the sound of the words, she imagined a dark-skinned man speaking that language, holding a black boot over her father's face, grinding his cheek against the broken lens of his glasses. He laughed and swung his leg back, aiming for her dad's nose. Then he said something in Spanish — *"Gracias por su selección."*

She dropped the phone and covered her face with her hands. If her visions hurt this badly, what did her dad feel? How were they ever supposed to forget that?

From the floor, the phone's speaker blared. "Thank you for your selection. Please note that our business hours are from 9 a.m. to 4 p.m., Monday through Thursday, and 10 a.m. to 3 p.m. on Fridays. If you are calling outside of regular business hours, please stay on the line to leave a message or call back during our regular business hours. *Gracias por su selección.*"

CHAPTER NINETEEN

Tuesday, April 8

THE SUMMONS ARRIVED IN HISTORY class. Mr. Parker had already reminded them their *Lonesome Dove* papers were due on Friday, and launched into a lecture about the boundary dispute over Oregon between England and America in the 1840s. "The slogan Fifty-Four Forty or Fight was a direct reflection of the belief that — " Then a student messenger opened the door. Mr. Parker stopped in mid-sentence, crossing his arms over his chest.

The messenger, a skinny Filipino kid wearing a T-shirt that came to his knees, gulped and handed him a slip of pink paper. He fled as soon as Mr. Parker's fingers had a firm grip on the note. Mr. Parker held it up to the light. "Emma West. They want you in the office." He leaned against the blackboard and re-crossed his arms.

Emma blinked. Notes from the office were never for her. Normal kids could go four years without seeing the inside of the main office, or rubbing shoulders with the stoners and gangbangers lining the walls of the principal's office. She swallowed heavily and shoved her binder into her backpack.

"You can copy my notes at lunch," Via whispered. "If you show up, that is."

Rachel turned in her seat. "It's not about your dad. He's fine, I know it."

Emma wanted to believe her, but Rachel couldn't know what had happened any more than she could. What if he'd had a blood clot or heart attack? What if he needed treatment they couldn't afford? Her parents weren't old enough to collect Social Security, and her mom had already complained about losing half the value of their 401(k) in tax penalties and early withdrawal fees.

Emma took a deep breath and hitched her backpack over her shoulder. Mr. Parker nodded when she took the summons, like a cowboy might when a woman passed him on the way to the general store. "See you tomorrow, West."

She tightened her lips and nodded back.

In the empty hallway, her footsteps thunked against the laminate floor. She wore her favorite boots, brown leather with a stacked heel. Her mom had taken them to the cobbler last year to put rubber on the soles to make them last longer. Emma would never have thought do to that. There was no way she was qualified to be a grown-up. She couldn't even take care of shoes.

As she walked, she tried to think of alternate explanations for the summons. Maybe this time it was her mom. They hadn't said a word to each other in the car that morning. Maybe, blinded by tears, her mom had missed a turn or crashed into a phone pole. Maybe her mom was hospitalized or already gone. In books and movies, the mother was always the first to go: Cinderella, Luke and Leia, Huck Finn, Cathy and Heathcliff.

She broke into a run.

At the end of the hallway, she turned left. The Cinco de Mayo murals blocked the hall's natural sunlight, shadowing everything in a wash of brown and red. Emma flung open the office door and stepped toward the big oak desk where the school secretary sat. "They gave me this," she panted, holding out the crumpled summons. "Is my family all right?"

"Have a seat, dear." The woman took the slip and adjusted the reading glasses on the bridge of her nose. "Oh, of course, Miss West. There's a policeman here to see you."

Emma froze. "What?"

A man sitting on a too-small chair in the corner of the office stood up. He wore a grey suit and a white button-down. He had no badge or lanyard visible to mark him as a civil servant of any kind. His face was pale and lean, with pitted acne scars above the cheekbones. His grey buzz cut had receded so far it almost wasn't visible looking at him head-on. "Miss West? I'm Detective Ivan Kobilinski. Can I have a word with you?"

"You're not here about my mom, are you?"

He shook his head. "Your mom's fine. Let's take a walk. Is that all right?"

"As long as you don't leave school grounds," the secretary said. "You could walk in the courtyard. It's a nice morning."

No, Emma thought. *It is not a nice morning.* "Isn't there a room we can go to?"

"You don't want to get some air?" the detective asked.

"I might want to sit down."

"Suit yourself." Kobilinski asked the secretary where they could go, and she offered them a room next to the guidance counselors' office. "Lead the way," Kobilinski said. "I don't know my way around."

Emma stumbled down the hall and around the corner. There was an empty room to the right, next to the counselors' office, with the door open and the lights off. "I guess this is it."

Kobilinski poked his head inside and the lights automatically came on. "Huh," he said, running his long fingers over the control panel, populated with clouded domes instead of switches. "That's new."

Emma sat at the far side of the rectangular table. Kobilinski closed the door and sat across from her. She wiped her palms on her jeans before clearing her throat. "Is my family all right?"

"I think so," he said, grey eyes gleaming as if he were a hungry wolf and she a fat squirrel. "Why do you ask?"

"No one gets called to the office unless it's something bad."

"I just want to talk for a minute, that's all." He reached into his jacket pocket and pulled out his badge. Emma leaned forward to examine it. It wasn't a seven-pointed star, like the badge the two officers who came to the house had had. This one was shaped like a shield, pointy at the bottom with the city seal in the center — a green field with the sun rising behind it. "Do my parents know you're here?"

The detective nodded. "Your mom said it would be okay."

"This is about what happened to my dad, right?"

"We're still looking for the people who hurt him."

"People?"

"Or person. We don't know, really."

Emma hated the thought of multiple men following and then attacking her father. She hated that the detective didn't know whether to use the singular or the plural. It meant no witnesses had come forward. It meant they had nothing. "Where's my dad's truck?"

"We haven't found it."

"Have you looked?"

"Why don't you let me ask the questions here?"

"Because you're doing a bad job."

Kobilinski reached into his pocket and retrieved a piece of paper torn from a spiral-bound notebook. Paper caterpillars curled over the edge of the page. "Do you know a kid named Alejandro Espinoza?"

If she consulted her yearbook, she could probably find a dozen kids named Alejandro Espinoza. If he were any good at his job, the detective would know that already. "No. Should I?"

Kobilinski shrugged. "It was a long shot."

"What year is he?"

"He's a junior, like you."

"I don't know him."

"Why don't you think about it for a minute? Let it really sink in. Is he in any of your classes?"

"I know who's in my classes."

"Have you ever heard that name before?"

"Not that I remember." She folded her left hand inside her right and put them in her lap so he wouldn't see her nails digging into the skin. "Did he have something to do with what happened to my dad?"

"We don't know."

"You have to know something or you wouldn't have even asked me about him."

"You wanna work for the police now?"

"I want you to find out who hurt my dad and stole his truck."

"We're doing that, Miss West."

"And then I want you to punish them."

Kobilinski looked up. His hungry eyes flickered over her face as if he hadn't bothered to see her until now. The skin under his eyes was a darker, shinier pink than the rest of his skin. "If we find out who did it, they'll go before a judge and a jury. You don't have a say in it."

Emma remembered the address she heard the policemen in her parents' room repeat back to her father. All they did was look up who lived there and send a detective to ask her about it. Couldn't they find a picture of Alejandro or his father or brother or whoever else lived there and show it to her father, to see if he recognized them?

"Why did you need to talk to me?" she asked. "I'm not a witness."

"We figured it couldn't hurt. Cover all the angles."

"Starting with obtuse."

He turned his head. "What was that?"

"It's from geometry class. Are you going to talk to my mom and my sister, too?"

"I don't know. Should I?"

"I don't even know why you're talking to me. Go find Alejandro Espinoza and talk to him."

"We don't know that he has anything to do with this."

"Then why did you bring him up?"

Kobilinski leaned back, balancing his chair on two legs. Part of his cheek moved, as if he were sucking it in. "You're a tough customer, kiddo."

Emma slapped her palm onto the table. "This is my *father*. Have you seen what they did to him? He couldn't stand. He couldn't see. Now he doesn't have a job, and we don't have any money. Is that tough enough for you?"

Kobilinski patted his pocket like he was looking for something. "I know this isn't easy, but a lot of bad stuff happens in this town. If your dad is still alive, he's one of the lucky ones."

"That doesn't make me feel better."

"Making you feel better isn't my job."

"No, your job is to keep people safe." She stared at him as hard as she could.

Kobilinski pushed his chair back. "I think we're done here." He reached into his back pocket and took out a business card. "Be a good kid and stay out of trouble. If you remember anything, give me a call." On his way out the door, he stopped at the lighting control panel, trying to push the cloudy domes.

"It's a motion detector," she said. "It turns off when no one's in the room."

"Huh." He looked from the lighting panel back to her. "You learn something new every day."

• • •

The secretary gave her a pass so she wouldn't get detention for being in the halls between classes. She went to her locker to exchange books, but they were jammed so close together she broke a fingernail trying to pull her chemistry book out from between French and pre-calc. When she looked at the convex curve of her nail, scooped out like ice cream, she realized what had just happened.

They thought she might be to blame. They thought someone might have attacked her dad over something that had to do with her.

All the swear words she knew flashed through her head, none of them enough to encompass or properly condemn the stupidity of the MVPD. Her dad had already been threatened by the people in East Malo Verde for looking like a cop. What more of a motive did they need?

Emma slammed her locker and trudged through the hall. Two weeks ago, she would have been angry about the grime on the floor, the flickering hallway lights, or the million other things wrong with the school that her parents' tax dollars should have fixed. Now, she stared at the floor and wondered how well the pockmarked linoleum absorbed blood. Was it better or worse than the cement walkway beside their front door?

Alejandro Espinosa.

She didn't know which of her five thousand fellow students bore the name, and of those, who might have been on El Camino Rojo that night. Was it even possible to find out? She sank to the floor outside her English classroom to wait, folding her thighs against her chest.

Down the hall, a lanky figure turned the corner near the locker bay. She recognized the turned-out limbs and bow-legged walk. Thunder rolled across her heart and she realized she needed him. He was the only way she could remember that not everything was bad.

She watched as he came toward her, dressed in his usual olive shorts, white T-shirt, and black flip-flops. His curly hair was flat on top, as if he'd worn a hat all day. "What are you doing here?" he asked, squatting beside her.

"I got pulled out of class to talk to a detective."

"How'd that go?"

"They think I have something to do with it."

He frowned. "Are you serious? Did they say that?"

"They said a name and asked if I recognized it. I think they expected me to say that we'd hated each other since the fourth grade or something."

"I thought that only happened in movies."

She shook her head. "The detective didn't even know how to work motion detector lights. I couldn't make this stuff up."

"Speaking of making stuff up, I have a present for you." He opened the drawstring of his backpack and pulled out a burgundy notebook, with a gold pencil tied to the spiral.

"Those are USC colors."

He smiled. "I thought with all the crazy stuff happening to you, you could write it down. When you're in class with Percival Everett, you'll have all your material ready and waiting."

Emma didn't think it was possible for her to forget the past two weeks — or that she'd want to relive it by writing about them. But then again, she hadn't been through many life-altering traumas. Maybe he had. Most of their conversations had been about her, and she realized how little she knew about him. *I'm an asshole*, she thought. *Again.*

"Thank you," she whispered.

"It's nothing. I just saw it and thought of you."

"That's not nothing."

Up close, his eyes were more olive than emerald, fringed with a blanket of lashes thicker than hers. His right hand moved to her face, fingertips resting against her cheek. "Then I guess it's something."

She leaned into his hand and the warmth of his skin made her want to melt. They were only connected by four small patches of skin, but the warmth of the entire world was concentrated inside of them. Four fingertips, four compass points, four seasons. The whole world was made of fours and now they were, too. She brought her hand up to cover his, pressing it to her face. "Thank you," she whispered again.

He leaned forward, the warmth of his breath bringing color to her cheeks. "You're — "

The bell shrieked its disapproval. The door of the classroom in front of them swung open.

" — welcome." He let his hand fall away as students poured into the hall. "Another time?"

"Another time," she said, wondering if he could see the pulse of her heart in her neck.

He grinned and headed for the locker bay. Emma watched him go, resting her cheek on her hand. Her heart felt sore, like a muscle stretched and contracted too violently during a workout. It opened to surround Dan and everything he brought her, then clenched shut when she thought about what had happened to her dad.

When the classroom emptied, she tucked Dan's gift into her backpack and zipped it closed. Via was only speaking to her because they hadn't talked about anything except her dad. If she rocked the boat, she'd have a war on two fronts to fight again. Much like the German High Command, she didn't have the resources for it.

"There you are," Via said, black hair haloing her face as she hurried into the classroom. "Why'd they call you to the office?"

Rachel followed, backpack slung over one shoulder. "Was it about your dad?"

Emma nodded. "A detective wanted to talk to me."

"A police detective?" asked Via.

"No, a pet detective," Rachel said.

"But why would they talk to *you*?"

"The detective asked me if I recognized a name. I didn't."

"Does that mean they know who did it?"

Emma shook her head. "I don't think they're going to help us at all."

Rachel snorted. "They pulled you out of history for that?"

"You missed the Underground Railroad," Via said. "The Civil War starts tomorrow."

Ryoki Sumitomo and Savannah Banks came into class practicing Spanish together. "*Dónde está la biblioteca?*" Ryoki asked.

"*En la piscina,*" answered Jen.

"How's your dad?" Rachel asked. "Is he getting any better?"

"He can sit up and eat. Mostly he's sleeping or reading old magazines." She didn't tell them that his left eye was still swollen shut, he had no glasses, and he hadn't been to a doctor.

"Is he handling it okay?"

Emma didn't know what "okay" would be. He was alive and he smiled at them. What went on inside him at night while he tried to sleep was something different. "I don't know," she said.

Mrs. Evans strode to the front of the class with a stack of papers in hand. "Take your seats, class. I'll return your Gatsby papers shortly."

Via and Rachel drifted into their seats as they awaited their fate. "I don't want mine back," Via said. "It was such a crock of shit."

Emma couldn't remember what she'd written and didn't care. When Mrs. Evans dropped her paper onto her desk, she shoved it in her binder without looking. On a fresh sheet of paper, instead of the day's date, she wrote "Alejandro Espinosa."

It didn't look threatening, not the way she wanted it to. She wrote it again, imitating her father's blocky scrawl, drawing the "j" as a long, solid line with a dot on top.

Better, she thought.

She tried again on a third line. This time, she used her right hand instead of her left. The "e" and "o" came out slanted, like they were drunk. Like *she* was drunk. Now it was back to being harmless.

She scribbled through the childish, malformed letters. This boy's name had to look like what he was, so everyone would know who was to blame.

She thought about Gatsby, dying in his swimming pool. About Myrtle, bleeding to death on the side of the road. About Lennie, crushing his puppy. About Curley's wife, dying because she was lonely. About George, shooting his best friend to save him. About Gus, who got killed by Indians because he couldn't settle down. About Donald Martin and Romeo and Juliet and Mercutio and Dimmesdale and Oedipus and Antigone and Hamlet and Ophelia. None of these characters died of cancer or leprosy or the plague. They were whole and healthy until they interacted with each other, until they *killed* each other, and kids were being taught that these were the greatest stories of all time.

• • •

Outside the locker room, Elvira reached up and pulled on her ponytail, tightening the bright pink elastic. It matched the wet-looking gloss on her lips. "Are you okay, *chica*? You were pretty upset last week."

"I'm doing better," Emma lied.

"Your lip is mostly healed. A little gloss and no one would even notice."

She'd forgotten all about the spaceship-shaped patch of raw skin on her bottom lip. No one else had mentioned it at all — Dan because he probably didn't want to embarrass her, and Via and Rachel because they probably didn't care. "Best to let it heal, I think."

The day's roster matched them up against Tina Wooster and Yvonne Matapang. On the court next to them, Rafael and Juan put on their usual show. Every time Rafael jumped to make a shot, Elvira's eyes wandered to the landscape of his chest, waiting for that moment when his shirt flew up high enough to give her a clear view of his six-pack.

"Enjoying the view?" she asked.

"Uh-huh," Elvira mumbled, drifting past the foul line of their court.

"Just serve already," Tina Wooster called.

Emma tossed the birdie and smacked it as hard as she could. As the strings of her racket bounced the birdie across the net, she thought about the sheet of paper in her binder with the culprit's name written on it.

Was a high-school junior really the one who beat up her dad and left him for dead? All she'd heard that night in the closet was the police officer repeating the address. Her dad hadn't given them any names because he didn't have any to give.

Who else lived at the Espinosa house besides Alejandro? There had to be something she could find, in public records or police reports online. She would start looking tonight, after her mom and Mattie went to bed.

When Mrs. Patterson dismissed them thirty minutes later, they were on a winning streak, with five unanswered points in a row. "Nice job, partner," Elvira said, raising her hand for a high-five. Emma tagged her palm and smiled back.

They dropped off their equipment in the bin by the gymnasium door, and headed back to the locker room. Before they got there, another girl hurried up to Elvira and grabbed her arm. She was taller than Elvira, with thinner eyebrows and more earrings, all the way from her lobe to the cartilage at the top of her ear. The girl ignored Emma. "*Carnala*, did you hear? There was a cop on campus this morning, asking questions."

Elvira shook her head. "What about?"

"Who's been in fights recently. Sergio told me last period, and I thought of Monica. Is she in trouble? Did that *chota* talk to her?"

Emma felt her heart stop in her chest. What was Kobilinski doing? Had he started asking more questions after he left the counselors' office? Did he summon Alejandro Espinosa, too?

"I don't know," Elvira said. "I haven't heard anything."

The other girl shrugged. "Sergio got the *gabacho*'s picture on his phone if Monica needs it."

Elvira looked from side to side. "Okay."

"Tell Monica not to worry. Hector will know what to do."

"I know. I'll tell her."

The other girl dashed off.

Emma put her hands in her sweatshirt pocket so Elvira wouldn't see them shake. "W — what was that about?"

"Letizia knows my cousin."

"Why would she need a picture of the cop?"

Elvira shrugged. "Don't ask me that, *chica*. You probably already know, anyway."

"They can't go beat up a cop to keep your cousin from getting in trouble."

"*Chica*, they thought your dad was a cop."

"Then where does it stop?"

"It doesn't. Blood in, blood out."

"Somewhere it has to stop."

"Would you stop? If it was your family?"

She remembered what Elvira had told her when she'd said a real family doesn't ask you to get beat up: *a real family doesn't have to ask.*

"It is my family," she said. Then she turned her back on Elvira and hurried into the locker room.

CHAPTER TWENTY

Tuesday, April 8

WHEN THE BUICK ROUNDED THE corner, Emma stepped out to the curb. "Hi," she said, flinging her backpack onto the floor mat. It was the first thing she'd said to her mom since the aborted dinner last night. Part of her wanted to hold that grudge like a blanket, pressing its silence to her chest until her mom pried it from her fingers. But if she did, she wouldn't find out what Kobilinski had said to them that morning.

Pride had to be sacrificed for the expediency of knowledge.

She sank into the vinyl seat and glanced sideways at her mom, dressed in a black T-shirt and black cardigan with jeans. As a little girl, Emma remembered her wearing reds and pinks and whites and purples, colors that looked so much better against her warm golden skin. She wanted to tell her mom that she looked beautiful in her memories.

"Did you have a good day?" her mom said.

"A detective talked to me at school."

"He came by the house and asked if he could see you. He promised it wouldn't take long."

"It didn't."

"Oh?" Her mom arched her knuckles over the steering wheel.

"I didn't know the person he asked about."

Her mom exhaled and loosened her grip. "I told him that's what would happen. I just wanted him to know we'd cooperate."

"Why wouldn't we?"

"We would. Of course we would."

Something in her voice told Emma the opposite was true. She made a mental note to get her dad's version of Kobilinski's visit. He would tell her the truth, especially if they were alone. "What's for dinner?"

"Hot dogs. Mattie requested them this morning."

"Can I see Dad?"

"After dinner. He'd just gone to sleep when I left."

When they got home, Emma spread her books out in the dining room and gathered quotes to use in her *Lonesome Dove* paper. Mattie came home later, dropped off by a friend's mom after a rehearsal for their class staging of *Romeo and Juliet*. "It's such a stupid play," Mattie said. "Who kills themself over someone they just met?"

"I take it you're not Juliet?" Emma said.

"I'm the nurse. Olivia Lee got to be Juliet."

"Fewer lines. That's a good thing, right?"

"Not when you want to be the star."

"Judi Dench won an Oscar for *Shakespeare in Love*."

"So?"

"She was only in it for, like, five minutes."

"Hmm," Mattie said. "Judi who?"

At 6:15 p.m., her mom called them for dinner and pointed at the row of hot dog condiments on the kitchen island. Emma picked up the mustard bottle. It was weightless in her hand. If she used it, there wouldn't be enough for her mom and Mattie.

She set it back down and reached for the ketchup bottle.

On TV, the news reported on a shooting and two related stabbings in East Malo Verde. "There's a power struggle going on," said Carlos Vasquez, the gang task force agent they always interviewed. "The FBI sting last fall sent four *Nuestra Familia* lieutenants to prison. They have replacements, but none of them are as strong. That leaves a power vacuum that the *Sureños* are trying to take advantage of. They send up a few soldiers to try and take over new turf, and the *Norteños* fight back."

Emma thought of Elvira's cousin, fighting a *Sureño* instead of going to class. What turf was so important that two girls needed to slug each other instead of learning how to write an essay or solve for x? Everyone in high school was dying to get away from it. It was like fighting for a piece of scorched earth or a dry well.

She bit into her hot dog. Ketchup oozed over the bun and stung the healing cut on her lip. When they finished eating, she helped her mom with the dishes and put away the condiments. "We're almost out of mustard," she said as she closed the refrigerator door.

"Put it on the grocery list," her mom replied.

Emma pulled out the drawer that contained a steno notebook with a mini-golf pencil tucked into the spiral. She wrote "mustard" beneath "pasta" and "bandages."

"You can go see your father now."

Emma closed the drawer and ran upstairs. She knocked on the closed bedroom door and waited for permission. When she heard his voice, she opened the door and smiled. "Hi, Dad. How do you feel today?"

"Better." A stack of old *Sports Illustrated* magazines lay on the nightstand, along with a bottle of ibuprofen and an empty glass. The bottle lay on its side with no lid. "I was up for a minute earlier."

"A whole minute?"

"One whole minute." His grey T-shirt matched his growing stubble, almost a short beard by now. She'd never seen him with so much facial hair. It was like he was an actor in costume. Only the deep brown of his eyes told her it was still him.

"Did you have a good day at school?"

"We got our Gatsby papers back."

"Did you get an A?"

"Yes," she said, even though she hadn't looked yet.

"I didn't even need to ask." He curled the corners of his lips without pulling on the crusted scabs. "I already knew."

No one in the world trusted her that much. *I don't deserve it*, she thought. She looked at her mom's dresser, topped with a square mirror framed in raw oak. Her most recent school photo, next to Mattie's, lay tucked into the frame. The whole room smelled faintly of the perfume her mom kept in the top drawer, something in a squat blue bottle. "I talked to a detective at school today."

"What did he want?"

"He asked if I knew someone named Alejandro Espinosa."

"Do you?"

"No."

"Don't let them bother you at school again."

"Mom said the detective came here first. She gave him permission."

"She didn't tell me. I would have said no."

"He didn't even talk to you?"

"No. And I don't want you to talk to him, either."

"But what if I can help?"

"You don't know what the other kids might see." He reached for her hand. The skin across his knuckles was spotted with scabs, a human relief map of a place with no contiguous land mass. His fingers tightened on hers and she understood that he was trying to tell her something.

She looked over her shoulder at the open bedroom door. "I don't think anyone but the secretary saw us. Why does it matter?"

"They know who we are."

"Who? The people who did this?"

Suddenly, her dad's breath shot out in a wheeze. He turned his head to cough, but couldn't get enough air and gasped as another spasm shook him.

Emma grabbed his glass and ran to the bathroom sink, clanking the rim against the faucet with her shaking hands. She dashed back and held the glass to his lips. His fingers grabbed hers in a first-time driver's grip. "It's going to be okay," she said.

He coughed once more and fell back against his pillows, exhausted. The bags under his eyes were thick and grey, two piles of ash from a fire long burnt out.

Emma set his glass on the nightstand. "We're all going to be okay."

"The truck," he whispered. "It had my registration in it. They took my badge, too. They know where we live, Em."

A blanket of lead descended onto her shoulders. "Did they say they'd come back?"

Her father tried to roll onto his side.

"Dad?"

He ignored her, pressing his face into the pillow. She wondered if those men were really coming back. Wouldn't her mom or Kobilinski have warned her? Maybe her dad had misunderstood.

Or maybe something else was going on.

Once, in history class, the fire alarm had gone off unexpectedly. She'd been staring at Mr. Parker's glasses, wondering how different a prescription he had from her dad. She saw the exact moment the fear took hold of him, when his brain registered the noise. His eyes went blank and the blood drained from his face. There was nothing left on it but a strange glow, a sick translucence only present to indicate an absence. Then Pedro Alvarez dropped his book and broke the spell. Mr. Parker shepherded them out to the practice field, where they lined up for a headcount like they were supposed to.

Mr. Parker had survived more than one ambush in Iraq. What it left behind inside him was more than she understood.

Emma looked down at the bedspread. "The police are doing everything they can. We'll be fine, I know it."

Her dad lifted his face from the pillow.

"We're going to be okay," she lied.

"T — tell me about school."

"I don't know, Dad."

"Tell me."

She'd already lied to him twice. She couldn't bear the thought of doing it again. "Do you really want to know?"

"I do."

"I don't know what I'm doing anymore. With school or college or any of it. Something happens every day that pushes it further away."

"What do you want to do?"

She turned her head to look at him. He was fifty-one now, with sinewy limbs and a head of hair that seemed grey before his time. How would he have answered that question at her age? No one grew up wanting to work in a seed-coating plant. "What did you want to do when you were my age?"

The corners of his lips curled. "I asked you first."

"I think I want to write."

"You need school for that, don't you?"

Emma nodded. "But the things they make us read . . . *Of Mice and Men* and *Gatsby* and *Romeo and Juliet* and *Hamlet*. What do they have in common?"

"All made into movies?"

"Dad." She rolled her eyes. "People die in the end."

"They're just stories, Em. It isn't real."

"Then why can't the greatest writers in the history of Western civilization think of another ending?"

"I know one that has a different ending."

"Which one?"

"*Field of Dreams.*"

"That's not a book, Dad."

"It is. Different title, though."

"The only reason no one dies in the end is because they're already dead."

"It counts."

She knew why he loved that story. His dad had played minor league baseball in the 1940s and dreamed of being called up to the majors, but that call never came. The best picture she'd ever seen of her grandpa was at his funeral, in a tarnished silver frame next to the punch bowl. He held a baseball. His skin was heartbreakingly smooth, his hair gelled into a pompadour. When she'd looked at his face, frozen in water-stained sepia, she realized it belonged to a person she didn't know. "All right," she said. "It counts."

"I'll get you to school, Em."

"Dad, stop."

"I promised I would."

"Dad, I don't even — "

"Help me, Em." He moved his hand and wrapped his long fingers around hers. "You have to have faith."

"I don't know what that is."

"It's believing in someone." His eyes swam with love and fear, the fear so dark it swallowed his pupils and widened his eyes. "Can you believe in me?"

She looked at his face. His cheeks had deflated, sagging into visible parentheses on either side of his mouth. *I did this*, she thought. *I took away his only escape.* She bent her head and lay down next to him, resting one palm on his shoulder. "I love you, Dad."

She watched his chest rise and fall, the way she had when she was younger and they'd taken naps together in the afternoon. She sat in the blue wheelbarrow while he pruned and mowed and edged the front yard. When he was done, he'd wheel her into the backyard, push her on the swing, then pick her up and carry her inside. He would lay on the floor or the couch, but never the bed. She would curl up on his chest or against his side, undisturbed by his snores.

He let her stay for a few minutes before reaching over with his right hand to smooth her hair. "Do you have homework?"

"Lots."

"You better get to it."

"I will." Emma's heart tightened, shrunken like fresh cotton in the dryer. None of this should have happened. Was it the fault of the men who beat him? Was it her fault, for refusing to consider Tennessee? Was it his fault for trusting her not to put her needs before his own?

Someone had to be responsible. And if she was the guilty party, she wanted to know just how much damage she'd done.

• • •

At 11:15 p.m., Emma heard her mom's footsteps on the stairs. Her mom went into the master bathroom, brushed her teeth, and crossed a squeaky patch in the floor to the bed. Emma waited for the brass bed to creak, then timed out an excruciating forty minutes.

At five minutes to midnight, she opened her bedroom door and crept down the hallway to the office. From her pajama pocket, she pulled out a tiny flashlight her dad had gotten for free with a coupon at a hardware store. In the closet, she teased open the top drawer of the filing cabinet. The manila file folders inside bore her mother's impossibly precise lettering: TAXES 2011, TAXES 2012, TAXES 2013, BANK STATEMENTS.

Emma pulled the out bank statements folder.

The current balance in her parents' account as of twelve days ago was $417.72. The current balance in their savings account was $560. She held the flashlight between her teeth and used her other hand to turn the page. There were two credits in the "deposit" section, payments from Christy for $388 each, and a whole page of debits.

On the final page of the statement, she saw the headline "Your Retirement Accounts." There were three account numbers listed, two with zero balances and one with less than $1,000 in it.

She flipped back to the debits and added them up, subtracting them from their total assets. They had less than one month's worth of money in the bank.

CHAPTER TWENTY-ONE

"BUFFER SOLUTIONS CONTAIN TWO PARTS," Mr. Lopez said. "Equal amounts of a weak acid and a conjugate base." He turned to write sample pKa and pH values on the board and Emma looked down at her homework. It wasn't finished, but she didn't care. Math was the only subject worth studying right now.

Every time she closed her eyes, she saw the numbers from her parents' bank statement. What was her mom planning to do . . . let them run out of money and wonder why there was no more bread or milk? If they had another source of money, it wasn't in that filing cabinet. She'd scanned the contents of a few more folders for anything that involved dollar signs. All she found was a bunch of owner's manuals for appliances they didn't even have anymore.

She looked back at the board and copied the formula Mr. Lopez had written. Beside her, Dan leaned back in a stretch, creaking the plastic seat of his desk. His outstretched hand dropped a folded piece of paper onto her desk. She jolted forward and put her hand over it.

It took her a moment to read his handwriting — all his e's, a's, and o's looked the same. *You. Me. Lunch on the bleachers. Be there or be square.*

She bit the inside of her lip to keep from smiling. No one smiled in AP Chemistry. No one smiled when their dad could barely breathe and thought they were all about to be attacked by a gang. But no person of the opposite sex had ever specifically requested she clear her schedule to be alone with him. Even if a meteor destroyed Earth later that night, at least she would die knowing Dan wanted to eat lunch with her.

• • •

After chemistry let out, Emma followed Via to PE. Via moved like water, slipping through cracks in the press of bodies filling the crowded hall between the courtyard and the entrance to the locker room. The best Emma could do was hunch her shoulders and draft behind her, like a cyclist or a racecar driver.

"Hey," Emma said, hurrying to catch up. "Can I ask you something?"

"Sure."

"It's kind of personal."

"I don't have anything to hide."

"How much money do you and your mom have left over after paying the bills?"

Via stopped in front of the locker room. She turned and held up a hand to shield her eyes from the late morning sun.

When she lifted her arm, her cropped flannel hoodie exposed a flat, hard stomach. "Jesus, that's not what I expected."

"What did you expect?"

"Something about loverboy tossing a note onto your desk in chemistry. Do the world a favor and never become a spy, okay?"

"I snuck into the office last night and looked at my parents' bank statement." Emma shifted her weight to her right leg. "It's really bad."

"And it reminded you of me? I'm flattered."

"The mustard was almost gone. I didn't want to be the one to finish it because I don't know if there'll be more."

Sandra Silva turned sideways and squeezed between them on her way into the locker room. Her backpack hit Emma in the chest.

"Don't go around us or anything," Via called after her.

"How much?"

"I don't know." Via shrugged. "Fifty bucks, maybe? Sometimes there's enough for a movie and fast food."

"How much does Rachel make at the Falafel Hut?"

"Eight bucks an hour."

Emma thought of the numbers in the "debit" column on her parents' bank statement. "That's not enough."

The red bell above the locker room entrance clanged its ear-splitting ring. "Goddamn," Via said, clapping her hands over her ears.

Emma followed her into the locker room, passing through a cloud of woodsy perfume. Via opened her locker and raised her arms to pull off her sweater. Emma looked away. She would have given ten IQ points to look more like Via and less like a Pillsbury marketing device.

"Look," Via said, folding her sweater into neat quarters. "My dad left. Rachel's dad left. Yours isn't going anywhere. If the worst thing that happens to you is that you have to get a job, it's not that bad."

Emma tossed her backpack to the floor. "The police pulled me out of class. My dad can barely breathe, and we don't have enough money to take him to the doctor to find out if he's got a broken rib or internal bleeding. What part isn't that bad?"

Via unbuttoned her jeans and slid them off, swapping them for sweat pants. "The part where you get to go home and tell him how much you love him."

"Wherever your dad is, he's still alive. You could find him."

Via snorted. "I could also buy meth from Mark Haworth and smoke it in front of the principal's office."

"Does it make you feel better to hate him?"

"Yes."

"Why?"

"Because it's too much work not to. Look, the universe will always devolve into entropy. It's the fucking law of nature and trying to stop that will only kill you. I have better things to do than die for someone who doesn't give a shit about me." Via slammed her locker shut. "Whatever you think 'hard' is, something worse has already happened to someone else. Try to keep that in mind, okay?"

Emma bent her head as Via brushed past her. Not so long ago, her biggest problem was the jealousy she felt when she saw the "xs" label peeking out from Via's sweatshirt.

She peeled off her jeans and stared at the worm-like brands on the sides of her thighs, pinched and reddened where the seams had dug into her flesh. Maybe Via was right. Maybe her family's problems were someone else's forgotten worries, dwarfed by the enormity of their own circumstances. If that were true, no one but the families of the dead and dying had anything to complain about. *And Dad's not dying,* she told herself. *So shut up and go to class.*

Elvira was already waiting at the locker room entrance. "How on earth do you do that?" Emma asked.

"Do what?"

"Get into the locker room, change, and get back out here without me seeing you."

"Magic." Elvira smiled and snapped her fingers. The pink polish had been replaced by purple with lime green polka dots.

"I could use some of that."

Elvira pushed up the sleeves of her sweatshirt, shaking a stack of gold bangles on her right arm. "When I was little, I thought anything with glitter in it was magic. Then my sister put glitter nail polish on my doll's hands. She told me that if I did anything bad, the doll would come to life and kill me, like Chucky."

Emma smiled. "That's genius."

"Yeah, until you're the one who spills strawberry soda on the carpet. I thought I was gonna die." Elvira looked up at her from beneath mascara-coated lashes. "You were kind of mad yesterday. Are we cool?"

"That stuff with the cop and your cousin freaked me out."

"Letizia and Monica are tight. They look out for each other."

"Can I ask you something about that?"

"Sure. You ready to go?"

Emma kept pace as Elvira headed for the gym. "Do you know a guy named Alejandro Espinosa?"

"Yeah." Elvira held her voice steady, like a pool cue she'd aimed at a tricky shot. "Why?"

A sequence of lies built itself in her mind, clicking together like a DNA double helix. "I heard some people talking about him in the hall."

"What'd they say?"

"He's in trouble with the police. Maybe that's what the cop on campus wanted yesterday."

"Wouldn't surprise me."

"Why not?"

Elvira stopped just outside the gymnasium door. Usually, it was propped open with the tarnished brass doorstop, but today, it was closed. Elvira looked over her shoulder before speaking. "They want his brother Hector. He's NF."

"Aren't lots of people in that gang?"

"Hector's a shot caller."

Emma shivered. "I don't know what that means."

"The shot caller gets the orders and then it's his job to make sure those orders get done."

"Who gives the orders?"

Elvira shrugged. "For a while, it was some guys up in Pelican Bay. Then it was some guy here in Malo Verde. It doesn't matter."

"Who does Hector give the orders to?"

"Everyone," Elvira said softly.

Emma shook her head. "So all the *Norteños* . . . they have to do what Hector says?"

"They're supposed to."

"Then why are the cops asking about Alejandro?"

"Hector has two strikes. He sends Alejandro to do a lot of his dirty work since the cops don't have anything on him." Elvira looked over her shoulder again and reached for the door handle. "But who cares about that *pinche cholo*? You ready to kick some ass?" Elvira flung open the door and stepped through, her bangs standing straight in the sudden rush of air.

So, Emma thought. Alejandro Espinosa was a legionnaire for his brother, Hector. Hector was a lieutenant answering to some sort of Praetorian Guard. The more she thought about it, the more sense it made. All the gang members she'd seen had one physical attribute in common.

The Romans had tattooed their soldiers, too.

• • •

The wind pushed cotton-ball clouds across a pale sky and Emma shivered. A group of black-clad stoner kids huddled at the opposite end of the bleacher, their backs turned to hide their conversation and the cigarette they passed around.

Emma reached into her backpack and pulled out her sack lunch. Two minutes later, she saw Dan's lanky frame emerge from the north end of the courtyard, carrying a cardboard box from the cafeteria. He hopped up the steps of the bleachers, holding the box in one hand. Emma smiled. "You have good balance."

He sat beside her and put the box on the bleacher in front of him. It held a juice box, grease-soaked chicken nuggets with dipping sauce, corn, and a brownie. Emma smelled the tang of salt and her mouth watered.

"So," he said, peeling the top off the container of ranch. "How's your day been?"

"Elvira and I won in badminton." She looked at his arms, bare to the wind, and waited to see if they got goosebumps. They didn't. "How do you stay warm?"

"Blood pressure."

"I don't have that."

"Do some pushups."

She looked at her peanut butter sandwich. "I'm eating."

"Can you even do one?"

"I don't know."

He chomped on a chicken nugget. "Let's find out. Show me what you got."

"I haven't done a push-up since middle school."

"It's easy. I'll show you." He hopped down the bleachers to the dry grass below.

"What are you doing?"

Dan wiped his fingers on his shorts and stretched out his arms in front of him. Then he rotated his arms all the way around, like a swimmer before a race, and started jogging in place. "Pace yourself. Fatigue is no laughing matter."

A couple of the stoner kids from the other end of the bleacher turned around. One of them exhaled in her direction and she breathed it in, wondering how much she needed for a contact high. "Are you serious right now?"

"As a heart attack." He whipped his hair back and dropped into position. "Okay, hands on the ground, like so. Back straight, like so. Then, using extreme care to keep that back straight, you go like this." He executed one perfect push-up. Once complete, he pulled his knees to his chest and hopped up. "We have to do thirty before we can get in the pool for practice. Now you try."

"No way. My hands will get dirty."

He held out both hands to her. "Come on."

"I don't — "

"You got this," he said, guiding her down the bleacher. "You can even do it girl-style, if you want."

"No way." She got down on all fours, feeling the soft blades of grass collapse under the weight of her palms. A black ant twirled its antennae, sensing the disturbance in its environment.

"Legs up," he said.

She lifted her knees and formed a plank.

"Back straight."

She dropped her knees a little, lowering her rear end.

"Now go."

On the exhale of her next breath, she unlocked her elbows. Instantly, her forearms started to shake. Her wrists felt brittle, like they'd buckle under the enormous pressure of her entire body weight. The ant crawled over the last blade of grass before her knuckle. It touched her with an antenna before climbing on, its legs tickling her as it crossed the thin strip of raised bone connecting wrist to knuckle.

Emma felt the blood rush to her face as she strained to push her wrists straight again. Somewhere in her temples, veins throbbed with the force of effort it took to make her body do what she wanted it to. She powered through the rest of the exercise, then fell to her knees, panting.

"That's my girl," Dan said, leaning down to give her a hand. She took it and he pulled her up easily. "That wasn't so hard, was it?"

The blood drained from her face, flowing through her body with a speed it rarely attained. For the first time in weeks, she felt alive. "No, it wasn't."

Dan kept his grip on her hand, pulling her closer and holding her against his chest. His right hand came up to touch her cheek and she leaned into it, just like she had in the hallway the other day. His hand was warm enough to erase the chill of the afternoon wind.

His eyes met hers, wide and warm and deep. "Hi."

"Hi," she whispered. The pulse in her throat knocked against every layer of her skin.

Tipped with silver, his thick lashes brushed his cheekbone every time he blinked. Until the time he didn't blink, because his mouth tilted toward hers. A buzzing cloud of blackness blanketed her as his lips pressed against hers. Or had she just closed her eyes, too?

Gently, like water from a slow stream, he kissed her. She felt his fingers on her back, splayed across her spine. All the places they were connected glowed, and she didn't even need to open her eyes to see it.

When he pulled away, she felt cold. She closed her mouth and pressed her lips inward, wondering if he tasted heat and salt, too. "Hi," he said.

She opened her eyes. "Hi."

His right eye was still half closed, as tilted as his smile.

I just kissed a boy, she thought. A tickle on her right knuckle made her twitch, and she looked down at the black ant circling the back of her hand. She held it up for him to see.

He smiled. "Did you know ants can fall from almost any distance and survive?"

"No."

"Make a wish, Em." He bent down and blew the ant off her hand, back to solid ground.

• • •

"Dinner's ready," her mom called. Her voice carried up the stairs and down the hallway. Emma heard it through the clack of her typing, halfway through the first page of her *Lonesome Dove* paper. She saved her work and scooted her chair out from under her desk.

Downstairs, her dad lay on the couch in the family room, watching TV with the remote clutched in his right hand. Without his glasses, Emma knew he couldn't see more than a few colorful blobs on the screen.

"Hi, Dad."

He turned to face her, gasping as he twisted his torso.

"Don't move! I'll come to you." She moved in front of the screen, comfortably within his line of sight.

He still hadn't shaved. Foggy white hair covered his cheeks and chin. "How was school?" he asked, panting on the exhale.

Earlier, she'd wondered how she was going to keep from smiling when she thought of Dan. Now she knew. "It was good," she said softly.

"What did you do?"

"Nothing special. How are you feeling?"

"I came downstairs."

"Mom helped you?"

He nodded.

"It looked like you were in pain a minute ago."

"I'm getting better." He held up the remote to change the channel. "See?"

"I do." Her heart clenched in her chest. "I'm going to see if Mom needs help with dinner."

"Good girl."

She turned and stepped into the kitchen. Her mom put the wok on the island and chopped up some veggies for stir fry on a plastic cutting board: a green pepper, which Emma hated, and some water chestnuts.

Her mom took a hunk of iceberg lettuce from the fridge and dug her nails into it, tearing out chunks several layers deep. The gold bands of her rings glinted as separated the leaves.

"Mom," Emma said.

"What?"

"Dad needs help."

"Emma, I'm making dinner."

When her mom finished the lettuce, she reached into the pantry for a can of garbanzo beans from the dollar store. She sprinkled a handful over the lettuce, poured the rest into a storage container, and tossed it back into the fridge.

"He needs help," Emma said again, a little louder to be heard over the whirring of the fridge. "Do you even care?"

Her mom pulled out three mostly empty salad dressing bottles and set them on a plastic plate. She carted it over to the empty place at the table and set it down. "Scoop your own salad. It's time to eat."

"What about Dad?"

"He'll eat on the couch."

"He'll spill and you'll get mad."

"Emma, for the love of God, just take some salad." She turned off the heat beneath the wok and leaned around the corner into the living room to call Mattie to the table.

Emma slipped her fingers through the red plastic serving tongs and scooped two clutches of iceberg lettuce and garbanzo beans onto her plate. On TV, the baseball game her dad was watching came back from commercial. The A's were losing to the Rangers by four runs in the bottom of the sixth inning.

Mattie wandered into the kitchen and leaned onto the island. "Are those green peppers?" she asked, hovering over the salad bowl. "I don't like those."

"Then pick them out." Her mom took a plate of salad to her father and came back to the table. "Sit down and let's say grace."

Emma put down her fork and folded her hands in her lap. Her mom started first. "Come, Lord Jesus, be our guest. Let these gifts to us be blessed. Amen."

"Amen." Emma picked up her fork and teased slices of green pepper away from the salad and noodles. Across the table, Mattie did the same.

Her mom glanced at their matching piles. "Someday you'll learn to like them."

"I don't think so," Emma said, just as Mattie said, "Maybe."

"You can't eat hamburgers and hot dogs every day."

"Lots of people do," Emma said, meeting her mother's gaze.

"And you think those people are happy or healthy?"

"More than we are."

Her mom threw a narrow-eyed glance at them, the same one they'd gotten as children if they begged for popsicles at the grocery store, or grabbed a department store rack to see who could hang from it the longest. If they'd protested, she would have dragged one or both of them out by the wrist, with a clearly enunciated monologue reminding them that "children who don't behave don't get to be in stores." Not once had it been an idle threat.

When kids are small, Emma thought, *all they want is to be beside their parents forever.*

She looked at her dad and felt the magma of hot tears rise behind her eyes. When other families fought, they used words, with meaning that wasn't buried so deep you needed an archaeologist to excavate it. She always thought her family would be different if the situation called for it, but they weren't. They were exactly the same as they'd always been, fossilized in sediment of their own making. She thought about Via and Rachel, and what they would do in her place. Via would fill a swear jar in ten seconds flat, and Rachel would wear down her opponent until she got what she wanted. It was time to decide what she would do.

She blinked and took a deep breath. "Dad needs help."

"Emma, what do you want me to do about it?"

"Take him to the doctor. He's in pain."

Her mom speared a bell pepper slice and a water chestnut. "They'll prescribe pain medication and send him home with a bill we can't pay."

"Or maybe they'll diagnose a broken rib or internal bleeding and save his life."

Mattie set down her fork and folded her hands in her lap, as if they were going to say grace all over again.

"Don't be dramatic," her mom said. "You'll scare your sister."

"She should be scared." Emma dropped her fork onto her plate. "You won't get him new glasses, so he can't see a thing. He can barely breathe, but you'd rather pretend everything's normal so making dinner is the worst thing you have to deal with."

"Stop it," Mattie said, blue eyes shining with unshed tears. "He can hear you."

Her mom's eyes darted to her father, but he didn't even turn his head. He watched the next batter, one of the A's, strike out on a fastball. *That's his third strikeout tonight*, the announcer said. *It's like his swing is off—he's just not reading the pitches the way he used to.*

Her dad leaned back against the sofa and sighed. The breath caught in his throat and he coughed. Then he gulped in a mouthful of air and coughed again. Emma heard his lungs straining to fill themselves, to get ahead of the cough. His face wrinkled into a grimace and he held his left side.

"Dad."

He couldn't answer her.

"Dad!" She jumped out of her chair and raced toward him.

He bent over and vomited blood onto the hardwood floor.

"Goddamn it." Her mom jumped up and grabbed the entire roll of paper towels from the counter, tossing it at Emma.

Emma tore off several sheets and floated them over the blood. The red and yellow mucous made fluffy cloud shapes as they soaked into the quilted paper.

"Stop looking at it and get it off the floor!" her mom yelled.

Emma looked down at the mass expunged from her father's body. She didn't know why she'd ever expected things to change.

She scooped the warm mess into a handful of paper towels as her mom bore down with a wet rag and sponge. Dark liquid shone in the thin gaps between each wooden slat. *It'll never go away*, Emma thought. *We'll always know it's there.*

Her mom got down on her hands and knees, dropping the wet rag against the floor. "You could help, you know."

Emma wadded the paper towels into a bloody ball and dropped them on the floor. "Now do you believe he needs a doctor?"

• • •

She left her plate on the table and went up to her room. Every inch of her tingled, like she was ready to run or scream or fight. But there was nowhere to run and no one to fight. She bunched her fist and slammed it into the foot of her mattress. It rattled the headboard against the far wall. She tried it with her other hand and got the same result. *I have to scream*, she thought. *I can't hold it in anymore.* Her hand shot out and grabbed one of the stuffed animals on her bed, a big blue elephant, and she pressed her face into its side. The scream tore from her throat, hot as a nuclear blast.

What had she been thinking, asking her dad to give up his job because she didn't make friends easily? She wasn't going to be an artist like Via, or a valedictorian like Rachel. Even Gatsby had died for a cause. What did she have, in comparison?

Across the floor, her backpack sat by her desk. In it was the maroon notebook Dan had given her. It wasn't green and it wasn't a light, but if there was anything worth striving for, it was Dan . . . and the vision of her that he saw. He'd seen her upset, he'd seen her cry, he'd seen her exhausted on virtually no sleep, and he still wanted to kiss her. Her fingers found their way to her lips, wishing there was something stronger than memory to pull her back into the warmth of his kiss.

Maybe there is, she thought.

She crawled across the floor and pulled the notebook out of her backpack. With the pencil from her nightstand, she began writing down all the things that were wrong in her house, all of the Miss Havisham decorations that had never changed, not since the day she was born. On the first blank line of the first blank page, she wrote, "The couch in the living room is older than I am. It's in every family photo I've ever seen. It has zebra stripes and fern fronds and bamboo stalks in a psychedelic mix of black and orange and rust and grey. The grey was white in the picture where I'm holding my second birthday present."

Forty minutes later, she'd filled three pages with complaints about their antiquated dishes, Tupperware, glassware, silverware, wall art, lamps, end tables, and other furniture. "Things," she wrote, "carry some essence of their owners."

She sat back and stretched her left hand, its outer edge now coated with a shimmery grey haze. There it was — the truest thing she'd ever written. Her fingertips slid down the page, feeling the fierce indentations in the paper. Anger made the words take shape, but only on paper. She'd never said any of them out loud. *Maybe*, she thought, *that was the whole problem*.

CHAPTER TWENTY-TWO

Thursday, April 10

HER MOM'S FEELINGS MADE THEMSELVES known through the contents of her lunch bag: a plastic cheese-and-cracker tray with a rectangular spreader, an orange (her least favorite fruit), and iced tea (her least favorite lunchtime beverage). It was the first time she'd opened her bag and not found a sandwich. Instead, her mother had entrusted her nutrition to the Keebler elves.

"Wow." Via ferried a tortilla chip sprinkled with hot sauce to her mouth and held her slim fingers in front of her lips while she spoke. "What did you do wrong?"

"Nothing." She didn't want to relive last night, in words or memory. She could still feel the heat rising from the pile of bloody vomit on the floor as it soaked through the paper towel in her hand.

A strand of red hair worked its way loose from Rachel's braid and whipped itself against her lip. "You must have done something," she said, peeling it off her shimmery gloss.

"Thanks for the vote of confidence."

"You get what you pay for," Via said.

Emma glared at her. She was the only one trying to fix things, and what did she get for it? Bitchy friends, the silent treatment in the car this morning, and processed cheese food in her lunch, the direst warning her mother could give her. Everyone wanted her to seal her feelings inside her heart, where they'd die without oxygen or water, like *The Cask of Amontillado.* "I was only trying to help my dad."

"Maybe you can't," Via said.

Emma shook her head. There was no point in talking to either of them. Their families were broken, unfixable, and they secretly wanted hers to be the same.

Her eyes floated over a group of Mexican kids in the courtyard, some dancing to the ranchero music. At the edge of the group, she saw a familiar profile with barrel-shaped bangs and gold hoop earrings. Elvira twirled and smiled, a red bandanna tied around her ponytail. One of the boys smiled and clapped, watching her hips sway from side to side. In chemistry today, she and Dan had smiled at each other and passed notes. He asked how things were at home, and she told him they were worse, but his notebook had inspired her to write about them. The smile it won her made her nerve endings fizz like a shaken soda can.

Rachel pulled a package of sour candy from her backpack. "If you're looking for a way to help your family, how about making your own lunch once in a while?"

"Mom would just get mad if I did that."

Via crumpled her tortilla chip bag. "No one's made lunch for me since I was seven."

"That's not how it works in my family."

"Then how does it work?"

Emma looked at the plastic container holding her cheese and crackers. "Food is control."

"Maybe it's just food." Rachel pulled one knee to her chest and rested her cheek on its surface. "It doesn't help that you're so angry now."

"I was always angry. I just hid it better."

"Jesus, why'd you stop?" Via slammed her chemistry binder shut. Tucked in its front pocket was a brochure for Amherst. It showed a group of students walking through a big iron gate, flanked by brick columns. Two of the four students had their arms raised above their heads in a cheer. The tuition for a single class would probably pay for a year's worth of any medical treatment her dad needed.

I don't know what I'm supposed to want anymore, Emma thought. She crumpled up her sack lunch. "I have to go."

"No, you don't." Rachel inspected her cuticles. Torn and bleeding, they were the only physical evidence that she wasn't perfect.

"I want to," she said, slinging her back-breaking pack over her shoulder.

The cold wind couldn't dampen the fire in her cheeks or the sweat in her armpits. Her own friends hated her. Her mom probably hated her, too. If she'd always been the real her, would they have hated her from the beginning?

Beyond the courtyard, she found a few splintery wooden benches still used by freshmen who found it amusing to carve their initials into school property. On one bench, a Filipino girl sat with her phone and a graphic novel. Emma heaved her backpack onto the second bench, littered with an abandoned soda bottle. She thwacked the bottle across its side with the flat of her hand. It tumbled off the table and clunked to the ground.

The Filipino girl looked up from her book. "Are you going to pick that up?"

Furious tears rose to the surface of her eyes. She couldn't even blow off steam without making someone angry. She picked up the soda bottle and walked it over to the rusted trashcan lined with a glossy black bag.

"They have recycling, you know," the girl called.

• • •

"*Alors, tout le monde, prenez votre cahiers et faites Exercise Trois.*" Monsieur Jordan wrote a page number on the board, along with the workbook's corresponding page numbers in the textbook. "*Levez la main si vous avez une question.*"

Emma opened her French workbook. The subjunctive was easy on paper. The whole French language was easy on paper. Ink made sense to her, no matter what shapes it made. Much like real life, she didn't get in trouble until she tried to speak.

Behind her, Juan Sanchez whispered to Griselda Gutierrez. "Hey, what's number two?"

"The fuck you ask me for? Just look in the book."

"I don't have my book."

"Why not?"

"I left all my shit at my cousin's last night. He and Sergio kicked us out when Hector got there."

Emma lifted her head. *Hector.*

"So it's really happening?" Griselda asked. "Like, tonight?"

"*Simón.*"

"Everyone?"

"Everyone they can find. RIP, *ese.*"

"Damn."

"Hey."

"What?"

"I still need the answer to number two."

Emma's heart thumped. What sort of gang-member holocaust did the Espinosas have planned? She closed her eyes, grateful her dad was home and not going door-to-door on El Camino Rojo. She'd never stopped to think that what happened to him might have been a blessing in disguise, a way of getting him out of harm's way before something harder than fists flew on the east side.

She tried to imagine what it felt like to die in a hailstorm of bullets. In the movies, people bounced like marionettes, jerking with each impact. An image of Rocio filled her mind, bullets slicing through her shelf of gold necklaces, tearing holes through the green calligraphy letters tattooed on her neck.

When she picked up her pen, she saw a big, blue puddle blotting out her response to question four. She'd held the tip of the pen to the page for too long without moving it. If Monsieur Jordan called on her, she'd have to hold the page up to the light or look at the indentations from the other side of the page to find it.

Maybe, she thought, *all the answers I need are like that.*

Maybe they'd been there all along, hidden beneath a layer of sameness that made them look invisible. All someone had to do was turn the page. Suddenly, no matter how angry her mom was, she couldn't wait to get home.

• • •

Emma dropped her backpack at the foot of the stairs. She had seven pages of her *Lonesome Dove* paper to write, but that could wait. She leaned into the family room to check on her dad. He was reclining on the couch, staring vacantly at the TV. An old afghan her mom had crocheted covered his lap.

"Hi, Dad." She stood in front of him so he wouldn't have to turn his head. "Are you feeling better today?"

He blinked and raised his eyes. "How — " He coughed and cleared his throat. "How was school?"

She realized he was avoiding her question, which meant the answer was no. Any other time, she'd have pressed him for more information. But now, to try and help, she had to ignore it. At least this time, she wouldn't have to lie to him. "It sucked."

His brows drew together, narrowing the slit of his purpled eye. "Why?"

"Want to come take a walk with me? Just for a minute."

"I don't — " He looked toward the ceiling. "Your mother said — "

"You could get some fresh air."

He paused.

"Mom won't mind. We'll just go onto the porch." She sighed. "And I'll tell you why my day sucked."

"Deal," he said, tossing back the afghan.

She took his arm and pulled him to a sitting position. "Still okay?"

"I think so." He looped his arm around her shoulders and shuffled beside her in his slippers. Each of his fingers pressed into her biceps and she wondered if she'd get bruises. She circled his waist with her arm to try and take some of the weight. "I'm sorry you had a bad day."

"I'm in high school. It's inevitable." She wanted to tell him that any number of bad days was worth it if it helped him get off the couch. "Here, I'll get the door. You'll be okay?"

He grabbed the hall bookcase to steady himself as Emma stepped forward to get the door. "Watch out for the doormat," she said, anchoring it with her foot. A gust of wind shook the wreath on the front door. She breathed it in, fresh with the scent of earth warmed in the sun, so different from the stale air floating like a miasma inside. "Doesn't that feel good?"

For the first time since that night, she saw something flicker in his eyes. His lips relaxed, parting enough for her to see his teeth. "It does. Thank you, Em."

We're turning the page, she thought. If she could keep him outside for a minute today, and two minutes tomorrow, and three minutes the next day, maybe he'd realize he was strong enough to stand even when she wasn't there.

She slipped her hand into his and he squeezed it. Together, they stepped over the threshold, onto her mom's heart-shaped coir doormat.

Just past the driveway, she heard a car engine gurgle like a garbage disposal. Slowly, the car came into view. It was black with raised chrome stripes and a long hood, like something from the car auctions her dad liked to watch on Sundays. "Look," she said.

But he was already looking. His eyes opened wide and his hand went slack in her grasp.

"Dad." She squeezed his hand, but he didn't respond.

She turned her head to follow his gaze. Two Mexican men sat in the front seat of the car, staring at them. One said something to the other and they nodded. The one in the passenger seat turned and pointed at them, his thumb and forefinger cocked like a gun.

Her dad jumped, turning his back to them and pressing her into the wall. Emma's head hit the stucco, teeth clamping on tongue with unexpected force. He panted, great gasps of air that might have been sobs. Clutched to his chest, she breathed the smell of stale sweat and vomit that clung to his bathrobe. "They're coming. Get back in the house," he said.

He pushed her across the threshold, then stumbled across himself. One heavy hand reached for the door handle. He flung it shut, clutching his ribs with the other hand. The door slammed, rattling every window in the house. "They found us," he said, wrapping his arms around her.

"Shh," she said, hugging him back. "Nothing happened."

Beneath her ribs, her heart knocked hard enough to register on the Richter scale. It didn't make sense. The Espinosas could have found them at any time — why now? The sweat on her back turned cold in an instant as she remembered what Juan had said in French class: *RIP, ese.*

From the corner of her eye, she saw her mom on the landing upstairs. "What the hell were you thinking?" her mom hissed, golden eyes flashing. "Are you trying to make things as hard as possible?"

Her eyes filled with tears. "I only meant to help."

From down the hall, Mattie's door opened and she peeked around the corner, rubbing sleepy eyes. "Who's slamming all the doors?"

Her dad rocked back and forth on slippered feet, face pressed into Emma's shoulder. "They found us," he whispered. "They found us."

• • •

In the upstairs bathroom, two of the eight bulbs in the lighting strip above the mirror were burnt out. Both sinks had raised rust pustules, multi-tonal and irregular in shape, exactly the way her mom's magazines described skin cancer. Emma opened the medicine cabinet and took out her toothbrush.

Until age nine, she'd swallowed all her toothpaste. Then a girl at a slumber party had told her that was wrong. All the other girls, in barrettes and wide-legged pajamas with ruffles at the hem, already knew how to spit. They'd laughed at her as she flung a mouthful of foam into the sink, desperately trying to sever the tensile string of drool that swung from her lower lip.

A second pair of footsteps came up the stairs as she brushed her teeth. Mattie turned into the bathroom and, for a moment, they stood side by side, staring at their reflections. "Do you remember that piece of toothpaste on the ceiling in the old house?" her sister said.

Years ago, they'd decided to see how long they could get away with not brushing their teeth. To remain undetected, they still had to make small amounts of toothpaste disappear. One night, Emma had disposed of her toothpaste by applying it to the brush and flinging the hunk of paste toward the ceiling. The grey-blue toothpaste had blended surprisingly well with the old popcorn ceiling. "I bet it's still there."

Mattie's lips smiled, but her eyes were shadowed by a glaze of tears. "How come we don't do stupid stuff like that anymore?"

"We're too old."

"No, we're not."

"Do you remember when we made witch soup?"

"That was gross." Mattie pushed her hair off her face with a headband and reached for her face wash. "And awesome."

Instead of dumping rainwater out of a yellow sand bucket in the backyard, they'd added mud, sand, chicken feathers blown in from the neighbor's yard, and a couple of lawn mushrooms. With the nervous excitement of evildoers, they had used their sand toys to scoop up dried cat poop (the neighbors *all* had cats) and dump the hard links into the brew. That was followed by a dried moth and spiderwebs from the corner of Emma's bedroom window, twirled around a stick.

Emma had pretended she and Mattie were witches, like Orddu, Orwen, and Orgoch in *The Black Cauldron*. She was almost sure there was no such thing as magic, but just in case, she'd squeezed two slats in her blinds apart each night and glanced into the backyard. As expected, no greenish haze indicated the rise of any Cauldron-Born.

This had gone on until their dad decided to trim the bottlebrush. He found the bucket, dumped it, washed it, and set it on the rim of the sandbox for them to play with again. "I hate the things that happen when you grow up," she said.

"I don't. I want to learn how to drive and wear makeup."

"You don't need any."

"That's not the point."

"I want you to be smart."

"You're already the smart one."

"So be smarter."

"Like that's possible."

"You can do it, Matt. You're better than me at everything."

Her sister met her eyes in the mirror. "Em, you have to be nicer to Mom. She thinks you don't care. She thinks you're making everything harder."

"Is that what you think?"

Mattie turned on the faucet and rinsed the excess face wash from her hands. "Just try, okay?"

"Something's not right, Matt. You have to feel it."

"Mom says everything'll be fine. I believe her."

Emma watched her sister splash her face with water. With her eyes still closed, Mattie reached for the towel hanging from the wall mount. "Me too," Emma lied.

A few minutes later, she put on her Daffy Duck pajamas and crawled into bed. Water rushed through pipes in the floor and she knew that someone, somewhere in the house, had flushed a toilet. *We're like ghosts*, she thought. *Communicating presence through plumbing and bad carpentry.*

Everything that was wrong could be traced back to that one terrible night, when a thread in the fabric of space and time had been snagged. It crumpled the air between them, creating rifts and canyons with their own storms and weather systems. What if those storms never went away? What if she and her mom grew apart, content to live on opposite sides of the tempest?

There was only one person who would tell her the truth. The piece of paper with his number was still in her desk drawer. She wondered if her dad's smartphone, the only one they had, was in its usual spot downstairs, on the built-in desk next to the laundry room. Emma flung back the covers, grabbed Dan's number from her desk, and crept out of her room.

The hall was dark. No light shone from beneath Mattie's door or her parents'. A solitary patch of moonlight fell through the skylight, illuminating the banister rail. She curved her palm over the rail and stepped down each stair. Two from the bottom, she stopped, the pulse pounding in her throat.

Her mom was downstairs.

Her mom was *talking* to someone.

"Hello, this is Sharon West," she said. "I submitted my application a week ago, and wanted to check on the status. I'm available for interviews any time this week." She paused. "I don't know if Christy mentioned anything, but this job is very important to me. I have two daughters and my husband isn't able to work right now and . . . we're . . . " There was another long pause. "I can work nights, weekends, overtime, graveyard shift, double shifts, anything. Please don't hesitate to call me at this number, 831-555-4589. I look forward to hearing from you."

Emma heard a soft plastic click. Two seconds later, she heard a gasp and the rough slide of a tissue being pulled from its box. Her mom took one deep breath then picked up the phone and dialed again.

"H — hello, this is Sharon West. I submitted my application a week ago."

CHAPTER TWENTY-THREE

WHEN EMMA CAME DOWNSTAIRS that morning, her dad was already at the table. Haloed with grey morning light, he stared at his folded hands. If he'd been kneeling, she could have mistaken him for a medieval monk, clad in a bathrobe instead of a habit.

"Dad, what are you doing? Shouldn't you be in bed?"

He turned his head to look at her, left eye still plum-purple and swollen. "I don't think I can sleep anymore."

She filled a bowl with store-brand bran flakes. She liked the way they got soggy all at once, releasing a faint metallic taste that made her think of holding a nickel in her mouth. "Do you need anything? I can make you some tea or get you some water."

He shook his head. "What will you do at school today?"

"Turn in my *Lonesome Dove* paper."

"What's it about?"

"*Lonesome Dove.*"

"What's it really about?"

"People who die because they can't adapt."

A faint smile lifted the corners of his lips and the silver beard surrounding them. "You're so smart, Em. I don't want you to do anything to ruin that."

"What would I do to ruin it?"

He unfolded his hands and bulbous blue veins rose on their backs, like worms taped to their surface. "When you were born, you didn't even have a name. Your nametag said 'Baby Girl West.' You were eight weeks early and had to stay in an incubator. The nurses put their hands in gloves and tried to rub you warm, but nothing worked. And then I realized it was because you didn't have a name." His eyes flickered sideways, moving from her head to her hands. "When my mother died, we found a box of baby girl's clothes in the back of her closet. It had five outfits in it, each with a tiny nametag sewn in — her grandmother's name. Your name. Instead, my mom had five boys."

"I never knew," she said softly.

"So that's the name I chose for you. The name of a baby someone wanted for years and never got."

"Dad, I — "

"I gave the nurses your new name. I watched them write your nametag from the hallway and I put my hands on the glass, even though they told me not to. I told you this name would make you strong." His lips curved in the echo of a smile. "I told you to fight to get well so I could come and meet you. And you listened."

Emma felt a sob bloom like a choking flower in her throat. She'd seen pictures of her dad in those days, with long hair, gold-rimmed glasses, baggy jeans, and big flannel shirts. She tried to imagine him having hopes and dreams that didn't involve her and Mattie, but she couldn't. He'd given them all up the day she arrived.

"You listened," he said again. "You twisted your body in the incubator, like you were trying to read your new nametag. You looked at it, you looked at me, and then you screamed. You were telling me you understood. And you've always understood, ever since."

"Except now."

"You're stubborn, Em. It was a good thing when you were in that incubator, but now . . . "

Emma tried to force her anger to displace everything else, but she couldn't. All she saw was a wrinkled red raisin of a girl, screaming because they kept her in a plastic box. He had loved her even then. At the heart of everything was love, always love.

"Dad, what did you want to be when you grew up?"

His dark eyes smiled so his lips didn't have to. "I wanted to be a dad." He got up and shuffled toward the stairs, one hand pressed to the base of his arched spine.

Emma felt that curve the way a fish feels a hook in its mouth. "Dad," she whispered. "I need help."

But he didn't hear her. He coughed and bent double, his throat dry from too much talking. Bruised and scabbed, his right hand gripped the banister until his knuckles glowed.

• • •

There were still twenty minutes to go in English class. In newer classrooms, like the portables, the clock's second hand twirled like a mechanized ballerina. In older classrooms, like this one, it thunked like an old man's cane. Emma liked the old ones better. Without even looking, you knew how much closer you were to getting out."

Today, Mrs. Evans wore a blue polka-dot dress with pantyhose and open-toed shoes. There was a ring on her left hand, a big black stone bound to the band with multiple strands of gold wire. It didn't look like a wedding ring, unless she'd gotten married in Middle Earth.

While Mrs. Evans read the daily bulletin, Emma reached for her binder. There was something she had to do today, before anything like last night happened again. She opened the zipper pouch and shoved the pens and pencils aside.

It wasn't there.

She didn't remember throwing the detective's card away, but it was the only explanation for why she couldn't find it. Emma zipped the pouch shut and tried to remember whether he'd also given a card to the school secretary.

"Okay, class," Mrs. Evans said. "Now that you've read *Of Mice and Men*, I want you think back to freshman year, where you read another book that ended with a controversial killing. Do you remember?"

Emma knew where this was going — Mrs. Evans wanted them to remember *The Ox-Bow Incident* and say that in *Ox-Bow*, the characters killed for their own good while in *Mice*, a character killed for the good of another. English teachers were the worst at asking questions that didn't telegraph the answer.

She reached into her backpack and pulled out the maroon notebook. She turned past the pages where she'd described her mom's Miss Havisham décor. On the next page, she'd written "Alejandro Espinosa," followed by the address she heard the policeman repeat to her father that night. Beneath the name and address, she'd already sketched a rough map of East Malo Verde, from Greenwood Boulevard to Vera Cruz Road, marking stoplights with X's. Now, beneath the map, she wrote the other name Elvira had given her: Hector Espinosa.

Which of them had smashed his fist into her father's nose? Whose bloody handprints were on his shirt? It had to be Hector. The name was compact and powerful, like a boxer. A punch from someone named Hector would hurt.

"Anybody?" Mrs. Evans asked. "Does anybody remember a book about a hanging?"

Emma bit her lip to keep from answering. It was habit now, the same way Rachel inspected her hair for split ends. She scraped the ridges of her two front teeth across the pale, slick skin where she'd punctured her lip. *I remember*, she thought. *And if real life were anything like that book, the Espinosas would have been hung a week ago.*

• • •

When class let out, she told Rachel and Via she had to go to the bathroom. For once, being on their shit list worked in her favor. They shrugged and she dashed off before either one could decide they'd go with her.

She ducked through the crowded main hallway, where football players twice her size held court surrounded by cheerleaders who looked half her size. For the first time, she absorbed the comparison without placing herself between them on the spectrum of female thinness. She had bigger problems now.

In the main office, the secretary asked how she could help. "I was here the other day," she said. "You called me in to talk to a detective."

"Oh, Miss West! Yes, I remember you."

"Do you have the business card the detective left? He gave me one, but I can't find it."

"I think it's around here somewhere." The secretary lifted her desk blotter to reveal an assortment of cards and gum wrappers. Emma's eyes scanned the logos, looking for the familiar star with a green field painted in its center.

"There." She pointed at a card with the badge printed on its left-hand side.

"Good eye." The secretary pulled out the card. "Is this what you're looking for?"

"Can I borrow it?"

"Of course." The woman handed it to her. "I have his name on the guest register."

Emma slid the card into her jeans pocket. "Thanks," she said, slipping back through the door and vanishing into the anonymity of the main hallway. There were still four minutes until the first bell. If she ran out of time, she'd be late for chemistry . . . and Dan. *It couldn't be helped*, she thought, remembering her dad's whisper: *They found us*. If the Espinosas really were coming back, someone had to do something.

She followed the main hall to the end of the building and exited the courtyard. Tucked into a corner was a small bay of payphones, left over from the days when no one had a cell phone. One day, when Mr. Parker had decided to lecture on government waste instead of King Phillip's War, he'd talked about blocking the school's plan to remove the phones because it would have cost $3,000 to contract out the work.

Emma said a silent thank-you to Mr. Parker's budgetary conscience and counted the change left over from an impulsive candy purchase. After three seconds in her palm, the coins gave off the heady metallic scent she loved best in the world. Two quarters bought her a dial tone.

His phone rang once, then twice, then three times. He picked up on the fourth ring. "This is Kobi."

"Detective Kobilinski? This is Emma West. You talked to me at school the other day about my father's case."

"I remember you, Miss West. What can I do for you? Did you remember something you want to tell me?"

"I'm calling to ask for an update. Have you found out anything new since last time?"

"Well, I'll be damned." She imagined him swinging his feet down off the desk. "Are you riding my ass?"

She stared at the silver and black phone box. Someone had written 14 VIDA in gold glitter pen on the top of it. Beneath it, someone else had written CHAP RIP in bloated bubble letters. Emma had seen that insult — *chapete* — in an online forum a few days ago, where forum posters bragged about their stockpiles of weapons in garages all over town. "If I were doing that, I'd have called you two days ago."

"Kid, what makes you think I'd tell you anything I knew?"

"My parents pay taxes."

"That doesn't mean I work for you."

"Have you figured out which Espinosa attacked my father? There are two of them, in case you didn't know."

"I did know, but I'm surprised you do." Kobilinski sighed. This time, she pictured him holding the phone against his right ear while he slipped his left arm out of his suit jacket. "Listen, even if I knew one of them was guilty, I couldn't tell you. Not until we make an arrest."

"Are you going to make an arrest?"

"No."

"Could you?"

"I know what you're trying to do, kid, but the law works this way for a reason. The evidence decides who is guilty."

"I thought it was the jury."

"Look, I can't tell you anything about an open investigation. End of story."

"What if someone gets shot tomorrow? You'll forget all about my dad. Our lives will still be ruined, and they'll get away with it."

"You're right. And I wish it could be different. But there are procedures I have to follow. If no one talks, there's no evidence and no one gets arrested."

"Then make them talk. Someone did this. Someone had to have seen it."

"What are they teaching you in school, kid? Gestapo 101?"

Heat blossomed in her cheeks. It traveled down her neck and deep into her chest, where it burrowed into the chambers of her pulpy heart. In a world where people went to jail for shooting burglars and rapists in their own homes, she shouldn't have expected anything different. "You're telling me we don't matter."

"I'm telling you your family doesn't matter any more or less than the Espinosa family. They have rights, too. I can't give you what you want, kid. I'm sorry."

She thought about asking to speak to his commanding officer, because that was what people did on cop shows, but she had no confidence that anyone else in the station would be more willing to help. She fired her last round of ammunition. "My dad said they're coming back. They have our address from the truck registration." She paused, and then decided her dad's version of events had a better chance of making waves. "We saw two of them last night, cruising past our house."

"Did anyone call and report it? Did you get a license plate on them?"

"No," Emma said slowly.

"Then I can't help you, kid."

"I read an online forum. There were *Norteños* and *Sureños*, bragging about how many guns they'd stockpiled. That's evidence, right?"

"Look, I got a stack on my desk a hundred cases high. At least eighty of them are armed robberies and forty-seven are weapons trafficking. Every *hefe* in East Malo Verde has a gun, a gun I can't trace because it's been stolen so many times even the gang members have lost count. The best I can do is go talk to the neighbors again and see if they heard or saw anything. If you see anything else that tells you you're in danger, get a license plate or a photo and give it to us. We'll do the rest."

"I thought that's what I was doing."

"Do your parents know you're talking to me?"

"Who do you think I'm doing this for?"

"Miss West," the detective said.

"What?"

"Study hard." Then he hung up.

Her stomach roiled with nerves, bile, and bitterness. Kobilinski wouldn't help because he didn't want to help. Flannery O'Connor was wrong. Good men weren't hard to find; they were just easy to ignore.

The second bell rang. She looked up at the cafeteria building, with its ugly rock exterior and huge wooden hanging depicting their mascot, the Minuteman. Dressed in a loose shirt rolled up to the elbows and tight knee-length breeches, he clasped a rifle in his right hand.

Emma sighed. Everyone in the whole goddamn town had a gun except for her.

• • •

As she stared at the mildewed grout on the locker room floor, she counted how many things she'd never done because she was afraid: try out for a sport, join a new club, eat lunch by herself on purpose. Most people at school pretended they weren't afraid of anything, like Tim and the boy he almost fought. Were they better at hiding it, or was there something abnormal about the fear she carried with her all day, every day?

She thought of the snowy TV screen she visualized to calm herself down when she was afraid. When most people looked at a snowy screen, they interpreted it as a signal to change the channel. She was the only one who interpreted it as a place to stay, a source of comfort.

She smoothed the cuffs of her PE shirt as she made her way to the entrance of the locker room. Elvira's cotton-candy gloss sparkled when she smiled. "Hey, partner. Is something wrong? You don't look so happy."

Emma glanced over her shoulder to make sure no one was there. "Do you want to go hang out behind the tennis courts?"

"Why, what happened? Is your dad okay?"

"I need to talk to you about something."

When Elvira nodded, Emma led her around the tennis courts to the practice field. The damp grass squished when Emma stepped on it. "Don't they know we're in the middle of a goddamn drought?"

"Now I know there's something wrong. You never swear."

"I swear in my head all the time. I just never let it out."

"That's not healthy. You're gonna have a heart attack."

They sat together on a damp set of bleachers. "So what did you want to talk to me about?" Elvira asked, leaning back.

"Remember when I asked you about the Espinosas?"

"Yeah." A cold wind gusted and Elvira snapped an elastic from her wrist, twirling it around her hair.

"How can I get a message to Hector Espinosa?"

Elvira let go of her ponytail. "You're kidding, right?"

"I don't know what else to do." Emma took a deep breath. "The men who attacked my dad said they'd be back. A car with two *Norteños* passed our house last night and he freaked out."

"This whole town is full of *Norteños*. That doesn't mean anything."

"I know," Emma said softly. "But what if he's right? The police can't do anything unless I have evidence. So I need Hector to give me some evidence. What about Letizia? Can she take him a message?"

"Holy shit, Emma, no, you can't do that." She reached out and gripped Emma's arm with more strength than she'd ever used to swing a badminton racket. "All those *pinche cholos* out there? That's his army. He tells one of them to go kill your whole family, they have to do it. You don't want to fuck with that."

Emma looked out at the far end of the field. The wind lashed her hair against her face, and she wished it was thick like Elvira's. "I don't know what else to do."

"Just leave it alone. It's not your job."

She turned her head and looked into Elvira's glitter-rimmed eyes. "No, it's not. But that's what you do when you love someone, isn't it? At least that's what you said about the gang members."

"That's different!"

"Why? I love my family more than they love their stupid gang." In her head, Kobilinski's retort played on eternal repeat: *Every hefe in East Malo Verde has a gun, a gun I can't trace because it's been stolen so many times even the gang members have lost count.* "You didn't see him. You didn't hear how scared he was. I tried to get the police to help, but they can't do anything."

"Maybe you just have to let it go."

"I can't." She blinked and the tears in her eyes made the horizon float and bob like a buoy adrift at sea. The world was full of water. She was drowning. They all were. "I need a gun."

"What? That's crazy. *You're* crazy."

"They broke his glasses. They kicked him in the stomach and the legs and the side of the head. They wrapped their hands around his throat and tried to choke him to death. They ground his face against the shards of his lenses. How much do you have to hate someone to do that to them?"

She looked down at her socks, splashed with muddy droplets of water. There was no shape or pattern to the drops, no curve or function she could graph to make sense of it all. "Am I supposed to let them do it again if they come to our house?"

"They won't."

"How do you know?"

Elvira looked at the ground. Smudged half-moons decorated the tops of her eyelids, where her thick eyeliner had rubbed off.

"What if it had been real, what my dad saw? My mom could have been outside getting the mail. My sister could have been getting dropped off at that very minute. We have a rosebush in the corner, by the front window." Something inside her clawed at her throat to get out. She coughed and pushed it back down. "My dad takes care of those roses."

"*Chica*—"

"Can your cousin get me a gun?"

"No. Tell me you aren't serious."

Emma put her face in her hands. There were too many words in the pit between her heart and her stomach. Everything she couldn't say at home had gotten stuck inside, and now her entire life was jumbled up, a grab-bag of Scrabble letters that were tangled and impossible to sort out. "I don't know."

"*I* know." Elvira put an arm around her shoulders.

Emma rested her head on Elvira's shoulder, grateful to have a place to put it. It was too heavy to hold up on its own. There were too many thoughts and too many people inside — Gatsby, Hamlet, Juliet, George, Lennie, Oedipus, Gus, Call, Clara, Mom, Dad, Mattie, Dan.

She imagined her *Lonesome Dove* paper, held sideways until all the letters fell off the page. The letters rearranged themselves in a landscape of mesas and ridges that Gus and Call rode through on horses made entirely of i's. A gun was just an L, clutched sideways.

"I need a gun," she whispered.

"*Madre de Dios*, Emma, do you hear yourself?"

"They're coming back. What would you do?"

"I can't do this. You know I can't."

Emma grabbed Elvira's arm, a forked bolt of fear stabbing her heart. "What if they come this weekend? What if I don't show up on Monday and you're the only one who knows why?"

Elvira sobbed. "Fuck, don't talk like that!"

Although it felt like lightning had struck her heart, it was her brain that raced, lit up by the blue-white pulse of power. "It'll work," she said quickly. "Listen, there aren't any metal detectors and no one's going to watch us in the locker room. I'll even meet you here before first period. You don't have to do anything except show up."

"What if you get caught?"

"I'll say I found it in a garbage can."

"They'll know it's not true."

"I've never done anything bad before. They'll believe me."

"No." Elvira swallowed heavily and stood up. "I can't."

"He coughs up blood! He was laid off a year and half ago and my mom cancelled our insurance and he can't go to the hospital, and I think something's really wrong. I can't fix that, but maybe I can keep something worse from happening, too."

Elvira sank back down to the bleacher. "You're talking about a gun, Emma. You could die. You could hurt someone."

She sank to the footboard, putting her eyes even with Elvira's. She opened her mouth to beg, and then caught sight of a gold chain beneath the neck of Elvira's T-shirt. She'd seen that necklace before; it was a medallion with a Catholic saint on it. "Listen to me," she said, reaching for Elvira's hands. "When Joan of Arc was fifteen, she led an army. She was defending a king, a man she didn't even know. How much harder do you think she'd have fought if it were for her dad?"

Elvira's eyes flooded with tears and she crossed herself. She pulled her golden medallion to her mouth and kissed it. "This is crazy. You know this is crazy."

"You're the only one who can help me." She looked up at Elvira from beneath wet star-tipped lashes. "Will you?"

• • •

After French class, she went to her locker to get everything she needed for the weekend. She felt like she was walking through a dream where the air was made of cotton. The harder you tried to scream, the more it filled your lungs. Instead of fighting it, you had to let it consume you. She slid her fingers down the fuzzy edge of her grocery bag book cover.

"Hey," a familiar voice said.

Emma jumped. "Goddamn it."

"Gotcha." Dan leaned his head against the locker bay. "Missed you in chem."

"I talked to the detective again."

"Did something happen?"

"Dad thinks the gang is coming back. I took him outside for a minute last night, but when a low-rider passed by with two gangbangers in it, he panicked."

"Jesus." He swept his hair back from his brow. "What did the police say? You reported it, right?"

"I tried. Since nothing actually happened, they can't do anything." She paused. "We're one family. We're easy to ignore."

He reached out and touched her arm, thumb stroking the tender skin of her inner elbow. "Who could ignore you?"

Goosebumps broke out across her shoulder blades. How did he always know what to say? "Dan, what if my dad's right?"

"Random gangsters aren't going to come into an unfamiliar neighborhood and start shooting."

"Of course not. They'll scout it out first, just like they did last night."

"Okay, it's scary when you say it like that." He stood up straight. "The cops seriously can't do anything?"

"Can't, won't, I don't know." She pulled her chemistry book and her pre-calculus book into her backpack. "I think it's time for Plan B."

"From outer space?"

"That's Plan 9."

"Then what's Plan B?"

"What's the waiting period for getting a gun?"

The smile fell from his face. "I don't know, but I don't think that's the answer."

"Not for me," she lied. "My parents could get one. For the house. Or for when they go out."

"And carry it with them all the time? That's no way to live."

"What about constantly fearing a drive-by? Or never knowing who's waiting to jump you when you leave the grocery store? How's that for a way to live?"

"Emma." His green eyes stared steadily into hers. "What did *you* see last night?"

She closed her eyes and tried to replay the scene in her mind. "I saw an old car. With two Mexican guys in it. The guy in the passenger seat pointed straight at us."

"Why would he do that? Was anyone behind you?"

"No. We were in front of the house. Dad got scared, and he pushed me into the wall to protect me, in case they started shooting."

"So couldn't they have been pointing at what looked like a man pushing a girl into a wall? Maybe they were really trying to help."

"No, it couldn't have been that. I saw their faces. They were laughing."

"To a lot of people, domestic violence is funny. Especially when it's happening to someone who looks like they have everything."

"Everything?" Emma said, stepping backward. "But they don't know anything about us! We don't even have enough money for real cheese."

"Then how's your family going to get enough money to buy a gun?"

"I don't know! I just want everything to go back to how it was!" She zipped up her backpack and slung it over her shoulder. "I have to go. I'll see you next week, unless we all get shot and killed this weekend."

"Emma," he said, reaching for her arm. "I'm sorry."

"Me too." She brushed past him and ran down the hallway toward the front gate.

CHAPTER TWENTY-FOUR

Saturday, April 12

CLOUDS SWAM IN THE BLUE ocean sky, framed by the family room's grid of windows. Emma sat in Great-Grandma Jennings's rocking chair, Dan's notebook open on her lap. *I'm sorry*, she wrote. *I got angry because I couldn't make you understand. I want to make you understand.* Then she crossed it all out. Mrs. Evans always told them to vary their sentence structure when writing. There had to be a better way to start an apology than with three "I" sentences in a row.

She got up and opened the sliding glass door that led to the backyard. Two dirty lawn chairs sat beneath the bottlebrush, shaded from the sun. Every side of the backyard was protected by a six-foot fence, with absolutely no street view. *Maybe*, she thought, *there are two apologies I can make today.*

She hosed the chairs off and wiped them down with old towels from the garage. Then she went upstairs and knocked softly on her parents' bedroom door.

"Come in," her dad said. He lay on the bed, dressed in a robe and sweats. "Did you come to read to me some more? I never found out what happened to George and Lennie."

"Mom and Mattie are at the grocery store, so I thought I'd sit outside and do some writing. Do you want to sit with me?"

"Outside?"

"In the backyard. I hosed off the lawn chairs and everything."

"I don't know." His eyes drifted down to the bedspread. "I'm tired, Em."

"I could make you a snack and some iced tea. The roses smell so good right now."

"I don't think — "

"Please, Dad."

He sighed. "You're doing homework?"

"Yes," she lied.

"All right, then." He nodded and she hurried to help him sit up before he changed his mind. He flattened his palms against the edge of the bed and leaned forward like a ski jumper. His back bent, as if it hurt too much to straighten it.

By the time he shuffled downstairs, she'd already put a few crackers and carrot sticks on a plate. "Ready?"

"I need a break," he wheezed, reaching for the kitchen island. He held on with his fingertips, like a kid in the deep end of the swimming pool. A minute later, he nodded. "Okay, I'm ready now."

She opened the sliding glass door and he stepped onto the redwood decking, squinting as the sun fell full upon him. His good eye narrowed and he raised his right hand to shield it. "It's warm out."

"I told you. Isn't it nice?"

He pointed at her maroon notebook. "What's that?"

"A present."

"From who?"

"My best friend," she said softly.

He shuffled to the closest lawn chair, reaching out with his fingertips like he had for the kitchen island. Before he could grasp it, a neighbor behind them opened a sliding glass door. "*Hola, cabrón, qué tal? Cuándo es la fiesta?*"

Her dad scanned the small backyard, panic widening his eyes. "What was that?"

"Dad, it's just the neighbor. He's on the phone."

"*Estaré allí a las nueves.*"

Her dad clapped his palms over his ears. "They said they'd come back. Em. We need to go inside *now*."

"Dad, it's okay. It's just Mr. Trujillo." She pointed at his rosebushes. "Look at Ingrid Bergman. Want to cut some blossoms for the dining room table?"

"We have to go, Em."

"You aren't even looking. Can't you even *try*?"

"Don't talk!" He pointed at the fence. "Now they know we're home." He hobbled to the sliding glass door, stepping inside and waiting for her to follow. Emma watched him in shock. This person wasn't her dad anymore. He was a wide-eyed, shaking, white-haired ghost she didn't even recognize.

"Fine," she said. "You want to go inside? We'll go inside." She picked up the plate of snacks and went back into the house, throwing all of it straight into the garbage can.

• • •

On Monday morning, Emma went straight to the locker room. Elvira was there, wearing a black tracksuit with white stripes down the sides. Her lips were dry and chapped, disappearing in the pale square of her face without their customary coat of gloss and glitter. It made her look older, like a grown-up who'd called in sick. "I saw it," Elvira whispered, sweeping her finger beneath her thin lower lashes. "In her drawer."

"Whose? Monica's?"

Elvira nodded, sitting down on the bench beside her gym locker. "She went down to the corner for some *ahorritos*. I told her I wanted some, even though I didn't."

"What happened?"

A thin blonde walked past them toward the showers. Elvira waited for her to turn out of sight. "We shouldn't be here."

"Tell me what happened and then we'll go."

"I didn't even know she had it. It was under an old shirt and a bottle of tequila. I just put my fingers on it and felt it. She brought that thing into our *house,* with my little brother."

"Did you take it?"

"I didn't even want to touch it."

"Just wrap it in a towel, and put it in a bag. That's all you have to do."

If Elvira brought her the gun, she could search online for a user's manual. Emma wondered if her parents' internet account would be flagged by such a search. Didn't writers do stuff like that all the time, though? Look up how to kill people, how to rob banks, how to build a bomb? *I was writing,* she'd say. *I was telling my own story.*

"If you bring me the gun, no one in your house will get hurt. Isn't that what you want?"

"*Sí*. But what about you?"

"No one in my house is going to get hurt, either."

"Monica will know I did it."

"She won't. How could she?"

"I'll get in trouble."

Emma dug her teeth into her lower lip. If Elvira's cousin was in a gang, her whole family was already in trouble. "Listen, all you have to do is get it to school. And then no one will know anything about it but me."

"I'm scared."

"I am, too." She reached for Elvira's hand and pictured the snowy TV screen, buzzing in perpetuity, keeping her from facing her deepest fear: a future where her father was always the scared, shaking man he'd been yesterday. "That's why I have to do this."

• • •

The main hallway glowed with red, green, and brown, the colors of the Cinco de Mayo murals on the other side of the glass. Emma watched the colors wash over her boots. She turned down a perpendicular hallway, where the glare of fluorescent tube lighting replaced the eggshell glow of the front windows.

At the other end of the hall, a group of four *cholas* turned the corner, walking shoulder to shoulder. The tallest walked in the middle, dressed in a red T-shirt and jeans that puddled over her shoes. Her lipstick looked like brewed coffee. When she saw Emma, she put her hand in her pocket and held it there.

They're coming, her dad had said. *They found us.*

But who was coming? And when? Were they just supposed to hide for the rest of their lives? She remembered her dad's hands as he'd reached out for the sliding glass door, fingers spread wide in panic. *I want to understand*, she thought. If she did, the grip of anger tightening her heart might loosen. But was it even possible? Every time Mr. Parker started to tell them about Iraq, he took off his glasses and wiped his eyes first. "The sand," he said, "it sticks to you like mud. When you go through a sandstorm, it chokes you, and the choke feels like — " But he never told them what it felt like. "Pray you never feel it," he said instead.

But I need to feel it, she thought. *I want to understand.*

Emma took a deep breath and stepped into the center of the hallway. All four *cholas* shuffled to a stop in front of her. Someone's tennis shoes shrieked against the dirty linoleum. "What the fuck," one of the shorter girls said.

"Move," the tallest said.

"No," Emma replied.

"You'll move." The tall *chola* shoved Emma's shoulder, pushing her back a few steps. "See?"

The three other girls laughed and hissed.

Now her armpits were wet, and the backs of her knees. She looked at the tall *chola*. The girl's eyes would be pretty even without the layers of black eyeliner and mascara. *I'm sorry*, she thought as she stepped into the center of the hallway. "I won't move," she said.

"What is this?" The tall *chola* tilted her head. "You wanna thrown down? Right here?"

"Bitch is crazy," one of the other girls said.

"Hella disrespect," said a third.

"For the last time," the tall *chola* said. "Move."

"No. Not for you."

"It's on," one of the other girls said. "Do it."

"Not for *me*?" The tall *chola's* eyes glittered like black sequins. "You don't even know me, bitch. But now you will."

She reached for Emma's hair. Pain sizzled across Emma's scalp as her head snapped sideways. The girl's leg swept a circle beneath her, knocking her feet out from under her. Emma hit the ground hip first, a shock wave forcing all breath from her lungs. Her body curled into a fetal position on instinct.

"Fight!" one of the kids in front of the Spanish class cried. Emma heard the squeal of sneakers on linoleum as almost every student within shouting range converged on the hallway.

Something big and heavy hit her in the side. *A foot*, she thought.

The floor smelled like rubber. She pressed her face into it and held her breath.

Another heavy thing hit her where her arms were crossed, over her chest. She closed her eyes.

Something long and thin raked across her left cheek.

I want to understand, she thought.

Then a deep male voice interrupted everything. "Break it up!" she heard. Then, closer, "Hold her."

"Don't touch me! I'll fucking kill you!"

"I said hold her."

Emma let out her breath. It blew dust and sand across the floor, onto the shoe of the man bending over her. She lifted her head and the red jacket of an assistant principal flooded her field of vision. The nametag on his jacket said ASSISTANT PRINCIPAL GALLEGOS. "Can you stand up?" he asked.

Emma released her arms and found them shaking. So were her legs, once she unfolded them from her fetal position. She pushed her palms to the filthy floor and pressed herself into a sitting position.

"All the way." Gallegos yanked her to her feet, keeping one hand clenched around her upper arm. She looked down at his knuckles, dotted with thick black hair.

"Emma?"

She looked up and saw Via standing behind the assistant principal. Mr. Parker was there, too, holding out his arms to keep the three other *cholas* from joining the fight. He looked worried, his eyebrows floating above the rim of his glasses.

Via ducked beneath Gallegos's outstretched arm. "What happened?"

Gallegos dropped his arm, forcing Via back. "Come on, you're going to the office."

A second assistant principal held the tall *chola*'s arms behind her back. "Are you gonna behave?" he asked.

She smiled and licked her lips. "Yeah, I'll behave."

Gallegos pointed down the hallway. "Get her out of here." The pair of them obeyed, the girl turning back to smile at her friends and mouth *you fucking bitch* to Emma. "I've never seen you before," Gallegos said. "Are you new here?"

"Junior," Emma croaked.

"Well, the nurse will clean you up and then I'll take you to the principal." He gave her a gentle push with his hand and she obeyed. Her hip hurt, and her back and her side. But she didn't see any blood on the floor beneath her. *When do I know if it worked?* she thought.

The crowd of students gathered to watch the fight parted for Assistant Principal Gallegos. He kept one warm hand on her shoulder to pilot her around the corner, back to the main hallway.

As Gallegos stepped in front of her to open the main office's door, Dan came around the corner from the chem hallway. He stopped dead, eyes wide. "Emma!"

"Keep moving," Gallegos said, ushering her inside and closing the door behind them.

Dan dashed to the window and pressed both hands to the glass, eyes traveling from Gallegos to her face to the *chola* already sitting on the bench in front of the principal's office. His mouth hung open, but his lips never shaped a word.

Emma let her eyes float back up to his. Wide and bright, they glowed like wet morning grass. *I'm sorry*, she mouthed.

He stood, hands pressed to the glass, until Gallegos took her into the nurse's office and closed the door behind them.

• • •

"Three seconds. *Three.* That's how lucky you are." Her mom sat across from her in the counselors' office, the same room Kobilinski had taken her to a few days ago. Under the artificial light, her mom's skin looked yellow instead of blue.

Emma pressed her cheek to her shoulder, feeling the strange rub of sweater against plastic. The nurse had put a rectangular bandage on her cheek where the other girl scratched her. "How is that lucky?"

"Let's get out of here, and then I'll deal with you."

Emma frowned. "Out?"

"The principal is coming to talk to us first."

Right on cue, Principal Brooks opened the door. His loose tie lay crooked beneath his shirt collar like a custom-striped noose. "Mrs. West?" he said, flipping open the file in his hand.

"I am Mrs. West." Her mom used her back-of-the-throat voice, the one she used with deliverymen and repairmen.

"I understand this is your daughter's first offense?"

"My daughter is a model student, and if that's her record you're looking at, you'll know she's the least of your problems right now."

Principal Brooks pulled out a chair between her and her mom and sat down facing her. "Emma, care to tell me what happened out there?"

Emma looked at the cracked skin on the backs of his hands. It flaked like dandruff, centering on the veins visible beneath his skin. How could someone whose worst problem was dry skin understand how she felt when she looked at her dad's sopping plum eye? "I always move," she said. "They never move for anyone, and I wanted them to see me, just once."

"Who are 'they'?"

Her mother coughed, but Emma ignored her warning. "The *cholas*."

"We've had some trouble lately," her mom said. "My husband was attacked by gang members, and I don't think Emma knows how to deal with that."

Principal Brooks shifted in his seat, facing her mother instead of her. "Are you saying the situation at home is the reason for her behavior?"

Her mom flushed in red blotches that traveled from beneath the neck of her cardigan to her cheeks. "The situation at home is one no college-bound teenage girl should have to deal with. But it exists, through no fault of her own."

"Regardless of what prompted it, she knows better." He glanced back at the folder. "Assistant Principal Gallegos noted that he broke up the fight three seconds before the bell rang. That being the case, I am going to suspend your daughter for one day. She can come back tomorrow."

"You can't do that. It'll go on her record."

"Ma'am, I can't do anything about that."

"She laid there and let them hit her without fighting back! Is that worthy of a suspension in your eyes?"

"I have three witnesses who said she pushed the other girl."

The other cholas, Emma thought.

"Emma wouldn't do that. She's never hurt anyone in her life."

Principal Brooks turned his wrist to look at a big gold watch. "Why don't you talk about this at home? Emma needs to leave school grounds immediately."

Her mom's eyes filled with tears. "Please, you don't understand. Isn't there anything we can do? She'll need scholarships. She needs a clean record."

"Good day, Mrs. West." He rose from his chair. "Emma, you may return to first period tomorrow morning."

"What kind of school are you running? Who punishes an innocent girl for being beaten up?"

Principal Brooks held the door open and stood next to it, waiting to usher them out. Emma's mom held her chin high, with all the fire of hell in her eyes. "I'll be writing to the school board. And the superintendent. And anyone else who cares about the good kids in this school system."

Emma slipped her sweaty palm into her mom's and squeezed it hard.

• • •

She dropped her backpack at the foot of the staircase. She ached in places she'd never felt before: the outside of her elbow, the curve of her waist. She slipped past her mom into the downstairs bathroom and closed the door, ripping off the bandage the nurse had put on. Turning her head, she saw two red lines bisect her cheek, thin as a fine-point Sharpie. The light streaming through the frosted bathroom window tinted her like an Instagram filter. She forced a smile, feeling the angry tear of tissue as she separated cells that had started to bond together again. She knew she was supposed to feel bad, like she'd lost something, but she didn't. She'd never seen the glow of morning light in the downstairs bathroom before.

When she opened the door, she saw her mom leaning on the kitchen island with her elbows, both palms covering her face. At the sound of the bathroom door, she stood up straight and wiped her index fingers beneath her eyes. "Emma, you can't keep doing this."

"Doing what?"

"Trying to fix things. Taking your father outside. Getting in fights at school. It's not helping."

"Nobody else is even trying."

"You don't know that."

Emma frowned. "I'm in school, and I'm the one who called the police to check on Dad's truck. How messed up is that?"

"I handled it. You're just making things worse."

"Dad can't see, he hasn't been to a doctor, and now he won't even go outside. What about that did you handle?"

Her mom's lower lip quivered. "It's on your record, Emma."

"I'm just a report card to you, aren't I? I could have a broken rib, but who gives a crap as long as Harvard doesn't know how I got it?"

"It's your future. You need to care about that."

"Maybe there's something I care about more."

"There is *nothing* I care about more." Her mom's eyes flashed with the force of a falling star, gravity pulling its pale fire into the atmosphere. "Go upstairs. I'll tell your father you came home sick."

• • •

The computer's glowing screen would tell her mom she was still awake, but Emma didn't care. She was convinced that nothing short of a pool of blood under the door would make her mom look her in the eye again that day. She'd eaten her squished sack lunch in her room at noon. At six, Mattie had come up with a tray. "I have to go back downstairs," her sister said. "I'm not supposed to stay."

"I know. It's okay, Matt."

Her sister's wide blue eyes blinked once. "Did you really fight someone?"

"Is that what Mom said?"

"Kayla's older sister texted her. She asked me in fifth period."

"I didn't fight. Maybe I should have."

"Did they hurt you?"

"A little."

"You're the smart one, you know."

"Mom already gave me the lecture."

"But you won't listen if it comes from her."

Emma looked up. "What do you mean?"

"You don't listen to anyone. Ever."

"That's not true."

"It is. Maybe that's the one thing you don't already know."

"So who should I listen to, Matt?"

"Until today, I would have said you." Mattie set the tray on the foot of Emma's bed and closed the door behind her.

Emma's breath caught like she'd been slapped. Now there was one more person she'd failed to make understand. First Rachel and Via, then her mom, then Elvira, now Mattie. They all asked her for answers, until they didn't like what they heard. Then they wanted her to be quiet and go away.

"Goddamn it," she said, leaving her desk and crouching at the foot of her bed. The tray held a dinner plate with a small pile of spaghetti and a crust of French bread, along with a small glass of milk. The crust of bread tasted better than every bite of spaghetti. When she finished, she put the tray on the floor and went back to her desk.

Four hours later, Emma felt the sharp pulse of a vein behind her eyes. She looked up from her chem homework, something about the reversible reaction of dissolving a solute in a solution. The headache had been there for at least an hour, but she managed to ignore it until it started tapping on her eyeball. "No one's home," she groaned. "Go away."

All night, she'd listened to the noise of movement and motion in the house: floors creaking, water pipes rushing, the plastic rumble of the dishwasher's top rack being rolled out. The neighbor's Corolla sputtered home and parked across the street. Someone walked a yippy dog. A kid rode by on a bike with noisemakers on its spokes.

She was the only one who wasn't making noise.

She pinched the blinds apart to look down at the street below. What if the happiest she'd ever be was walking a small dog after work, feeling it pull on the leash while she held her hand over her eyes to shield them from the thick fog? She thought about how long it would take for her to be that person. Five years — one more of high school and four of college. She didn't get to make a single selfish choice for the next five years. Instead, she'd get an IV drip full of stress, a third-world nation's worth of student loan debt, and the burden of paying it all back while finding a place to live and a job that didn't make her feel like Edward Norton in *Fight Club*. And she hated *Fight Club*, because it was a lie, a trick, a cheat.

She shoved her chem book off her tiny desk and turned on her computer instead. As soon as the hard drive stopped grinding, she signed into chat. Immediately, *Redhead_Rachel* messaged her.

Redhead_Rachel: Emma!! Is that you? You okay?

BookGirl14: Fine. My head hurts.

Redhead_Rachel: How long are you suspended?

BookGirl14: It's already over. I can come back tomorrow.

Redhead_Rachel: What happened? Did you really swing at that girl?

BookGirl14: No. I wish I did.

Redhead_Rachel: I'm glad you didn't. You know what they say. Violence isn't the answer.

BookGirl14: Tell that to the people who beat up my dad.

Redhead_Rachel: I can talk to my dad for you.

BookGirl14: Why?

Redhead_Rachel: So you can go to prom. You can't go if you have a suspension, remember.

BookGirl14: I'm not going to the prom.

Redhead_Rachel: Dan looked miserable in chemistry. Just so you know.

BookGirl14: When did your mom leave your dad?

Redhead_Rachel: What does that have to do with anything?

BookGirl14: When?

Redhead_Rachel: October 12.

BookGirl14: Would you have given a shit if prom happened on October 13?

Redhead_Rachel: Emma, you're doing it again.

BookGirl14: What?

Redhead_Rachel: Being weird. Angry.

Emma wanted to type *sorry not sorry*, but figured she'd caused enough trouble for one day. She imagined a character, just like her, who wanted to make everyone happy. What would Jesus type? *I'll get better*, she wrote.

Then, smiling, *I want to get better.*

CHAPTER TWENTY-FIVE

Tuesday, April 15

EMMA WALKED INTO THE LOCKER room with her backpack slung over both shoulders instead of just one. Her body ached too much to let all that weight sit awkwardly on one side. She'd tapped her elbow against the shower door that morning and felt a kick of pain shoot up her right arm. Although her mom hadn't said anything in the car, Emma felt her eyes roving over her body, looking at the scratches on her cheek (already fading), analyzing her movements to see if she was really hurt (a bit late). Her dad hadn't questioned the story about her being sick, and she had no idea how her mom had explained the scratches. Maybe he'd never even asked.

Emma looked down at her watch. 7:51 a.m.

She didn't know if Elvira would come, or if she knew what had happened yesterday, or if she'd ever talk to her again. That thought hurt more than the red welt on her side, where the *chola's* first kick had landed.

She watched the second hand fly around the dial. Girls tossed their backpacks into lockers and gave her strange looks over their shoulders. No one hung out in the girls' locker room for fun.

7:53 a.m.

She pushed her weight onto her other foot. Two more minutes and she'd have to run all the way through the courtyard and the main building to Mr. Parker's class. She leaned her head back against the cold cement wall. Somewhere behind her forehead, that same vein was throbbing. *This is stupid*, she thought, pushing herself off the wall. *I'm stupid. She's not coming.*

She hurried to the locker room entrance and crashed into Elvira. Sweat beaded her friend's brow beneath the barrel-roll bangs. Her cotton candy gloss was smudged below her bottom lip. "I did it."

Emma gulped. A nervous stab in her stomach dwarfed the pain in her head. *It's really happening*, she thought, glancing at her watch.

7:55 a.m.

"Let's go." She grabbed Elvira's arm and pulled her to the bench beside her PE locker. Elvira eased her backpack off her shoulder, setting it down gently, as if it contained a bomb. Emma clenched her stomach muscles as she twirled her combination lock.

Elvira pulled a shopping bag from her backpack, something from a bath store, red with white candy canes on it. She handed it to Emma, fingertips turning white where they grasped the handles.

"I don't know where she got it. It's probably stolen."

"They all are," Emma said, gauging the weight of the bag. It felt like a full soda bottle, not a two-liter, but the size that cost $1.50 in the vending machine. "The cop told me that much."

Elvira zipped her backpack and stood up. "Emma, I only did this — "

"It's okay," Emma said softly. "I know why."

"Don't get in any more fights, okay?"

"I won't."

"So I'll see you in PE?"

Emma nodded. "Thank you. You're the only person who understands what family means. What it *should* mean."

Elvira smiled wanly and turned to go. Emma set the red bag down on the floor and dropped her backpack next to it.

7:56 a.m.

She pulled out a piece of scratch paper with last week's grocery list on it. On the other side, she'd scrawled a quick diagram of a handgun, copied from an online store. There were four of them, the top sellers on the site, with the safety marked in red colored pencil on each. According to the website, the safety temporarily disengaged the firing pin. The gun couldn't go off in her locker or backpack as long as she set it correctly.

She looked over her shoulder.

Two girls stood at the end of the aisle, their backs to her, gossiping about a third girl. As long as she could hear their voices, she was safe.

Emma picked up the bag and set it on top of the pile of clothes in her locker. Carefully, she reached inside. Her fingers touched the soft cotton of a crumpled white T-shirt. She splayed her fingers over it, feeling out the contours of the gun.

When she'd established the handle and muzzle, she slid her fingers underneath the T-shirt.

The gun was heavier than she thought it would be. The ones on TV looked so light. People did rolls, flips, and slides while pointing and shooting with complete accuracy. Emma knew it wasn't possible, at least not for her. The weight alone would wear on her arm after more than a few seconds.

She tilted it downward. It looked fake, like a cheap piece of plastic. The article she'd read said that different kinds of guns had different safety mechanisms. The trick was in deciding whether this was a revolver, a semi-automatic pistol, or a kind of weapon not mentioned in the article. She'd studied images of the different types over the weekend. Just as she'd suspected, a revolver looked exactly like it was depicted in the game of *Clue*. This was not a revolver.

It looked like a semi-automatic.

She held the muzzle up and looked at the side of the gun. *Glock*. There were numbers along the side of the gun, too: 19, gen4, and 9x19. She didn't know what they meant, but now that she knew she had a Glock, she could figure it out.

She flipped over her paper, where she'd written something down about Glocks, Smith & Wessons, Sig Sauers, and Rugers. For a Glock, the YouTube video said, you just had to make sure the trigger safety was in the "forward" position. If it was, the gun wouldn't fire without a significant amount of trigger pressure.

She tilted the gun and felt the satin slickness of sweat-soaked skin. Her armpits would be dripping by the time she finished. It couldn't be helped.

7:58 a.m.

In the trigger hold, she saw two levers sticking out, looking like the tiny scissors in her mom's Swiss Army knife. According to the YouTube video, this meant the trigger safety was engaged.

Emma let out a shaky breath and slipped the gun back into the bag, settling the T-shirt on top of it. She slammed her locker, twirled the combination lock, and sprinted for Mr. Parker's class.

• • •

"Take your stations," Mr. Lopez said. "You have forty-five minutes to complete the lab."

"Ready, partner?" Dan asked.

Emma didn't answer. *There's a gun in my locker*, she thought.

She grabbed the printout with the lab instructions and followed Dan to their workstation. He handed her the required safety goggles, enormous plastic windshields that left red suction marks across her forehead and the bridge of her nose.

She tried to read the lab directions through the plastic haze, but the words were all blurry. Every time she thought about what was in her locker, goosebumps raced down her legs and she had to start all over. "Hand me those test tubes," Dan said.

Emma obeyed.

As he took them, he brushed his knuckles against hers. She looked down at his hands, lightly freckled, covered with long golden hairs. She wondered why his knuckle hair was blonde instead of dark, like the hair on his head. "Em, are you all right? You didn't call yesterday. I kind of thought you might."

Emma reached for her pencil. "Things are weird right now."

"I can see that." He pipetted $PbCrO_4$ into $BaSO_4$. "You're stroking your thumbnail against your index finger like you're petting a dog."

"That doesn't mean anything."

"Classic nervous tic." He looked down at their notes and circled the trial K_{sp}. "You're doing it again."

"Shit." She pressed her hands flat against the lab table.

Dan put down the pipette and sighed. "Em, you're starting to scare me. A fight?"

Her eyes drifted to the note he'd marked with his finger: *trial K_{sp} is used to determine whether a precipitate will form when two solutions are mixed.* K_{sp} was a constant representing the solubility product. But how could there be such a thing as a constant if the universe was descending into entropy? Wouldn't that preclude a constant in the first place?

"I didn't fight. I just curled up and let her hit me."

"That doesn't make me feel any better."

"What am I supposed to do?"

"I can't tell you that, Em. It just doesn't seem like a fight is something the real you would do."

"The real me." No one wanted to see the real her. They wanted her to box it up and take it back, like a Christmas gift that didn't fit. "I don't even know who that is anymore."

"You're more Anakin than Vader, I can tell you that."

"Things change."

"Not all things. Not the Force."

"The Force is made up. It doesn't count."

"Look, when you're feeling bad, it's easy to convince yourself everything is bad. I don't want you to do that. Don't let this thing get bigger than you."

"What if it already is?"

"It's not," he said, stepping closer to her.

"How do you know?"

He leaned over her shoulder and whispered into her ear. "Because it has to go through me first."

She turned her head away, afraid of what he would see if he looked in her eyes. *There's a gun in my locker*, she thought.

• • •

At the end of the day, Emma hurried back to the locker room. Most of the sixth-period girls were gone or finishing up: lacing boots, reapplying lip gloss, smoothing hair ruffled by the wind. She squeezed herself along the wall, unsure whether to look at them, past them, or at the floor. Every choice seemed wrong. They'd take one look at her and then they'd know and then they'd turn her in.

She wondered what would happen if they called her mom to come get her from the principal's office again. Would she even come? Where did they put kids so bad their own parents wouldn't come and get them anymore? She didn't want to eat dinner in her room again, missing Mattie's smile and her dad's warm eyes.

"Excuse me," she said, shouldering through a line of girls. When she looked up, she found herself face-to-face with Via. White-hot panic flooded through her.

"Jesus," Via said. "Overreact much?"

"What are you doing here?" Emma asked.

"I wore my PE shoes because my boots were pinching. What are *you* doing here?"

"I stepped in a puddle," Emma lied.

Via glanced at Emma's jeans. "You look fine to me."

"I was in my PE clothes. Now I have to wash the pants."

"You're going to do laundry?" Via snorted. "I'll believe it when I see it."

Via's skin was smooth and dark, with a luminous glow even though she only drank soda, never water. Her irises were almost the same color as her pupils, big drops of ink blotting out the truth in the beautiful parchment of her face.

Emma took a deep breath. If Via wouldn't say it, maybe it was time she did. "All you ever do is tell me what I can't do."

"That's not true."

She set down her backpack, feeling a strange pang in her stomach. It wasn't hunger or pre-test nerves. It was something sharper and faster, a stab from an exquisite knife. "Since freshman year, you've called me 294 times, 263 of them to ask what the homework is. You knew I liked Will Decker and you went after him anyway. You got angry when Dan started paying attention to me because you can't stand the idea that someone might want to date me instead of you." She paused, looking for a reaction. It wasn't there. "What is it about me that makes you hate me so much?"

"This is such bullshit." Via rolled her eyes. "Isn't your mom waiting for you or something?"

"I only ever wanted to be your friend."

"Friends need to have something in common first."

"Don't we?"

"Emma, you're just — "

"What? What am I?"

"Selfish. You're so oblivious about anything that happens in the real world. I can't fucking stand it."

Emma thought about the blood on the walkway leading up to the door, the vomit stain on the hardwood floor by the sofa, the cracked leather of the badge holder Kobilinski had flipped open in the counselors' office. "Oblivious," she said. "Is that what you call this?"

"One bad thing happens to you, and it's like the world is ending. You bitch about everything, but you never do anything to fix it. School, grades, boys, college, nothing is ever your fault."

"I thought those were things we all felt. I thought we were helping each other." Emma looked up at the buzzing tube light above her head. "Aren't you tired of making decisions that affect the rest of your life before you even know what that means?"

"Come on, Emma, what do you think it means?" Via evil-eyed Marci Pitman, who did a 180-degree turn and walked the other way. "I have a job, Rachel has a job, and we go after the things we want. That's how the world works, and you're the only one who can't figure it out."

"Like you went after Will Decker?"

"Are you still in love with him?"

"No, but I thought I was. You knew that."

"Then you should have fought for him." She shifted her backpack on her shoulder, looking at Emma from the sides of her eyes. "Grow the fuck up and do something without help for once in your life. The rest of us might die of shock." Via brushed past Emma, a waft of rain-scented shampoo trailing behind her.

Emma sighed. Parts of her body felt like they were on fire: her cheeks, her heart, her belly. Pieces of the conversation echoed in her head, the words bumping into raw nerves and veins. *Selfish. Complain. Fault.* She tried to memorize them so she could save them for later, when she had time to figure out who was right. There was still a gun in her locker and she still had to get it out without being caught.

She shuffled over to her locker and opened the combination lock. Inside, on top of her wadded PE clothes, sat the red bag. She lifted it by the handles and snatched the clothes out from under it. Then she rolled up the clothes and tried to remember which way the gun pointed. What if she covered the gun with the clothes, but the fabric snagged the trigger and pulled it? What if she shot herself, or her mom, or Mattie?

She stared into the bag, at the white T-shirt Elvira had probably also stolen from her cousin. She could leave it all here and go home like nothing happened. Tomorrow, too. But then she'd spend every day tiptoeing around the locker room, wondering if she had the guts to touch the bag ever again.

She set her PE clothes on top of the gun and looped one finger through the bag's raffia handles. A bead of sweat dripped from her bra band to her belly button. She held the bag away from her body as she walked toward the school's main entrance.

When her mom pulled up, she shrugged her backpack off and tossed it onto the floor of the front seat. She held the bag in her right hand, moving slowly to keep it steady.

"What's that?" her mom asked, flipping on her blinker.

"A bag for my PE clothes. I borrowed it from Elvira."

"Who is Elvira?"

Shit. If anything went wrong, her mom had a name to give the cops. "Some girl in the locker room. I don't even know her."

"Didn't I just wash your PE clothes this weekend?"

"I got them dirty again."

"Emma."

"I know," she said softly. "I make a mess of everything."

"You'll eat in your room again tonight."

"Mom, I —"

"If you want to eat with the rest of us, you have to behave like the rest of us."

Like an ostrich? she wanted to say.

But just for tonight, maybe it was for the best. She had a gun to hide and manufacturer's diagrams to find. It would be easier to do all of that without having to look her dad in the eye and answer questions about what she did at school that day.

• • •

Emma went straight upstairs and turned on her computer, blinds shut tight against the prying eyes of the outside world. Her hands shook where she held them over the keyboard. The gun was less than three feet away. She'd stowed the red bag and everything in it on a stack of crates in her closet, behind her hanging clothes. It was the safest place she could think of. Under the bed was too obvious, as were her desk and dresser drawers.

She'd have all afternoon and evening to figure out how to load it and fire it once she finished her chem lab write-up. She wouldn't have bothered with homework at all, except that the write-up counted for Dan's grade as well as hers. He was depending on her, and he was one of the only people who hadn't let her down.

She opened the doc for the write-up, typing out the complicated chemical equations and solving for the trial K_{sp}: $[.25][.10] = .025 = 2.5 \times 10^{-2}$, which was greater than the actual K_{sp}, 6.3×10^{-7}. *The result*, she typed, *proves there will be a precipitate.*

She stared at the blinking cursor. Why wasn't there an equation to tell her whether a friend was real or fake? She thought of all the days at the lunch table when she and Via had sat next to each other, thighs touching in companionable silence. All that time, Via had wanted her to be someone else. Now it seemed like her mom did, too.

There were other things she was supposed to do: a French essay, pre-calculus problems, a take-home quiz in English, two chapters to read for history. Emma glanced at her backpack. Nothing in it could help her put her life back together. She scooted her chair out from the desk and decided to get a glass of water. Her mom hadn't forbidden her to do *that* yet.

Downstairs, the kitchen was empty. Mattie wasn't home yet, and her parents were nowhere to be seen. Emma grabbed a glass and filled it with water. A whiff of chlorine wafted from the tap. Through the kitchen window, she saw the slick green leaves of the rosebushes glowing in the late afternoon sun. She wondered if her dad would ever tend to them again. There wasn't anywhere in the whole town you could go outside and not hear Spanish.

She went back upstairs and headed toward her room. At the end of the hall, she saw her door ajar. White lightning forked across her heart. She knew she'd closed that door.

Emma tiptoed forward, avoiding the creak in the hall floor, and pushed the door open. Her mom stood in front of her closet, pushing the row of hanging clothes aside.

"Mom," she snapped. "What are you doing?"

Her mom gasped and spun around.

"What are you doing in my closet?"

A forced smile widened the parentheses around her mom's mouth. "Looking for your PE clothes. The ones you brought home for me to wash."

They were in the red bag with the gun, inches from her mom's fingertips. She'd forgotten to take them out before she hid the bag. Emma's heart beat fast enough to make her see spots. "I already took them downstairs."

Her mom tilted her head. "Where?"

"The floor of the laundry room."

"I looked there a minute ago. I didn't see anything."

"Mom, I told you, they're downstairs."

"Do you have anything you want to say to me, Emma?"

"The clothes are downstairs, Mom."

"That's all you have to say?"

Emma felt her mom's eyes roam over her face, looking for a sign of weakness. She clamped her lips shut until her mom let go of her hanging clothes, reaching instead to tuck her hair behind her ear with her right hand.

Her bare right hand.

"Mom." Emma felt the floor sway beneath her feet. "Where's your ring?"

"I said I'd handle things, didn't I? But you didn't believe me. One thing you'll understand when you get older . . . there are consequences for everything, Em. If I could make you understand anything, it would be that."

She'd never seen her mom without that ring, not since the day they'd cleaned out her grandmother's empty house. Her mom had sat in the passenger seat, clutching a single canvas tote to her chest and sobbing.

Her mom let her hand fall to her side. "Where is that bag, Emma Christina?"

"It's just a bag, Mom," she said softly. "It's nothing."

"You're lying to me." A tear fell down her mother's pale cheek. "Why would you do that, Em? I'm not trying to hurt you. I've *never* tried to hurt you."

"Mom, I was only doing my homework." She pointed to the computer screen, still displaying her lab write-up. "I just want to do my homework."

"Be careful what you wish for, Em." A false smile twisted her lips. "You can come downstairs again when you're ready to tell me the truth. Until then, your sister will bring you a tray for dinner."

Emma bent her head, ready to feel her mother's lips or her hand as she passed. Neither came. Her mom turned sideways and slipped through the door, a faint whisper of floral perfume trailing behind her.

She sank to her knees, grabbing her desk for support. Was love so fragile it could be destroyed by just a few words? Once her mom went downstairs and saw the clothes weren't there, she'd never get that love back. That's what her mom had been trying to tell her, wasn't it? But she couldn't change anything now. She made a choice to protect her family, whether they wanted it or not. If they were truly in danger, her way was the only way.

She got up and closed the door, then sat down at her desk. She opened a browser window and searched for the name and numbers on the side of the gun. Glock, she remembered. 19. Gen4. 9x19. A sporting-goods store came up first in the search results. She clicked through and read the description of the gun. In a few minutes, she managed to find instructions for loading, care, and cleaning, as well as a diagram of the gun's parts.

Emma reached into her backpack and pulled out Dan's notebook. She made a sketch and a few notes on loading and firing. She wasn't brave enough to retrieve the gun and compare it to the diagram on the screen in front of her.

When she finished, she deleted the browser history, cookies, and cache. She moved her mouse over the menu with the "Shut Down" command and a chat window popped up.

Redhead_Rachel: Were you even going to tell me about what happened with Via?

She deleted the message and shut down her computer. Then she slid open the closet door and pushed her clothes to the left. The bag sat on top of her stack of crates. Gently, she pulled the roll of PE clothes from the top of the bag and slid the coats and blouses back into place. The only way to keep her mom from finding the bag was to take it with her to school, but she had no intention of doing that. If her mom wanted to find it that badly, she'd find it and there was nothing she could do about it.

Part of her wanted to go downstairs and throw the bag into the green yard waste can in the garage. No one would ever look in there, and the gun would end up in a landfill, tied up in a plastic bag with leaves and sticks.

But then she imagined a *Norteño*, maybe even one of the Espinosas, coming to their door and kicking it in. What if that man came upstairs? What if that man started opening bedroom doors, and found her dad? Her gun was the only thing that might save him, or her sister, or her mom. She couldn't abandon it. It was all she had.

She slid the closet door closed and laid down on her bed, crying for the ring neither she nor Mattie would ever wear.

CHAPTER TWENTY-SIX

Wednesday, April 16

THE HALLWAYS TEEMED WITH PEOPLE who suddenly knew who she was. Hot glances seared the skin between her shoulder blades and whispers spread like a virus as she passed.

That's the girl who fought Claudia Morales.

Claudia said she'd fucking kill her. She looks alive to me.

My friend saw everything. This girl started it, stupid bitch.

Claudia's going to get her back, I heard her say so.

Emma raised a hand to the scratches on her cheek: two raised lines, dotted with scabs like stitches in the hem of a dress. For the space of a single breath, she wished she'd brought the gun with her to school. Instantly, she dismissed the idea. Even if Claudia wanted another try, all she'd have to do is take another beating until Claudia was satisfied. Saving herself some blood and bruises wasn't worth the chance that she'd accidentally hurt someone. If she hurt someone, she wanted them to know she meant it.

She trudged down the hallway toward her locker. Near the junior locker bay at the end of the hall, she heard a familiar voice. "She's clearly insane," Via said. "I mean, blaming me for stealing Will Decker freshman year? Get a fucking grip." Emma stopped, pressing against the wall to stay out of Via's sight.

"She doesn't care about him," Rachel said. "She likes Dan."

"Could have fooled me. I bet she has a shrine to Will in her room or stalks him on Facebook. I should message him so he knows. Safety first, you know?"

"For the longest time, I thought she might be a lesbian. I introduced her to a guy at youth group and she practically ran away from him."

"Great. Do you realize how many lesbian scholarships there are out there? As if she hasn't had enough of a free ride already."

"Can she still qualify for valedictorian? You know, with a suspension on her record."

"She'll self-destruct before we ever get there. She cuts class all the time now anyway."

"It's sad," Rachel said. "Don't you kind of miss the old Emma?"

Emma didn't wait for Via's answer. She turned and ran . . . or at least, she intended to. Instead, she crashed straight into Mr. Parker. "I'm s — sorry," she stuttered, stumbling backward.

"West." He put out a hand to steady her. Then he bent his head, eyeing her through the lenses of his wire-rimmed glasses. "Are you all right?"

"No," she whispered, feeling her chin start to shake.

"Come on, then." He led her into his classroom and closed the door behind them, locking it from the inside.

• • •

She blew her nose and sniffed again immediately. Mr. Parker leaned against the chalkboard and crossed his arms over his striped cowboy shirt. He'd placed a box of tissues on the desk beside her and stood, staring at her.

Emma glanced at the locked door. "You're probably not supposed to do that."

Mr. Parker shrugged. "Wasn't supposed to lose half my pension to that embezzling son of a bitch in the district office, either."

Her eyes floated to the huge bookcase on her right. All the books were hardbacks, with titles like *Armies and Warfare in Europe, 1648-1789* or *The Rise and Fall of the Third Reich*. She reached for a tissue and blew her nose again. He pointed at the pile she'd amassed on the desk. "Does this have anything to do with why you were called to the office last week? Or what happened on Monday?"

Emma looked up at him. She knew nothing about his life, his real life, away from school. He didn't wear a wedding ring and he'd never mentioned a home or family. His eyes were the same rain-colored grey as the wire rim of his glasses. "Have you ever tried to help someone but everything got ruined instead?"

Mr. Parker unfolded his arms. "I was in Iraq, Miss West."

"I know. You told us about it."

"No, you don't." He shook his head. "If I told you what really happened, they'd fire me and you'd have nightmares for the rest of your life."

"I thought I'd be able to understand if it happened to me. But it didn't work like that." She'd fallen asleep at 11:30 p.m. last night and the night before, sleeping through until her morning alarm both times. "I still don't know how to stop it."

"Stop what?"

"Thinking it's going to happen all over again."

"No one knows how to stop that."

"Then what do you do if you know someone that's happening to?" She met his gaze and he gave her a hard look. "It's not me."

"Are you sure?"

Emma tried to smile. "She didn't even knock me out. I'm a little tougher than that."

"I know," he said. "I read your *Lonesome Dove* paper."

Emma shook her head. Writing that paper felt like years ago, when things like introductions and conclusions had mattered, before blood and guns and rings and money. "I don't remember what I wrote."

"You blamed every single character for the mess they made. You didn't give anyone a pass, not even Gus. Most students really like Gus."

"Gus is a jerk. He should have stayed with Clara."

Mr. Parker nodded. "He couldn't settle down. He couldn't change. Can you?"

She looked up. "What?"

"Whatever's going on in your life, you can't let it beat you. Gus let it beat him. Call let it beat him. They didn't think hard enough about the choices they had. I don't want to see a smart kid like you make the same mistakes." The doorknob jiggled and Mr. Parker looked up at the clock. "Well, it's almost eight. You ready to let them in?"

"Just a sec." She got up and tossed her pile of tissues in the trash. One deep breath later, she turned to Mr. Parker. "So you're telling me I got an A on the paper?"

He nodded. "Only one in the class who did."

"Okay. You can let them in now."

• • •

Via ignored her in history and English. Rachel offered a single glance as she entered the classroom. Sitting between them was like being sandwiched between glaciers. It was bad enough knowing Via hated her, but if she'd turned Rachel against her, too, she'd be left with no one.

No, she thought. *Not no one.*

When English let out, she hurried to Mr. Lopez's room. Her eyes flew straight to Dan's desk. It was empty. Ryoki Sumitomo and Savannah Banks were the only ones there, talking about an upcoming SCORE club trip to Humboldt State.

Emma shuffled to her desk and took out their joint lab report. After a grade dispute last year, Mr. Lopez required both partners to sign the report along with a special cover sheet he printed out for them. She pretended to read it again, so her eyes wouldn't be facing the doorway when Via and Rachel walked in.

She felt it the second Dan opened the door. The amount of light his silhouette blocked, the shape of it, even the flop of his hair: recognition sent a thunderclap of longing across her heart. When she saw his lopsided grin, something in her heart caved in.

Three long strides carried him to her desk, where he held out his hand. "Come on. Time is of the essence."

"What are you talking about?"

He glanced over his shoulder as Via and Rachel slipped through the door. Their heads were bent together, lips moving, and it didn't take a genius to figure out what they were saying. "Mr. Lopez is in the copy room, making more cover sheets. He's going to be there for a while."

"Why?"

"I jammed the paper tray."

"Okay, but why?"

"So we could have a minute."

She shook her head. "How did you even do that?"

"You have to load a piece of — wait, I can't give that away. It's a trade secret."

"Where did you learn about copiers?"

"My dad hated his boss. When I was a kid and had minimum days, he brought me to his office and turned me loose."

"Let me guess. You copied your butt."

"And dialed 9-1-1 through the fax machine. The cops show up when you do that. It's really cool when you're six." He glanced over his shoulder. "Em, come on. It's a jam of epic proportions. The secretary is going to yell at him for at least ten minutes. We have time."

She glanced down at her bag.

"Leave it," he said. "Just take my hand."

She looked at the lines tracing his palm, long and dark and forked. She slid her fingers against them and he closed his hand over hers.

"Where are we going?" she asked as he pulled her out of the classroom.

He tightened his grip on her hand as he led her down the hall and through a door, onto the school's front lawn. She followed, dimly aware that it was against school rules to leave the building while class was in session.

The sunlight, cold and bright, bounced off the concrete walkway. Emma raised her hand to shield her eyes. "It's so bright out here."

"Emma West, will you go to the prom with me?"

Her eyes hadn't adjusted yet. When she looked up at him, all she saw was a big black oval. "What did you say?"

"You heard me," he said, squeezing her hand. "Will you go to the prom with me?"

"That's what you wanted to come outside for?"

Dan jerked a thumb over his shoulder. "You want me to ask you in front of that gang of assholes, all ready and waiting to mind their own business?"

"No," she said, smiling. "And yes."

A smile, small and Gatsby-like, eased onto his face. "I thought you might say that."

"But I don't even know if I can go to prom. My suspension, remember?"

"I thought of that. Which is why I took the liberty of reserving the banquet room at my cousin's pizza place. I'm not gonna let some school tell me I can't take you to the prom. We'll have our own if they won't let us into theirs."

Emma blinked. Here she was, standing in the cold April sunlight, as warm as she'd ever been in front of a blazing fire. "This is like a movie. You didn't have to do this."

"I know. That's why I did it."

She met his gaze, so firmly focused on her face. He didn't see the same things she did: the scars left by volcanic zits, the cowlick in the middle of her forehead, the purple bags under her lower lashes. His eyes never flicked to the opposite side of the room, the way Rachel's did when Emma said something that bored her. He saw her, the deepest part lodged in the marrow of her bones, the part still trying to resist entropy.

"Em," he said, reaching out to take both of her hands in his. "You're not alone, okay? I just want you to know that."

"I do." The warmth of his hands made her palms sweat, just like they had when she'd gripped the textured handle of the Glock in the girls' locker room.

"Good." He pulled her close, resting his lips gently on hers. She opened her mouth just enough to feel their breath, together, warming a space that hadn't been warm before.

"Now," he said, pulling away just far enough to speak. "You have exactly three days to pick the color of your corsage. My aunt works in a flower shop and has promised to steal only the best for us."

"Steal?"

His lip curled. "I'm a sophomore. I can't drive and I don't have a work permit. But with a week's lead time, I can get you any flower in the world you want. That's worth something, right?"

"It's worth everything."

• • •

Emma took her wrinkled PE clothes out of her backpack and changed as fast as she could. Her chem notes for the day were a bust — all she did was stare at the page, reliving the kiss over and over. She tried to remember how close they'd been standing and how she'd known when to open her mouth. It had all just *happened*, which was wonderful, but it meant she had no idea what to do when it happened again.

She pulled off her jeans and slid into her sweats. In world-record time, she shoved her backpack and clothes into the locker, slammed it shut, and hurried out to the front of the locker room to wait for Elvira. Whatever else happened, she never wanted to change next to Via again. Her cheeks flamed as she remembered her so-called friends mulling over her sexual identity, like it was an equation they could solve if they plugged in the right variables.

"Hey," someone behind her said. She turned around and saw Elvira, white-faced, without foundation or mascara. Her uncurled bangs flopped low over her eyes. Even her voice sounded different, deeper and scratchy, like after something with a lot of yelling — a concert or football game.

"You look different," Emma said. "Is everything okay?"

"I can't stop thinking about it."

A pang of guilt scraped Emma's gut. She glanced around to make sure Mrs. Patterson wasn't within earshot. "Do you want to go somewhere and talk?"

"I don't want to do anything bad anymore."

Emma fell in step beside her as they walked down the long hallway to the gymnasium. "I'm sorry I got you involved."

"It wasn't you."

"You're the only one who didn't expect me to be anything else, not even good at badminton. I shouldn't have expected you to be someone else just to help me."

Elvira's chin quivered. "*Chica*, you don't know, do you?"

"Know what?"

"It was on the news." Elvira's face contorted into a sob. "Monica's dead."

"What?" Emma pulled Elvira into her arms and hugged her. "I'm so sorry. Are you okay?"

"I was at the mall with Letizia. Monica was watching my little brother."

"It happened at your *house*?"

"A drive-by," Elvira sobbed.

"What about your brother?"

"Monica hid him under the bed. Then she went to get the — " Elvira stopped, her muscles suddenly tense beneath Emma's arms.

In an instant, Emma knew exactly what Elvira was going to say. The world opened up in front of her like a ravine, newly split and spreading further apart with every breath. She was on one side. Everyone else was on the other.

"It's my fault." She rested her forehead on Elvira's shoulder. "This is all my fault."

Elvira's arms snaked around her, but her lips stayed shut. They sobbed against each other's shoulders until the first bell, then walked into the gymnasium, tear-streaked and grim-faced.

CHAPTER TWENTY-SEVEN

Wednesday, April 16

THE WIND HAD WHIPPED COLOR into her cheeks. She couldn't see it, but she could feel it. They still stung, hours after the lunch she'd spent outside alone, crying for a girl she'd only seen once.

It was Monica's gun she'd asked Elvira to steal. What if that gun had been in the nightstand when the drive-by happened? What if Monica had shot back? Maybe the shooter's car would have moved on a little faster, a little sooner, when Monica was a little more alive.

Emma put a hand on her forehead. It radiated heat, like the surface of the toaster oven after Mattie made a Pop-Tart. Across the street, she heard the rattle of the busted-ass Corolla's loose muffler. It seemed strange that other people could go on with their lives, never knowing how things had changed forever just a few feet away.

Suddenly, she understood why school had to be completed while you were young. When you grew up and had real problems to deal with, there was no way you'd tolerate being asked to graph a function. People were hungry and hurt and dying everywhere in the world, and some stupid college thought it was important that she understand when the limit would approach zero.

There's a gun in my closet.

She slammed her math book shut and walked down the hall to the spare bedroom, snatching the cordless phone from its cradle. Rachel's cell was easy to remember. The last four digits were 1814, the year of Napoleon's exile to Elba. She dialed as she closed the bedroom door behind her.

It rang three times before Rachel's breathy voice answered. "Hi, Emma."

"I wasn't sure you'd pick up."

"Neither was I. Where were you at lunch today?"

"I needed to be alone. Something bad happened."

"Are you okay? Is it your dad?"

"Do they let you go to church anytime you want?"

Rachel paused. "The chapel's open until ten. But there's also a youth service tonight."

"I need to get out of here."

"Emma, you sound terrible. Are you crying?"

Her eyes drifted to the closet door. It had no real handle, just a grab-hole with a brass-plated fixture. Within a month of moving in, her sweaty fingers had permanently darkened the metal. "I did something stupid and someone got hurt."

"What are you talking about?"

"Can you come get me? I know things are weird right now, but I need you to take me to church."

"Emma, this is serious, isn't it?"

"I don't know what else to do."

"Hold on, okay? I'll be there soon."

When they hung up, Emma went downstairs. Her mom, dad, and Mattie sat in the family room, watching a talk show. The blinds tilted inward, darkening the room. Her dad was in his bathrobe, a napkin spread across his lap. "Hi, Dad."

He craned his neck and pressed his dry, white lips in greeting. "Em, you've been hiding from us."

I would never hide from you, she thought. "Mom, Rachel's coming to get me. I asked if she'd take me to church with her. Is that okay?"

"Yes," her mom said, letting out her breath. "That's more than okay."

"I won't be late. I still have homework."

"You always have homework," Mattie said.

"That's why she'll make the big bucks," her dad said, pulling his dry lips into a smile.

Her mom got up and opened the fridge, pulling out some lunchmeat and a brown hunk of iceberg lettuce. She reached for a spreader and cast a thin sheen of mayonnaise across a slice of wheat bread. "They won't feed you there, will they?"

"I don't think so."

Her mom squeezed a bit of mustard onto the turkey. "Are you sure this is what you want?"

"I don't know. That's why I have to try."

Her mom handed her a plastic bag with a sandwich inside. When Rachel came to the door, her mom followed her, standing at the long, narrow window beside the front door as they drove away.

• • •

It was cold and foggy when Rachel pulled into the church parking lot. They got out of the car and Emma looked up at the droplets of mist swirling in the breeze, their windswept stops and starts visible in the stream of orange streetlight. "We're in a Van Gogh."

"Uh-huh," Rachel said.

Emma looked sideways at her. "You don't see it, do you?"

"It's mist." Rachel's eyes flickered toward the door. Even though the temperature was in the low fifties, Rachel wore plaid flannel shorts, a white T-shirt, and flip-flops. "Let's just go inside."

Emma followed her friend's perfect ponytail past the gymnasium, into a vestibule. A sign over a door on the left said CHAPEL and Emma started toward it. "Not that way," Rachel said. "Youth service is in the rec room."

Emma groaned. There was nothing holy about a rec room.

"Come on." Rachel pulled her through a wide doorway. Across the room, Tim leaned against a wall with one leg turned out. He wore narrow-leg jeans and a Western shirt with pearly buttons. He smiled at them as they approached.

Rachel took his hand and let go of Emma's. "You remember my friend Emma?"

Tim nodded. "I do. How are you?"

Rachel squeezed his hand and smiled brightly. He cleared his throat, which apparently meant he rescinded the question. Emma's eyes floated across the room. Some of the same girls she'd met last time were here again — Madison, and the blue-skinned girl whose name she couldn't remember. Behind them, in a corner, stood Owen.

I come here so I'll know what I'm up against, he'd said.

Whatever he meant by that, she didn't think he'd find it here. This place looked like any other conference room, with folding chairs arranged in rows and thin industrial carpet on the floor. Bloated ductwork hung from the ceiling, creeping like inchworms around the perimeter.

The mullet-wearing youth leader stood at the podium in front of the room. "Take a seat, you guys," he said, waving them in. Everyone filed into the room and bunched into the seats in the back. Emma caught a whiff of several different perfumes and colognes, along with someone's day-old sweat. She hunkered down in her seat as the pastor began to talk about peer pressure. He talked with his hands, and after a few minutes, tiny beads of sweat began to glisten on his forehead.

Beside her, Rachel and Tim kept their eyes downcast. Emma glanced around the room and saw the blue-skinned girl curl her fingers to inspect her nails. One boy had a cell phone tipped out of his pocket, angled to read the message on the screen.

The pastor reached into a cubbyhole in the lectern. "Now, if you brought your Bible, please share with a neighbor and turn to Matthew 16:21. Let's look at what happened when Jesus faced peer pressure."

Rachel and Tim made no move to find a person with a Bible. Emma stared at the floor.

"Here, Peter pressured Jesus not to go to Jerusalem, where he would surely be killed. But Jesus refused. He told Peter it had to be that way, and he wouldn't bow to the pressure of his disciples to save himself."

Emma wondered how a few busted-ass fishermen and shepherds counted as peers for the Son of God. On her left, she saw Rachel's hand sneak into Tim's. He curled his fingers around hers, letting their joined hands swing between their chairs. Emma closed her eyes and wondered whether Monica had had a boyfriend.

When the youth pastor stopped talking, Rachel and Tim lingered in their chairs, fingers still entwined. It made Emma long to be home with her family. The comfort Rachel found here had nothing to do with God or the Bible. It had to do with Tim and her dad.

Everything led back to a father in the end.

"I want to go home," she said.

"Just one more minute," Rachel said. "Please?"

Emma sighed, remembering the feel of Dan's lips on hers, and his warm hands on her arms. She hadn't even told Rachel that he'd asked her to the prom. It didn't matter now, not while she had a dead girl's soul on her conscience. "Can I go into the chapel? I'll wait there, or by the car."

Rachel nodded. "The chapel's open. Down the hall, through the double doors."

Emma followed her directions. At the end of the hallway, she saw oak double doors with brass plated handles. She pulled one open and entered the chapel.

The ceiling was higher than any room she'd ever been in. Oval stained-glass windows ran the length of the walls. The aisle led to an altar draped in white cloth. She breathed in, feeling the weight of air perfumed by heavy, waxy flowers.

Halfway down the aisle, she sat in a pew. The stained-glass window on her left depicted a man with a halo, raising his right hand and holding a book in his left. *Are you there, God? It's me, Emma,* she thought. *But you can call me Margaret if that makes things easier.* She folded her hands and rested them on the pew in front of her. She knew she wouldn't get an answer, but she asked anyway. *Would Monica have lived if she had her gun? Would she still be alive if it weren't for me?*

The HVAC system kicked on, blowing a draft across her ankles. She wondered how anyone in a modern church knew what was a sign and what wasn't.

Suddenly, the door creaked behind her. "Didn't think this is where you'd be," a familiar voice said.

She turned to see Owen's shaggy head poking through the doorway. He looked at her down the long, flat bridge of his nose. "Why'd you come back? People only do that when they want something or when something bad happens."

"Something bad happened."

"And you thought you'd be forgiven if you sat in an empty room for a few minutes?"

Emma shook her head. "I don't know what I thought."

"Then why are you here?"

"Why are *you* here?"

"I don't have anywhere else to go." His clear grey eyes met hers head-on. "You?"

"I think I helped kill someone."

"Well, there you go." He slipped through the door and eased it shut so it wouldn't make a noise. With silent footsteps, he walked down the aisle and edged into the pew beside her. "You didn't have these last time," he said, pointing to her cheek.

Emma shrugged. "Temporary tattoo."

"You sure about that?"

"Why do you hang around a church and not a library?"

"Library's never open. Budget cuts."

"How do you know Rachel?"

"I've been coming here about a year."

"How long has she been coming here?"

"You're her friend. You should know these things."

"Girls don't always tell each other the truth about things." Emma sighed. "I'm only here so she and Tim can make out for a few minutes before we leave."

"You'd rather be somewhere else?"

"Home."

"I can take you."

"You have a car?"

He nodded.

"But I thought you said — "

"I said I didn't have anywhere to go. Never said I couldn't get there if I did."

Emma looked up. Beneath the cross, electric candles cast their unbending light on the polyester altar cloth. "Coming here didn't help."

"If you wanted forgiveness, you should have tried a Catholic church."

"Do they forgive you for beating a census worker nearly to death? Or for shooting a girl who's babysitting her cousin?"

Owen shrugged. "I just sleep here." Then he glanced back at her. "You didn't do those things, did you?"

She blinked and was surprised to feel her lashes grow heavy with moisture. "I don't know."

"Come on. You can tell me about it in the car."

• • •

The streetlight closest to the church's side door was burnt out. Emma reached into her purse for a pen and some scratch paper.

She scrawled a quick note for Rachel and went to slip it under her wipers. A quick survey of the rec room hadn't turned up a single glimpse of her or Tim. "One sec," she told Owen, jogging into the misty night toward Rachel's car.

"What the hell were you thinking?" a man's voice called.

Emma jumped. She pulled her hand back from Rachel's windshield and turned around.

There was no one there.

"Dad, I—"

"You can't explain it away, not this time."

The girl's voice belonged to Rachel. Emma's eyes scanned the parking lot. She spotted them near the side of the building. Rachel leaned against the wall, hands clasped behind her back. Her dad stood over her, pointing and yelling. Richard Cooper wore a dress shirt, tie, and slacks, like he'd come straight from the office.

"You impersonated me and forged my signature, Rachel. What you did is illegal!"

Rachel tilted her face toward him. "I asked for your help and you ignored me."

"I was in Atlanta, working on a case."

"You didn't answer me!"

Mr. Cooper sighed. "Just because I don't answer you right away doesn't mean I'm not listening."

"How am I supposed to know that?"

"You're supposed to know it because I'm your father. Do you really think that because I have to go across the country for a few weeks that I'm going to forget you? You're my daughter, Rachel. Can you *please* try to remember that for more than a day at a time?"

Emma blinked. *Forgery?* The only thing Rachel had mentioned was the note that got Tim cleared to go to prom. *Oh my God*, she thought. *It couldn't be.*

"Family doesn't forget, Rachel. Not in good times or bad."

He put one hand on her shoulder and Rachel shrugged it off. "Are you going to tell Mom?"

"This could have real legal repercussions, Rachel."

"It was just a stupid piece of paper."

"No, it wasn't. You lied to get what you want, and you used me to do it. I've never been so disappointed in your behavior."

"Hey," Owen said, walking up behind her. "Are you ready?"

Emma spun, putting her finger to her lips, but it was too late. Rachel's head snapped toward the new voice. She found Emma's eyes and met them with a glare that would have turned Medusa to stone, her angry eyes and tear-stained cheeks glowing in the foglight. She would never believe that Emma didn't mean to eavesdrop. *I'm sorry*, Emma mouthed.

Rachel pressed her lips together.

"Come on," Owen said, pulling Emma away. "It's cold."

He guided her to the other side of the parking lot, to a dirty black Volkswagen bug. "*Mi casa es su casa*. It's not locked."

Emma opened the door and sat on the cold vinyl seat. She shivered and rubbed her palms against her arms. The left one, covered with a swampy kick-bruise, throbbed under her touch. Everything hurt, everything was wrong. Church hadn't worked, and now Rachel would hate her the same way Via did.

"So that was weird," Owen said, turning the key.

"She'll hate me for seeing that." Emma looked down at her hands, folded in her lap. "Why aren't we going anywhere?"

"Car needs to warm up. You ever been in an old car before?"

"No."

"You probably won't like it."

"Why are you doing this? You don't even know me."

He curled his thin upper lip. "You trying to tell me you're dangerous or something?"

"My mom would kill me if she knew I got in a car with you."

"I just left two witnesses behind. I'm sure they'd come forward if someone found you in a ditch tomorrow morning."

Emma snorted. "One of them would."

"What is it with the way girls all secretly hate each other?" He put the car in reverse and backed out of his parking space without looking over his shoulder. Carefully, with one foot on the brake, he eased it over the steep curb to the street.

"Boys see things for what they are. We only see what we want things to be." Emma paused. "It eats us alive."

"You seem to be surviving."

"I was." A green traffic light cast a phantom glow on the hood of the car. She touched her fingertips to the scratches on her cheek. "But I don't have any friends anymore. You shouldn't listen to me."

"Where do you live? I don't even know where I'm going."

She gave him directions and closed her eyes, letting her body sway with the movement of the car. It was louder than her mom's Buick or her dad's pickup truck. The whole vehicle felt thin and rough, like it had to work just to take a breath.

Twenty minutes later, he pulled into her driveway and put the car in park. Its gurgling engine sputtered and coughed, louder than a lifelong smoker. "It's this one?"

She opened her eyes, wishing the ride could have lasted longer. Her mom would ask how Rachel was, and she'd have to decide whether to lie. She unbuckled her lap belt and looked at Owen. "Why did you really come into the chapel earlier?"

He shrugged. "They don't look very hard before locking the door at night."

"Where are you going to sleep now?"

He patted the torn vinyl of his dashboard. "I know a place."

"If you go back, tell them you claim sanctuary."

He drew his brows together. "Does that work?"

"It used to. Thanks for the ride." She pulled the door handle and a cold breath of air whooshed into the car.

"Emma."

"Yeah?"

"Nothing's so bad you can't fix it."

Her lips pressed into a toothless smile, the only kind she felt she could give. She closed the door behind her and stepped up to the porch. According to her watch, it was only nine. She was safe.

The motion detector turned on the porch light as she approached. Owen waited until he saw it to back out of the driveway. Emma closed the front door behind her as fast as she could to block the noise as he roared away.

Somewhere down the block, a dog barked.

"Who was that?"

Emma jumped. She saw her mom standing alone in the shadows of the dining room. "Mom! You scared me. What are you doing?"

"That wasn't Rachel. Who was that?"

"A friend of Rachel's."

"Em, how could you?"

"Mom, what's wrong? I'm home on time."

"I heard that car pull into our driveway." Her mom stepped from the shadows, her hand wrapped around the phone with a grip so tight her knuckles shone. "I heard it from the family room. I grabbed the phone and ran to the window, hoping I'd recognize the car."

"I don't understand."

"My fingers were on the buttons, Emma. 9, 1, 1. What was I supposed to think? You *knew* what your father said about those men coming back."

The blood in her veins turned to lead once she realized what her mom was talking about. Then the words tumbled out of her mouth, as if speed could make up for ignorance. "I'm sorry. I didn't think. Rachel's dad was there, and he was yelling at her, and I had to find another way home, and — "

"I'm done, Em. You may not care what happens to this family, but I do and I will not have it disrupted. You are not to leave this house except for school."

The words hit her like clods of dirt, tossed onto a casket in the ground. "Mom, this family is all I care about."

"Everyone else is doing their part." Her mom's eyes drifted toward her empty right ring finger. "Why do you want to make things harder?"

"I'm only trying to help."

Her mother shook her head. The skin under her eyes glimmered with unabsorbed facial cream, the kind that smelled like milk and honey. "What's happened to you, Em? You're not the same anymore."

"I'm still *me*. Why can't anyone see that?" She looked down at her feet, bathed in moonlight from the far window. That window was shaped with a rectangle on the bottom and a half-circle on top: two basic shapes used to create a new one. She thought that maybe their lives could be like that. The shape of *before* was the rectangle, no different from any other window. The half-circle was *after*, a cautious shape, smaller and bent inward.

They both let in light.

And they could both be broken by the same rock.

"Go upstairs," her mom said. "Tomorrow I'll decide whether to tell your father."

CHAPTER TWENTY-EIGHT

Thursday, April 17

MALO VERDE'S SEASONS DIDN'T PAY attention to the calendar, and spring was no exception. The car's chilled vinyl seat was no match for Emma's thin denim. She shivered as she latched her seat belt. In the driver's seat, her mom gripped the steering wheel and said nothing during the entire trip to school.

Emma waited for a word, or even a look, to tell her things could still be normal. It didn't come. She cleared her throat each time they hit a red light on Carver Boulevard, trying to work up the courage to say the word "mom." Each time, something stopped her. If she said the wrong thing and made it worse, her mom might break her silence and tell her dad everything. The worst thing Emma could imagine would be to have her dad misunderstand her the way her mom had. How could they think, after sixteen years of being a good daughter, she would suddenly become the opposite of what they needed?

When her mom pulled up to the curb, Emma got out quickly, without a wave or a goodbye. She trudged through the front gate, looking at the black galaxies of bubble gum on the cement. She wondered what it would take to disappear inside one. Every part of this day would be hell. Rachel and Via were in three of her morning classes, with Elvira in the fourth. All morning, she'd be reminded of how badly she failed the people around her. Dan was the only person she hadn't failed yet, and that was just because he was new. Give her time, and she'd find a way to screw that up, too.

She kept her head down in the halls. Even the people who didn't know about her fight with Claudia Morales stared at the scratches on her cheek. All those extra stares had weight — she felt them like extra books in her backpack. When she stopped at her locker, she tilted her shoulder and let her backpack fall to the filthy floor.

Her fingers gripped the combination lock's ridged edges. *Twirl, stop, twirl, stop, twirl, stop, lift.* When she bent down to unzip her backpack, she saw a familiar pair of black flip-flops. The first smile of the day bubbled up inside her like a geyser, pushing through the layers of salt and tears. "I'm so glad it's you," she said.

But the face she saw wasn't the one she was so used to seeing. The ease around the lips and the warmth in his eyes were gone. Dan looked colder and harder, like a replica made of wax or stone. "What's wrong?" she asked. "Did something happen?"

"I was coming to ask you the same thing."

"I don't understand."

He reached into his pocket and held up a folded piece of paper. "I found this in my locker this morning."

Emma took the note and unfolded it with clumsy fingers. Her stomach churned as she recognized the handwriting. This was a whole new level of sabotage, something she never would have done. "I would have kept her secret forever," she whispered. "I was never going to tell."

"What secret?" Dan snatched back the note. "What's going on, Em? Is it true?"

She grasped the side of her locker door and let the rough metal bite into the sides of her fingers. The note, written in Rachel's childish balloon letters, told Dan that Emma had left church last night with a boy she barely knew. *They were holding hands*, the note said, *and she left with him, alone, even though I was the one who drove her there. Just thought you should know.*

"It didn't happen that way," she said.

"So you didn't hold hands with some guy and leave with him in his car?"

"It wasn't holding hands." She bent her head against the locker door, needing its coolness on her forehead now, too. *Think*, she told herself. *You have to say this right or he'll walk away and he might never walk back.*

"Emma, who is he? I thought you wanted to be with me."

"I do," she said, looking into his eyes. "You know I do. I don't even know Owen. He's someone Rachel knows from her youth group."

"Did he touch you? Why did Rachel think you were holding hands with someone you don't even know?"

"Fuck," she said, slamming her locker. Every part of that question was a trap. It ended with her as the villain, any way she played it. Either she revealed Rachel's secret, which was a shitty thing for a friend to do, or she kept it, which was a shitty thing for a prom date to do.

"Just answer the question."

"I was leaving a note for Rachel. Owen pulled me away because there was something going on Rachel didn't want me to see."

"Did he pull you straight into his car?"

"Well, someone had to give me a ride home."

He tilted his head back. "Em, that doesn't add up. Either you know him better than you say you do, or you did something really dangerous."

"That's the least dangerous thing I've done lately," she snapped. "My mom grounded me for it, she might tell my dad, Via hates me, Rachel's mad, I can't look Elvira in the eye, and you're all that's left to keep me going."

Dan nodded and made a grunting noise deep in his throat. "All that's left, huh?"

"I didn't mean it like that."

"You have some serious shit going on, and I get that. I've told you over and over that I can help you. I *want* to help you. But when you start getting in strange guys' cars . . . that's not just ignoring my words. That's ignoring me. Maybe I should take a hint."

Anger flushed her cheeks, spreading from the black hole in her heart. "Everyone wants me to be someone else, but you know what? Just because you want something doesn't mean you get it."

"I can see that," he said, pushing himself off the locker bay and walking down the hall.

• • •

After history class, she walked straight through the main building, across the courtyard, and out the hallway that led to the locker room. She'd wanted to run the minute Dan walked away from her, but she knew what Mr. Parker would think if he saw her empty chair. He'd think she wasn't so tough, that maybe she didn't deserve that A.

I deserve it, she thought. *And I'm going to prove it.*

She ducked behind the row of math portables she and Elvira had hidden behind after Monica's fight. No one would find her here, if only because no one would be looking. The grass was cold and wet, so she set her backpack on the ground and used it as a cushion.

There had to be a way to fix this. If she could solve an equation for the superpositions of left- and right-moving waves during the quantum mechanics unit in chemistry, she could find a way to repair the domino damage that had buried her in the past week. The worst parts of that damage had happened at home. How could she show her dad that it was okay to leave the house? What would it take to make him feel safe?

The people who hurt him — who threatened to come back and do it again — had to go away. The only ones who could make that happen were the cops, but they had no evidence and no witnesses.

Then she would get them evidence and witnesses.

She stood up and pulled the maroon notebook out of her backpack. She let her fingers slide down its cover slowly, as if Dan would feel her touch on his face. What would he do if he knew she'd stolen a gun? Probably never talk to her again, just like Rachel and Via.

She took a deep breath to keep the tears back, wiped her nose with her hand, and flipped open the notebook. In the beginning, she'd written about her mom's Miss Havisham decorations. Then she'd drawn maps of East Malo Verde, noted the cross streets of El Camino Rojo, copied what little she'd been able to find on the Espinosas from news sites, sketched gang signs, and noted the names of known *Norteño* lieutenants.

It was all there, just like writing a paper: Read the source material, gather quotes, make a thesis, and plug the quotes into supporting points. It was the only thing she'd ever been good at, and the only chance she had to stop the dominoes from falling.

The first bell rang and she uncapped her pen. The second bell rang and she started writing.

• • •

The cul-de-sac's curb hadn't been the color of cement in years. Blackened by its brushes with tires, it was now the color of a cheerleader's smoky eye makeup. The Buick was there right on time, its tires never having contributed to the cloudy coloration.

Emma got in and clutched her backpack in her lap. The two feet between them felt like the twenty thousand leagues separating surface from sea floor. She stared ahead, afraid to look at her mom or turn her head. At school, she at least had the option of flight.

Maybe in a day or two, if she behaved, she could convince her mom not to ground her. She hadn't even told her about Dan or the prom. Maybe that was for the best, since it didn't look like Dan wanted to be around her any more, either.

She was toxic, like asbestos and lead paint.

Emma sighed with relief when her mom pressed the garage door opener and turned into their driveway. She decided to go upstairs and stay there as long as she could. Her mom would send Mattie with a tray, and maybe a night without her would remind them that they missed her. She slung her backpack over her shoulder and went up to her room.

Smoky grey light fell through the skylight over the stairs. She walked straight through it, wishing it could make her invisible. The hallway smelled like lemon cleaner, all bleach and citrus, and she wondered if her dad had thrown up blood again.

At the end of the hall, her door was closed.

She never closed her door, not even with the gun in her room, because she never had before and doing so now would tell them all she had something to hide.

She reached for the brass doorknob, newly caked with fingerprints. Her next breath seared her lungs. If Kobilinski or the other cops were waiting for her behind it, she'd tell them she only ever wanted to help.

The knob turned and she opened the door.

It wasn't the police. It was worse.

It was her dad.

He sat on her bed, his spine curved like a boomerang. The blue robe was gone, replaced by an afghan her mom had crocheted a couple years ago. His eye was still ringed with glossy purple skin, although the swelling had gone down. The snowy beard had grown another inch.

Emma looked at him and felt the same way she had when she saw the pictures of her grandfather at his funeral. "Dad," she said, partly to convince herself this sad, bowed creature with hair whiter than sifted flour was really him.

In the SeedCorp days, he'd done a lot of the plant's hiring and firing. He knew all the tricks for getting workers to confess they'd clocked in high or lied about that sick day yesterday. It took her a moment to realize he was using them on her. *Don't speak*, he'd said. *That's rule number one. Make them think you know everything.*

She sat in her desk chair, facing him. It took all her will-power not to look at her closet door and see if it was closed all the way. Behind him, on the bed, her row of stuffed animals looked at her with bleak button eyes. "How are you feeling?"

"Not so good." His voice was rough and tight, like muscles that hadn't been stretched before a run.

"What's wrong?"

"I think you know."

"Mom sends me upstairs all the time now. I don't know anything."

"She told me what you did, Em. All of it."

"The fight," she said slowly, turning her cheek so he could see the scratches.

He shivered and pulled the blanket around his shoulders. "Why did you do it?"

"To show them they didn't win."

"That's not what you did."

"It feels like that's exactly what I did."

"You lost the chance to show them you're better than that."

"What happened to telling me to fight? It's what you wanted when I was a baby."

He blinked his one good eye, still pink around the iris. "That means something different now."

"It means exactly the same thing," she snapped.

"For me, maybe." He breathed deeply and touched his ribs with his right hand. "I always wanted to live on a farm, with fruit trees and irrigation ditches and wide blue skies. But the job was here, so we stayed. The only thing that made it better was knowing you were smart enough to get out."

"School isn't any good for the real world, Dad. It doesn't mean anything."

"It means something to me."

Emma turned her head. "Why does everyone want me to be something I'm not?"

"You can't stop, Em. You've come this far."

"Dad, why didn't you go to Tennessee?"

He sighed. "I know it's not easy for you to make friends, Em. I watched you struggle with it all these years. You found people you like here, who like you. I'd never take that away from you."

"I wish you had," she said softly. She wished he'd told her to shut up and pack, like Via's dad or Rachel's dad might have done. *I ruined everything*, she thought. *And I did it by being me.*

"Things should have been different," she said.

He shook his head. "I wouldn't trade one day with this family for anything. You make me happy, Em, you and your sister. That's all I need. I need you to know that."

She slid out of her chair and sat next to him on the bed. He put his arms around her, so gently she could barely feel them. She rested her cheek on his shoulder, feeling the hard, calcified rope of his collarbone beneath her skin.

CHAPTER TWENTY-NINE

Friday, April 18

AFTER A FEW MINUTES, THE gun felt normal in her hand. It was like holding a hairdryer. You just had to get your arm used to supporting the weight. She held it in her hand and moved her arm around, up, down, in circles, from hanging at her side to pointing out in front of her.

When her arm started tingling, she set it down and took a break. When the blood had run back into her fingers, she picked it up and ran through the same set of drills. She consulted her notebook diagrams and practiced flicking the safety on and off. The diagrams also told her how to disengage the magazine and check to make sure there were bullets.

There were.

Monica had been ready.

Detective Kobilinski had said they needed evidence to charge the Espinosas with attacking her father. If he couldn't get it on his own, she would give it to him. Everything bad that had happened stemmed from that night. If she could repair that damage, she could start working on everything else, too, like running a film reel backward. Nothing would be all right unless she could make sure her dad never had to fear the people who hurt him. If her family could heal itself, she would work on Via, Rachel, and Dan.

She looked at the tray her sister had brought to her, untouched, sitting on the foot of her bed. The plastic plate held a turkey sandwich and a few chips, the plain kind, without any flavor powder. She wondered what they were eating downstairs and why she couldn't have any.

Her dad had always told her that doing things for other people made you a good person. But sometimes doing those things meant knowing what other people couldn't find the words to ask for.

She swaddled the gun in Monica's T-shirt, the one Elvira had brought it to school in. Then she slipped it into her purse and set her purse by the bed.

• • •

On Saturday morning, she woke to sunlight streaming into her room. The concentrated rays made her sweat beneath the sheets and she threw back her covers. The clock radio said 9:45 a.m.

She lay uncovered for a few more minutes, feeling her skin tingle as it adjusted to the cooler temperature outside her sheets. When she was little, it had seemed so natural to wake up at 7 a.m. and go into the living room to watch cartoons. Kids still thought there was a reason to get up, that something good might happen if they did.

Grown-ups — and teenagers — knew better.

During the night, Wellington had fallen onto the floor between her bed and her nightstand. She picked him up, smoothed his fur, and set him back on the bed. "I'm sorry I dropped you." After a pause, she added, "I'm sorry every time I drop you." She picked him up, crushed him to her, and kissed his fuzzy forehead.

She reached for her favorite jeans and a plain white T-shirt, one of the few she hadn't spilled anything on yet, and headed for the shower. Even though she'd never done it before, she followed the directions on the shampoo bottle: Lather. Rinse. Repeat. After the "repeat," her hair squeaked when she slid two fingers down the too-slick strands.

As she dried off, she noticed that the hand towel hanging next to Mattie's sink was wet. Darker patches had imprinted like a Rorschach test on the pink terry cloth. Mattie usually slept until 11 a.m. on weekends. What was she doing up?

Emma slid a plastic comb through her hair, massaged zit cream into her chin, and grabbed her purse from the bedroom. Holding it by the bag instead of the strap, she carried it down the hall. The carpet was finally getting soft again, after the multiple rounds of cleaning solution, and she wriggled her bare toes over it. She paused on the landing and wished everything could move backward in time, so that anyone who was in the kitchen would smile at her instead of just wanting her to go away.

Her feet made no sound on the tile floor as she set her purse near the door to the garage. There were only two items missing, but she'd have to wait for both of them.

Mattie and her mom stood together in the kitchen. Mattie held a wooden spoon in a death grip as she stirred something in a silver mixing bowl. She wore flannel PJs and her skin still had that dewy morning glow, like a baby's. Emma closed her eyes and made a wish. *Please*, she prayed, *don't let her lose that.*

"What are you guys doing?" she asked.

"We're making muffins," Mattie said. "Lemon poppyseed."

"That's my favorite."

Her sister smiled. "I know."

Emma glanced at her mom, who shrugged and looked away quickly. "It's your sister's doing."

"Thanks, Matt."

"It was supposed to be a surprise. What are you even doing up so early?"

"I guess I knew you were up to something."

"Forsooth," Mattie said.

Emma put her elbows on the kitchen island and watched her mom put muffin cups in the tin. She rotated the colors, pink and blue and yellow, so that an even number of each color was represented. "About done mixing?"

"How would I know?"

Her mom leaned over Mattie's shoulder. "No lumps."

"Here, you pour. I always mess up."

Her mom took the silver bowl and poured each muffin cup half full of batter. Just like she did with waffle batter, she tilted the bowl to control the flow and didn't spill a drop on the counter or the muffin tray. Emma looked at her sister's face, with three faint wrinkles pulling to the surface of her forehead. She wished she could tell Mattie that she'd measure up, that there was plenty of time.

As soon as the muffins were in the oven, her mom moved into the dining room, to the table where Emma did homework every other day of the week. She pulled a sheaf of newspaper from a stack in the middle of the table and opened it to the crossword puzzle.

Mattie stayed in the family room and turned on the TV.

Emma followed her mom, sitting at the far end of the table, pretending to look at the ads in the Saturday paper. Over the crenellated top of the Target ad, she watched her mom scratch through one of the clues as she solved it. She pursed her lips as she read the next clue, tapping the pencil eraser against her cheek. A moment later, she entered her response and drew a line through the clue, straight and dark. The hand that held the pencil was bare.

How long, Emma wondered, *would that sight feel like a stab in the gut?* "Is Dad upstairs?"

Her mom nodded. "It took him a long time to get to sleep after he went to bed last night."

"Me too," she said. Once her dad woke up, her mom would go check on him and help him wash up. As soon as she heard water running, it would be time to go.

She pretended to read the rest of the ads until the kitchen timer went off. "They smell done," her mom said, scooting her chair out and going into the kitchen. Emma heard the creak of the oven door, then the squeak of the cabinet next to the microwave, where her mom kept the toothpicks.

A rich, lemony smell wafted through the dining room. Emma closed her eyes and breathed it in. *Don't ever forget this smell,* she told herself.

Her mom carried two muffins on a plate to Mattie in the family room and brought four into the dining room for herself and Emma. She'd sliced all four and buttered each individual half. The tiny pats of margarine melted before her eyes, dissolving into amoeba-like shapes beneath visible trails of steam. Emma opened her mouth and was surprised to find her voice choked with a cobweb of tears.

The four of them were everything to each other: earth, air, water, and fire. Her mother was the fire. Her father was the earth. Her sister was the air. That left only water for her, although she couldn't figure out what that meant.

Once, swimming in the ocean at Santa Cruz, she'd slipped under a wave as she took a breath. She'd kicked for the surface as salt water flooded her lungs. The sun above the water had looked like the moon, smaller and dimmer and whiter than she'd remembered. She broke the surface of the water and coughed, hating the burn of the salt in her throat and in her eyes. The cough had stayed inside her for a week. She'd never gone into the ocean again.

They weren't the kind of family that said "I love you." They were the kind that showed it. They wrote it, baked it, sewed it, bought it, nurtured it, taught it, and breathed it. She understood that now, and she understood she had to reply in kind.

"Mom, let me get you a napkin." She scooted out her chair and grabbed a napkin, folding it in half to tuck under the side of the plate the way her mom always did.

"Thank you, baby," her mom said.

The word *baby* struck her heart, laying open the whole pulpy mess. She realized how much she needed to hear her mom's voice. The silent car rides, the dinner trays delivered by her sister . . . they left her starved, like a plant trying to grow under the dense canopy of a thousand-year oak.

"I missed you, Mom."

"I missed you, too." Her mom's lower lip quivered. "Don't go away again, okay?"

For a minute, she considered changing everything. She could stay and watch TV with Mattie. Help Mom with dinner. Tell Dad what Mr. Parker said about her *Lonesome Dove* paper. They'd stay inside, breathing the same air, as if the house were a womb that could nurture them until they were ready to face the outside world.

Emma pressed her finger into a crumb that lay on the plate. She put the crumb in her mouth and sucked on it, tasting the salt of the margarine. How long would it take, she wondered, before that salt came out again in tears? Only as long as it took for Dad to throw up blood again, which would make Mom mad, which would make her mad, which would make Mattie mad. She looked at her mom's empty right ring finger. Grandma Jennings's wedding ring was supposed to buy them another chance, but so far, nothing had changed.

In that moment, she understood why she was water, and the other members of her family were earth, air, and fire. Water had patience. Water carved canyons through rocks hundreds of millions of years old. Water wore down everything, even fear.

• • •

An hour and three muffins later, she heard a door open and close upstairs. *Dad*, she thought. He'd gone from the bedroom to the bathroom. Her mom snapped to attention at the sound, putting down her pencil and looking up at the ceiling. "I'd better go see if your father needs any help." A smile teased the corners of her lips. "Save him a muffin, okay?"

"More than one," Emma said.

Her mom pushed out her chair and walked to the stairs.

"Mom?"

"Yes?" Rays from the skylight fell on her hair, turning the brown and grey into red and gold.

Emma's throat ran dry and the words stuck inside it. "I'm sorry," she whispered.

"I just want you to be happy." Her mom smiled. "Nothing else matters."

Emma felt a swell of love inside her, threatening to split her ribs to make room for her heart. *I love you, Mom*, she thought. She stared at her, dimly aware that it might not be possible to do so again. *It isn't the last time. It can't be.*

Her mom turned and went up the stairs. Emma waited until she heard the door of her parents' room close. Six hurried footsteps carried her to the door that led to the garage. She picked her purse up from the floor, and snatched her dad's smartphone and the extra set of car keys hanging in the cupboard next to the door.

"Hey, are you going somewhere?" Mattie called from the couch. "I thought you were grounded."

She forced her lips to smile so her voice would sound normal, even while her heart hammered in her chest. "Just to the garage. I think my old yearbooks are out here."

"Why do you need car keys to find your yearbook?"

"Be good, Matt," she said, slipping through the door.

There was no going back now. She had to open the garage door to get out. As soon as someone pressed the button, the door clanked like a medieval drawbridge, shaking the floor of her bedroom upstairs. It was so loud that her parents tried to reserve weekend errands and yard work for late morning, so as not to wake her up. She didn't deserve that.

Emma shuffled down the narrow walkway between a row of boxes and the car. Mattie's old chalkboard easel, shoved into the corner by the water heater, proclaimed, "Today is not March 23, 1962."

The driver's seat was cold as she slid inside and put the key in the ignition. One click of the rectangular remote clipped to the visor and the garage door rattled its way up, so slowly that Emma knew she'd get caught.

Mattie would get Mom. It would take her at least a few seconds to explain, and another few for her mom to run downstairs. She kept her eyes trained on the steering wheel, not wanting to see the look on any face that came through the door.

The garage door rattled its way open. Emma threw the car in reverse and zoomed into the driveway. When her tires hit the sidewalk, she pressed the button again to close the garage door. It came down rickety and slow, cutting off her view of the boxes that still held her childhood toys. On top of the boxes sat a basket that held her old lace-up roller skates, a jump rope, and a plastic ring toss. It was the last thing she saw before she sped down the block.

• • •

There was one stop to make before heading into East Malo Verde. She turned into the gas station four miles down the street, the one that was always crowded. No one would notice a white Buick, especially one that only stopped for a few minutes.

She parked next to the food mart and pulled her purse from the passenger seat. Clutching it to her chest, she locked the car and walked up to the ancient payphone beside the front door. Her dad's smartphone would be traceable; plus, she needed every second of battery life.

She fumbled for the ridged sides of the quarters she'd dropped into her purse last night. As the phone rang, she counted "one-Mississippi" in her head, even though she had no idea what Mississippi looked like.

Dan answered on the second ring. "Hello?"

"Two Mississippi."

"What does that mean?"

"It means I wasn't sure you'd pick up."

"The caller ID didn't say who it was. Is this really your number? It's not the one you gave me before."

"No, it's not."

"Em, what's going on?"

"I really wanted to hear your voice."

"You've never called me before. What's the occasion?"

"My mom made muffins this morning."

"I'm jealous."

"What are you doing right now?"

"Washing my dad's truck."

"Why?"

"Because he'll give me ten bucks."

"Wouldn't a carwash be cheaper?"

"I don't get the money that way. I have prom tickets to finance, if you remember."

She bent her head against the shell of the payphone kiosk. The metal felt like ice against her brow. "Dan?"

"Yeah."

"Thank you."

"For what?"

"Seeing me."

"Lots of people did. I was the only one smart enough to do anything about it."

Her stomach lurched. "I won't forget."

"You can pay me back by putting me in a story. Just don't make me look like a dick in front of Percival Everett." He paused. "Well, you can make me look like a dick when you write about yesterday. I'm so sorry, Em. I was an asshole to you and you didn't deserve it."

Her hand clutched the phone, squeezing it until her fingers left dents in the rubber coating. "You remembered."

"It's your dream. That's not something I'm going to forget."

"My dream," she whispered.

"Em, you sound weird. Did something happen?"

"No." She cleared her throat and forced her lips to curve like the prow of a Viking ship. "No, everything's fine."

"Do you want me to meet you somewhere?"

"Keep washing that truck. We need every penny, right?"

"Em —"

"I have to go."

" — I miss you."

"I'm still here."

"Then can you imagine how bad I'd miss you if you were really gone?"

She closed her eyes. Every word she could say now would be a lie, and he had never lied to her.

"Em, just tell me what's going on."

"Goodbye, Dan," she said, replacing the handle of the phone in its silver cradle.

CHAPTER THIRTY

Saturday, April 19

THE MARQUEE BENEATH THE FAST food sign contained a message in Spanish she couldn't read. In the parking lot, she saw a Mexican family piling into a minivan with a rust-flecked hood. The mother looked fifty but she held a new baby, with five small children clustered around her. The father looked thirty, dressed in tight black Wranglers, a striped long-sleeved shirt, and a cowboy hat.

Emma drove past them and turned onto the next block. She tucked a flyaway hair behind her ear to stop it from tickling her cheek. Her hand smelled like the gummy black coating on the payphone's handle.

The payphone.

There was still time to turn around. She could order a soda from the drive-through, paid for with the stash of change her mom always kept in the center console. But what would it solve? Everything was still ruined, and she was still herself. Even though her heart pounded in her chest, drenching her spine with sweat, she had to keep going. Stalling would only give the razor-winged butterflies in her stomach more time to fly.

With her foot off the gas, she idled down Sobrante Street at ten miles an hour. According to the map she'd drawn in her maroon notebook, El Camino Rojo was less than a quarter-mile away. She tried to pick out landmarks as she passed, but all the houses looked the same — small stucco boxes with a two-step front porch, a living room window to the right, and a one-car garage to the left. Some bled rust from window corners or a spinning roof vent. Most of the front yards held plastic toys or play gyms, bleaching like bones in the sun. None of them had grass. They were all filled in with dirt or rocks or sand. Even the weeds couldn't get a break.

Two blocks later, she found it: El Camino Rojo, its street sign bent as if someone tried to run it over with a car. The name plate had two holes shot through it.

She told her hands to turn the wheel. They wouldn't.

Instead, they turned onto the next block, Rossano Road. Her sweaty palms slid over the steering wheel as she leaned forward. Cars lined the curb like ants on a log. There wasn't an empty space in sight.

She idled along, braking over the intersection's deep gutters. Three and a half blocks later, she found an empty spot between a lowered green Civic and an Aerostar with no paint on the hood or the roof. It was five blocks from the address she'd written down. If something went wrong and she had to run, five blocks was an eternity. *It'll work*, she thought, meeting her own gaze in the rearview mirror. *It has to.*

She pulled up even with the Civic, shifted into reverse, and cranked the wheel to the right. Her rear tires slapped the curb before she started to straighten out. She swore and shifted into drive, walloping the wheel in the opposite direction. Beside the street, two kids played in a chain-linked yard, scooping dirt into a cracked sand bucket. They squatted in the dust and stared at her, plastic shovels held in mid-air.

This time, when her rear tires were even with the Civic's, she shifted into reverse again. *Gently*, she thought, remembering her dad's lessons on parallel parking. What was it he'd said? *Be nice to the steering wheel.*

It was all he'd ever asked of anyone.

And somewhere nearby, the Espinosas launched fists and feet into his body, breaking bones and blood vessels and other things inside him. She closed her eyes, her nose instantly full of the smell of iron and blood. She wondered what happened to the clothes they'd worn that night. Everything from shirts to pants to socks had been smeared with blood. They went into the hamper and never reappeared.

Just like us, she thought. The darkness had swallowed them, too, and they still hadn't found a way out. Maybe there wasn't one.

Patches of sweat blossomed beneath her arms and behind her knees. She turned the wheel and took her foot off the brake. When the car slid into the spot without hitting the curb, she straightened it out and sighed with relief. It was only the fourth time she'd parallel parked.

She turned off the car and looped the long strap of her cross-body purse over her head. When she got out, the little boy in the fenced yard laughed and pointed at her. "Go inside," she said, but he and his sister ignored her. Emma pressed her purse to her hip to feel the outline of the gun.

"I warned you," she said.

• • •

The house at 16305 El Camino Rojo was small and off-white, with a tile roof and metal bars over the windows. The exterior was smooth, not stucco, with rounded corners instead of piercingly straight ones. *Adobe*, she thought. *Like the Alamo.*

Emma took a deep breath and looked up at the sky. The air felt warmer and thicker here, without the salty tang of the offshore breeze that blew through her neighborhood. She couldn't remember if it had been cloudy or sunny the day her dad saw this same patch of sky, when he'd come to ask how many people lived in the house. All he'd needed was a number, and they couldn't give it to him. Instead, they opened up his skin to let out his blood.

She wondered what she'd see if she looked down at the gutter and the grate over the drain. Dried blood, broken glass, missing buttons, the plastic sleeve of his census badge? She forced her eyes to focus on the dark, scuffed door of the little house across the sidewalk. Her right hand lifted the flap of her purse and curled around the handle of the gun. She left it there, letting her fingers slide up and down the handle, warming it to the touch.

Two steps carried her onto the driveway.

Another four brought her onto the porch.

Under the overhang, a daddy-long-legs spider defied gravity, its legs pointed toward the roof. A doormat full of cracked green tines with a plastic daisy in the corner decomposed one sunrise at a time.

She clamped her fingers around the handle of the gun and slid it from her bag. With her left hand, she banged on the door.

There wasn't a peephole or doorknocker, just a dull metal knob that sagged beneath its own weight. Someone grasped it from the other side. Her lower lip shook with the weight of the fear she couldn't force down.

The door opened and an old woman looked up at her from the other side. Small and bent, she had black eyebrows and white hair. One wrinkled hand held a crocheted shawl around her shoulders. "*No te conozco.*"

Emma raised the gun. "Is Alejandro here?"

The old woman breathed in sharply. "No, no, no."

Emma pushed past her and turned sideways, keeping the gun pointed at the old woman's chest. "Where are they? I want to see Alejandro and Hector."

"*No hablo Inglés. Por favor, no me tire.*"

"Where did they go? Are they at the store, at someone's house, down the street, where?"

The woman whispered something that sounded familiar. Emma bit her lip and forced her brain to think in French. Sometimes, when she spoke French and Rachel spoke Spanish, they could understand each other. "Again," she said.

The old woman repeated the word.

Église. The word sounded like *église.* She tried to remember the words on the sign in front of the Catholic church on Calle Real. There was a statue of Jesus out front, his arms and hands outstretched in a shape she knew well. *Graph the function of this parabola,* she thought. *Find the limit so you'll know who goes to Heaven and who goes to Hell.*

"Are they at church?" she asked. "*Á l'église?*"

"*Sí*." The old woman nodded slowly. "*Iglesia*."

"Close the door."

The woman understood. She pushed it closed without locking it. "*Señorita, no hagas esto*."

"I don't know what you're saying." Emma glanced around the room. A red brick fireplace dominated the far wall. On the mantel sat three bottles of tequila and two prayer candles. Light flooded through the front windows, illuminating the diamond-bright sparkles in the popcorn ceiling.

Something in a pan on the stove snapped and hissed. For the first time, Emma noticed the smell emanating from the tiny kitchen. It was warm and thick, like pastry, or something that went into pastry. She pointed the gun toward the stove. "Do you need to go check on that?"

"Ay," the woman moaned.

Emma moved toward the living room, where she could point the gun at the old woman in the kitchen or whoever walked in the front door. She fought the urge to lean against the waist-high counter separating the living room from the kitchen. The gun was already heavy in her grasp, but she didn't want to get sloppy. The first third of her plan had succeeded.

She was in the house and no one had been hurt.

The old woman flung her shawl onto the counter and hustled into the kitchen. She used a pair of tongs to lift a tortilla out of the pan. It shredded in her grasp, the bottom half sticking to the pan. She muttered and used the tongs to scrape at the stuck tortilla.

Emma saw her hand slip once, bringing the flat of her hand in contact with the hot pan. She didn't flinch.

On the counter, a black cell phone sat like a paperweight on a stack of bills. Emma put her hand over the phone and slipped it into her purse while the old woman's back was turned. "When will they be back?" she asked. "From *iglesia*?"

The old woman shrugged.

"*Quand est-ce que votre famille retournent de l'église? Vous comprenez le français?*"

"*No entiendo.*"

Emma felt bubbles pop and hiss in her bloodstream. "What's wrong with you? Why don't you speak English?"

The old woman met her eyes and flexed the muscles in her jaw. "No."

Emma stormed into the kitchen and slammed the muzzle of the gun into the microwave's digital display. "Clock. It's called a clock. I want to hear you say it."

The old woman closed her mouth.

"Say it!"

"Clock," the woman mumbled.

Emma pointed the gun at the first number in the digital readout. "Ten." Then she moved the muzzle to the minutes. "Twenty-five. It's 10:25 a.m. When will Alejandro and Hector be back?"

The old woman lifted her shoulders.

"What time?" She pressed the "timer" button and entered 11:00 on the keypad. "Is this when they'll be back?"

"*No sabe, señorita.*"

Her heartbeat pulsed in her ears. A drop of sweat traced its way down the base of her skull. Emma stepped to her left, away from the hot stove. She looked at the burnt tortilla, its spotted carcass dropped like an animal hide on the counter. "You do know. You knew when to start the tortillas."

The old woman heard it first. The muscles in her jaw relaxed and her gaze shifted to the front door. Emma held her breath as a car door slammed outside. She waved the old woman further into the kitchen. "Be quiet. *Silencez-vous.*"

With her left hand, she fumbled in the purse for her dad's phone. It shook in her hand as she pulled it out and swiped to unlock it. Her sweaty thumb clouded the screen as she tapped to turn on the recorder. A rectangular battery icon flashed red.

One bar.

"Fuck," she whispered, shoving the phone in her pocket.

Someone's shoe scuffed against the step outside, and a bone-deep moan rose from the dark cavern of her throat. Her heartbeat felt like it would flood her chest with blood, more than the weak chambers of her heart could hold.

I'm scared, she thought. *Daddy, help me.*

The old woman's lips moved in silence and Emma wondered who she was praying to. She wiped her palms against her jeans and used her left arm to brace her right, tightening her grip on the gun.

A pair of masculine voices grew louder, joking in a mixture of English and Spanish. Someone's hand grasped the doorknob and turned. When the door opened, a short boy wearing boots, jeans, and a tucked-in T-shirt stepped over the threshold. "What the fuck," he said, stumbling backward when he saw her.

"Are you Alejandro Espinosa?"

"Don't shoot!" He raised his arms and turned his head to look over his shoulder. Emma saw a mole on his left cheek.

I know him, she thought. *How do I know him?*

The second person on the porch pushed Alejandro aside. Taller and paler, he had a yellow cast to his skin that made him look like he belonged in a hospital. His black hair flopped over his eyebrows, just like Dan's, falling to his cheekbones in gel-crisp curls. Beneath the taller man's brows, the dark eyes set deep in his skull absorbed everything and reflected nothing. "Put your fucking hands down," he said, slapping at the other boy's arms.

"You're Hector," she said.

"*La puerta*," the old woman cried. "*La puerta!*"

Alejandro closed the door.

The old woman sighed behind her. The rush of breath stirred Emma's hair, sending a flood of goosebumps down her spine. "You're Hector," she said again.

If he was surprised, he didn't show it. His eyes searched her face, stripping it of soul and love and meaning. "Do I know you, *gabacha*?"

"I came here to ask you a question."

"You break in my fucking house, you wave a fucking gun at me, and you think I'm gonna answer a fucking question?"

"I didn't break in. I knocked politely and your grandma let me in."

"She knows better," Hector said softly. "Don't you, *mi abuelita*?"

The old woman clutched the spoon to her chest.

"I've seen you before," Alejandro said, stepping away from his brother. "You go to my school, don't you?"

"That's what the cop said." Emma looked him in the eye. "But I don't know you."

"What cop?"

Hector pushed his brother into the door. "The one Letizia heard asking too many questions at your school, *bruto*."

Emma tried to match Alejandro's slim frame to one of the brown shadows in her memory. He leaned his head against the door and she saw once more the black oval on his cheek. *A lizard belt*, she thought. *A girl whose bare skin he almost touched.*

A drop of sweat slid into the center of her bra. "I saw you," she said. "In the courtyard, at lunch. You wore pointy boots and danced with a girl."

Alejandro nodded. "You eat with the smart girls by the front gate. You never look happy."

"You don't know anything about me."

His eyes flickered over the gun, clutched in both her hands. "Why did you come here?"

"I want to know why you did it."

"Did what?"

"Beat my father half to death."

"I didn't do that." Alejandro's cheeks paled. "I don't know what you're talking about."

Emma watched his eyes widen in alarm. Once, Mr. Parker had told them about interrogating insurgents in Iraq. *If they nod every time they say yes and shake their head every time they say no, they're lying to you.* But Alejandro's head didn't move.

She shifted the barrel of the gun toward Hector. "Then it was you. You beat my father and left him for dead and I want to know why." She imagined the wet thump of Hector's fist breaking her dad's nose. One glance at his hands, held loosely at his sides, revealed a collection of tattoos she couldn't decipher. *I should have told you, Dad. I should have told you it was a war zone. I'm so sorry.*

Hector smiled. "You ask too many questions. Does that mean you're a cop, too?"

"He wasn't a cop! He was a census worker. They count how many people live here so the government can give you money for schools and things. My dad was trying to *help* you. He never did anything to hurt you."

A haze of fear and nausea clouded her vision. It would overwhelm her if she let it, traveling in waves from her gut to her forehead, pricking her skin with sweat. She heard her own breath, coming in short, ragged gasps. Her fingers were wet where they held the gun.

"Hector," Alejandro said. "Did you do it?"

"He did." Emma felt hot tears spill from the corners of her eyes. "He did it, I know he did. He broke my dad's nose and cracked his ribs and ground his face into a pile of crushed glass."

Alejandro's gaze drifted down to his brother's black boots. "Hector."

Something in her ears began to roar. At first she thought it was an earthquake or a car crash, but it wasn't. She tried to take a breath but there was no air. Then she knew. She was under the waves again, in Santa Cruz, kicking for the surface and the sun.

Hector tossed his head, shaking his hair out of his eyes. "Why did you come here, *gabacha*?"

"You don't even know what kind of person he is," she sobbed. "You can't just hurt people when you don't know how good they are."

"I hurt everyone who comes into my territory asking questions."

Emma tried to swallow, but her throat was closed. She sputtered and choked, her finger sliding down the trigger.

"You should go," Alejandro said.

The old woman in the kitchen shuffled her feet. "*Vete ya.*"

The sound of rushing water blocked out the old woman's mutter. It roared in her ears like a roller coaster. "I can't. I can't go back until I make things better."

Alejandro held out his hands. "You don't want to do this."

"Joan didn't want to be burned alive. The people in the Alamo didn't want to die." This house was poisoned. These people were poisoned. Hector Espinosa's eyes were poisoned. They were oil and she was water. It had to end, and it could only end when her dad was safe. He was the reason she'd come, the reason she had to try and undo all the damage she'd done. "Say you did it," she cried, sliding her finger up the trigger.

Hector snaked his right hand around his back.

"No!" Alejandro cried.

Hector whipped out a gun, small and plastic-looking like hers, and aimed it at her heart. "You made a mistake, *gabacha.* Maybe I did, too. But I know how to fix my mistakes. I know how to bury them."

"Hector," Alejandro said. "Shut the fuck up."

"I won't let you near my family," she sobbed.

"*Gabacha,*" Hector said, clicking off the safety. "You won't be here."

Emma thought of her mom, skimping on milk to make pudding for her after a hard day. Of Mattie, telling Mom she wouldn't go to college if that made it easier for Emma. She imagined her dad, white-haired and bathrobe-clad, shuffling between rooms without front-facing windows for the next thirty years. He wouldn't wait up by the door to make sure Mattie came home from a date on time. He wouldn't go to her track meets. He wouldn't go see her when she played the lead in *Romeo and Juliet*. They'd pretend it was some sort of normal, a problem swept under a rug the size and shape of all their years together.

No, she thought. She would tell them she loved them the only way she knew how.

"Neither will you," she said, and pulled the trigger.

Alejandro jerked the muzzle of his brother's gun as Hector fired back. A spray of red blossomed on Hector's blue flannel shirt. He fell backward against his brother, both knocked to the floor by the impact. The old woman screamed in the kitchen.

"Hector!" Alejandro cried, laying his brother down. "Hector!"

Emma sobbed. *I did it*, she thought. *Dad, I did it.*

Alejandro looked up at her with sun-bright anger in his eyes. As he looked at her, though, his face began to change. The anger faded like a sudden twilight, all its brightness descending into grey. "Go," he said. "This is over."

Something smelled like burnt cardboard. The old woman had forgotten something else in the oven. Emma let her right arm fall. She lifted the flap of her purse to slip the gun inside. When she pulled her hand away from the bag, her sleeve was wet. She gasped and looked back at Alejandro.

"Go," he said.

She stumbled toward the door, smearing the knob with red as she threw it open. *That's not my hand*, she thought. *My hand is not that color.*

Outside, the sun had risen hot and high in the sky. She held up her right hand to shade her eyes. Her mom's car had air-conditioning. She'd be fine once she got in the car.

But as she looked around at the strange pastel houses, she couldn't remember where she was. *I don't know this street*, she thought, looking at the fences with broken pickets or rusted chain link.

She stumbled down to the sidewalk and brushed against a peeling picket fence. The pickets turned red and she felt something sting in her midsection. She grabbed at the pickets and used them to pull herself down the sidewalk.

Five pickets later, her shirt caught on a broken slat. She tried to move, but the picket held her fast. She swung her left arm for momentum and her wristwatch caught the sun. It was after 11:00 a.m. Her mom would be starting lunch and she would probably be late.

She was always supposed to call if she was going to be late.

Her right hand gripped the fence post while her left snaked inside her pocket. She pulled out her dad's smartphone and held it up. The battery was dead. Her wrist began to shake and her fingers couldn't hold onto the phone. The screen shattered on impact when it hit the sidewalk.

I'll fix it, she thought. She reached into her purse, rummaging for the second phone, the one she'd stolen. It was a flip phone, small and black, with a tiny number pad.

She stared at the numbers, wondering why where were too many. She closed her eyes and counted by feel, sliding her fingernails into the spaces between the numbers as she read them out loud. She pressed all the numbers that meant home and held the box to her ear.

"Hello?" her mother answered. "Em, is that you?"

"Mom." Her voice sounded strange, like it was rolled up in a carpet.

"Em! Where are you? Are you all right?"

"I think I am." She tried to move — the sun was so *hot* — but her shirt was still caught on the fence post.

"Where are you? Tell me where you are."

"The car's here. I'm going to find it and then I'm going to come home."

"Em, tell me where you are. I'm coming to get you."

A field of purple spots floated over the sidewalk in front of her. She blinked, but they didn't go away. *Not yet*, she thought. *I'm not ready yet.* "Mom, tell Dad everything's all right now."

"What are you talking about? Baby, where are you?"

"Tell him he doesn't have to be afraid anymore. He can go see Mattie in her play or when she runs."

"Em, I'm scared. What are you talking about? Where are you?"

"I did it for you," she whispered. The sun was too hot. Parts of her felt like they were already burned. She should have worn a hat or put on sunscreen. Her mom was always nagging her to put on sunscreen. "Because I love you."

"Emma! What did you do? Oh, God, Em, tell me you're okay."

"Mom, I have to find the car. I have to go."

"Emma, don't you hang up! Where are you? Emma, I need you, baby. Where are you?"

"I'll be late," she whispered. "You don't have to wait for me."

"Emma Christina," her mother said. Now her voice was hidden under carpet, too.

"But maybe we could say grace? We always say grace."

She heard a sob and a crash on the other end of the line.

"Mom?" She wanted to tell her mom to put her lunch in the fridge, but her hand was so slippery it dropped this phone, too.

The black box fell to the ground and she couldn't bend down to get it. Something would hurt if she did that. The sun would burn her back. She'd forgotten her sunscreen.

That was all right.

She hadn't forgotten what mattered most.

She coughed to clear her throat — something hot and thick had gotten stuck inside it — and recited the Swedish blessing her dad had taught her. "Come, Lord Jesus, be our guest. Let these gifts to use be blessed." She tried to say the last word loud enough so that her mom could hear it, too: *Amen*.

AUTHOR'S NOTE

Thank you for taking a chance on this book. *The Red Road* has more real-life elements than I usually incorporate in a story, which made it hard to write and even harder to send out into the world. I have more grey hair than I used to, but it was worth it if you enjoyed the book. I'd love to hear what you thought! You can write to me at jenni@jenniwiltz.com or use the contact form on my website, JenniWiltz.com.

If you enjoyed the book, I'd be grateful for an honest review — even a quick star rating can help get the word out! Thank you for reading *The Red Road* and spending time with characters who are all such a big part of me.

ABOUT THE AUTHOR

Author photo by Ryan Donahue

Jenni Wiltz writes fiction and creative nonfiction. She has won national writing awards for romantic suspense and creative nonfiction. Her short stories have appeared in *Gargoyle*, *The Portland Review*, and several small-press anthologies. When she's not writing, she enjoys sewing, running, and genealogical research. She lives in Pilot Hill, California. Visit her online at JenniWiltz.com.

www.ingramcontent.com/pod-product-compliance
Lightning Source LLC
Chambersburg PA
CBHW031309210726
48287CB00005B/1484